The SWEETGUM Knit Lit Society

Center Point Large Print

**This Large Print Book carries the
Seal of Approval of N.A.V.H.**

The SWEETGUM Knit Lit Society

Beth Pattillo

CENTER POINT PUBLISHING
THORNDIKE, MAINE

This Center Point Large Print edition
is published in the year 2008 by arrangement with
WaterBrook Press, a division of Random House, Inc.

Copyright © 2008 by Beth Pattillo.

The text of this Large Print edition is unabridged. In other
aspects, this book may vary from the original edition.
Printed in the United States of America.
Set in 16-point Times New Roman type.

ISBN: 978-1-60285-262-4

Library of Congress Cataloging-in-Publication Data

Pattillo, Beth.
  The Sweetgum Knit Lit Society / Beth Pattillo.
    p. cm.
  ISBN 978-1-60285-262-4 (library binding : alk. paper)
  1. Knitters (Persons)—Fiction. 2. Knitting—Fiction. 3. Book clubs (Discussion
groups)—Fiction. 4. Female friendship—Fiction. 5. Teenagers and adults—Fiction.
6. Tennessee—Fiction. 7. Domestic fiction. 8. Large type books. I. Title.

  PS3616.A925S94 2008b
  813'.6—dc22
  2008018698

For Randy,
for everything

One

Over the top of her reading glasses, Eugenie Pierce eyed the teenage girl sprawled across two chairs at the long table in the Sweetgum Public Library's reading area. Late afternoon sunlight spilled through the tall windows and fell like a spotlight on the youthful offender. The city council could make noises about forcing Eugenie to retire in six months' time, but that didn't mean she would neglect her library in the interim. Not that it was her library personally. It belonged to the good citizens of Sweetgum, Tennessee. But the library had been in her care for almost forty years, and no teenager since the Nixon administration had put his or her feet anywhere but on the floor, where they belonged.

Eugenie moved a step closer to the girl and continued to stare. Usually her narrowed gaze moved mountains—or at least wayward adolescent limbs. But this child was not so easily motivated. Another two steps, sensible pumps tapping against the tile floor, and now Eugenie stood within three feet of the girl.

"Ahem." She resorted to clearing her throat. Still the girl did not respond. Eugenie moved closer. She tapped the table in front of the girl and cleared her throat again.

"What?" The girl looked up, rolled her eyes, and slumped even lower. She had those white wires hanging from her ears, which meant she wasn't reading but listening to that awful rap music. The girl finally pulled one of the buds from her ear. "I said, 'What?'"

"Please take your feet off the chair," Eugenie replied, snipping each word. She lowered her glasses to the tip of her nose and looked pointedly at the girl's cheap plastic flip-flops and black-lacquered toenails. True, none of the furniture in the Sweetgum Public Library was anywhere near new, but every stick of it was in pristine condition.

"I'm not hurting anything." The girl spoke too loudly because of the remaining bud wedged in her right ear.

"Shh. You're disturbing the other patrons."

Granted, the only other people in the library at the moment were Mr. and Mrs. Hornbuckle, who couldn't hear a train wreck between them, but it was the principle of the thing that mattered. A library was a holy place, like church, and you wouldn't find people sitting in a house of worship with their feet on the pews and headphones jammed in their ears. At least not in Sweetgum.

The girl looked around, saw the Hornbuckles, and laughed. "You'd have to shoot off a cannon to disturb them."

Eugenie sighed. She wasn't up for this. Maybe Homer Flint and his cronies were right. Maybe it truly was time for her to retire. She'd had the same conversation with four decades' worth of teenagers. Her track record, of course, spoke for itself. She'd steered any number of wayward youth onto the straight and narrow, although lately not as many as she used to.

"Library patrons do not put their feet in the chairs. And please turn down the volume on your CD player. Others may not share your taste in music."

The girl bristled. "It's an iPod."

"A what?"

"An iPod. Not a CD player." The scorn in her voice shouldn't have bothered Eugenie. But she was tired of people who treated her as if she was an ignorant civil servant instead of a well-educated woman with a master's degree in library science.

And then she saw the book lying on the table in front of the girl.

Knitting for Beginners.

Eugenie eyed the girl again. "Do you knit?" she asked in a slightly kinder tone. Eugenie was a firm believer in productive activities, and if this girl was a knitter, perhaps she wasn't such a lost cause after all.

"Huh?" Finally, the girl removed the remaining bud from her other ear. "What'd you say?"

"Are you a knitter?" Eugenie gestured toward the book on the table.

The girl stiffened, her mouth tightening as if she'd bitten into a lemon. "Why do you care?"

"Well, if you knit," Eugenie said patiently, "you might be interested in a group that meets the third Friday of every month at the Christian church. The Sweetgum Knit Lit Society. All knitters are welcome." Although she silently wondered just how welcome the other women would make this grungy girl feel. The ties that bound the group were tenuous at best, yet Eugenie managed to hold them together by sheer dint of will.

The girl shoved the book away. "I was just looking at it." The angry defensiveness of the girl's reply caught Eugenie off guard.

"I merely intended to—" But she stopped herself before she could utter the fateful word.

Help. I merely intended to help. The unfinished sentence lay between them, unspoken but entirely present. The girl's blue eyes narrowed in her round face. She shoved a hank of dirty blond hair off her forehead with one hand. "I don't need your help."

And then Eugenie heard the telltale rustle of paper from underneath the table.

"What's that?"

More rustling. The girl's face turned red. "Nothing."

Eugenie reached out and took the knitting book. With practiced efficiency, she flipped through the pages. She saw immediately where the little heathen had defaced *Knitting for Beginners.*

"You've ruined it." Disgusted by the jagged edges

where the pages had been ripped from the binding, Eugenie snapped the book closed. "You'll pay to replace it."

But despite the iPod—Eugenie had heard they were quite expensive—the girl didn't look like she had enough money to buy a decent pair of shoes, much less replace a hardback book.

"I didn't do it. It was already like that." The girl spoke too loudly, not because of her headphones but because she was lying.

Eugenie extended one hand. "The pages, please."

The girl stared back, mutinous, before finally giving in. "Here." She pulled the wad of glossy paper from beneath the table and thrust it at Eugenie, who took the pages, glancing down to see what the girl had torn from the book.

A pattern for a scarf. Why hadn't she simply checked out the book if she wanted the pattern?

"I'll look up the price and let you know what this will cost. There are processing fees in addition to the cost of the book."

"It doesn't matter." The girl slumped farther still in the chair. "I don't have any money."

"What's your name?" Eugenie asked. "I'll need your parents' names as well." She knew the girl heard her question because her cheeks went pale beneath the smear of blush that failed to cover the thicket of freckles.

"I don't have any parents."

Again, Eugenie could tell she was lying. "Then

who is responsible for you? A relative?"

The girl turned her head away. A library was also similar to a church in that it often provided shelter for lost souls. Temporary shelter for the most part, but Eugenie had found that everyone from latchkey children to battered wives and lonely senior citizens might wander into her library on any given day.

"If you can't give me the name of the adult who's responsible for you, I'll have to call Theda Farley over at Family Services."

The girl's head whipped back around to Eugenie. "Don't you dare." She scrambled out of the chair. Eugenie might be old enough to retire, but she was still spry. With a quick snag, she caught the girl's arm.

"Hey! You can't touch me!"

"Young lady, in my library, I can do as I see fit."

"This is child abuse!"

"You've ruined one of my books. You don't have the money to pay for it, and you won't tell me who you are. Perhaps I should call the police."

The girl's kohl-smeared eyes widened. "All right. All right. I'll tell you my name. Just no cops."

Eugenie held in a sigh of relief. She wouldn't have called the police anyway, not for so minor an infraction, but the girl didn't have to know that.

"So what is your name?" Eugenie demanded, releasing the girl's arm.

"Hannah."

"Hannah what?"

"Hannah Simmons."

The name rang a bell. "You're Tracy Simmons's daughter?" She knew Tracy. Wild. Promiscuous. She'd had her first child, this child, at sixteen. That was the thing about a small town like Sweetgum. Everyone knew everyone else's business, unless of course you knew how to be very, very discreet. Tracy Simmons had been the antithesis of discreet.

"Tracy's my mom. So what?"

Well, that explained the tattoos the child had drawn up and down her arms with ballpoint pen, the too-tight tank top, and the cheap flip-flops. She was definitely her mother's daughter.

And then Eugenie remembered something else. A hazy picture of Tracy Simmons when she was eight years old, sitting on the floor between the stacks in the juvenile section of the library, her dirty blond head buried in a book. Her mother would drop her off at the library for hours at a time, at least until Tracy had entered junior high school, developed a figure, and been left elsewhere to fend off the attention of adolescent boys. Within a couple years, she'd become one of those girls who rode around the town square on a Saturday night in the back of a pickup, a bottle in a plain brown bag in one hand and a cigarette in the other. By then it had been a long time since she'd darkened the door of the library. Tracy was one of the few who had escaped Eugenie's influence. The memory startled Eugenie, and it changed her mind about how to handle Hannah's debt.

"If you can't pay for the book, you'll have to work off the cost."

"What?" Hannah had chewed off most of her metallic pink lipstick, leaving only a rough stain around the edges of her mouth.

"You'll have to do some work for me here at the library to pay for the book."

Her eyebrows shot up. "You can't make me work. I'm thirteen. What about child labor laws?"

Eugenie smiled. "Well, you're welcome to call the police if you think I'm violating the law."

Hannah's shoulders slumped. "You're evil."

Now Eugenie could laugh. "No, Hannah. I'm not evil." She paused for effect. "I'm a librarian."

"So what do I have to do?" Hannah demanded, one hand on a bony hip that jutted out. "Shelve books, sweep, stuff like that?"

"For today, yes."

Hannah scowled. "I have to work for more than a day?"

"We'll start with an hour a day on weekdays and a half-day on Saturday."

"You're kidding. For how long?"

"For as long as it takes."

The girl grumbled, but she didn't protest further. Eugenie thought she looked secretly relieved. Something to do after school. A way to get out of the house on Saturday. Both were probably a blessing to Tracy Simmons's daughter.

14

"And one other thing." Eugenie looked down at the torn pages in her hand. "You have to participate in the Knit Lit Society."

"I don't want to be in your nitwit society."

"And I don't think you have a choice."

"They won't want me."

"Of course they will," Eugenie answered, but she spoke with more confidence than she felt. "They'll help you learn to knit as well as broaden your mind through reading."

Eugenie's words were met with silence.

"What do you like to read?"

Again silence.

"What were your favorites when you were younger?" she persisted. *"Little Women? The Wonderful Wizard of Oz?"* She couldn't remember this Hannah coming to the library before, now that she thought about it.

"I never read any of those."

"A Little Princess? Pollyanna?" Eugenie asked with rising incredulity.

Hannah shook her head. "I tried that one about the girl on the mountain. You know, the one where her mother died and she went to live with her grandfather."

Eugenie was afraid she could see the appeal *Heidi* might have held for Hannah. "Well then, I think I know what the Knit Lit Society will be reading next." She turned toward the information desk and motioned Hannah to follow. "Come on. We'll start with some dusting. After I close up, we can walk over to Munden's Five-and-Dime to buy some yarn and needles."

"I told you I don't have any money."

"You can work the needles and yarn off as well. Besides, the Knit Lit Society meets tomorrow evening, so you'll need them."

"My mom won't let me come down here on a Friday night."

Eugenie doubted that Tracy Simmons cared about Hannah's whereabouts on a Friday night. Or any other night for that matter. The last Eugenie had heard, Tracy worked as a cocktail waitress at a seedy bar on the outskirts of Sweetgum.

"You leave that to me," was all she said in response to the girl's protest. She stepped behind the circulation desk and reached into a cubby for a dust cloth. "Here." She held it out to Hannah. "Start in the fiction section over there with the A's. And when you see *Little Women* by Louisa May Alcott, pull it out. That will be our first book."

Hannah's eyes widened. "I can't read that by tomorrow night."

"Of course not. That will be next month's selection. Tomorrow you'll just meet the other members of the society. And learn to knit."

Hannah looked skeptical. "Whatever." But in spite of her resistance, she took the dust cloth.

"Don't forget the lower shelves," Eugenie admonished as she walked away.

Half an hour later, Eugenie looked around to find Hannah Simmons sitting on the floor between the stacks of the Sweetgum Public Library, her head buried in a copy of *Little Women*, a forgotten dust cloth on the floor beside her. Eugenie watched the girl from behind the information desk and allowed herself a small, satisfied smile.

Now all she had to do was convince the Sweetgum Knit Lit Society to welcome their newest member.

Two

Merry McGavin slid her minivan into a parking space near the main doors of the Sweetgum Christian Church and shoved the gear lever into park. The clock on the dashboard showed ten minutes past the hour. She scrambled from the van, grateful for the shade of the town's namesake trees, and yanked open the sliding door to the rear seats. Empty water bottles, Happy Meal toys, and crumpled Wet Wipes littered the vehicle's floor. Her knitting bag had toppled over when she rounded the last corner at Spring Street, so it took her a few moments to shove the jumble of yarn, needles, and books back into her quilted tote. The plastic water bottles and other detritus she ignored.

Merry hated being late, but that's all she ever was anymore. Late to teach Sunday school. Late getting Courtney to her orthodontist appointment. Late picking Jake up from soccer practice. Late retrieving Sarah from preschool. Late, late, late.

"Merry!"

She looked over her shoulder to see Ruthie Allen jogging down the sidewalk toward her, golden September light forming a halo around the older woman's head. The Sweetgum Christian Church sat directly behind the east side of the town square on Spring Street, two blocks down from the public library. Ruthie, the never-married church secretary, had probably run over to Tallulah's Café for a bite of supper after the church office closed. Merry wished she could eat a meal at the café's counter in blissful solitude. Most of her meals were consumed standing up at her kitchen counter while she baked, washed, fried, or cried.

Merry forced a smile. Ruthie was a rather plump woman of fifty-five, twenty years Merry's senior, and she really shouldn't be jogging in public. Not at her age. And certainly not without proper undergarment support above the waist.

"Hey, Ruthie," Merry said. "I'm glad I'm not the only one who's late. Now I don't have to face the wrath of Eugenie alone."

Ruthie grinned. She was wearing tight purple yoga pants, a sweatshirt that said "Love Your Mother" with a picture of the earth emblazoned on the front, and a worn pair of running shoes.

"You can hide behind me," Ruthie answered, hoisting her see-through plastic carryall higher on her shoulder. "I'm used to 'the wrath of Eugenie' as you so aptly put it."

Merry wished her smile was as genuine as Ruthie's broad, toothy grin. Even though she thought the older woman was a bit too free-spirited, she envied her naturally sunny disposition. Merry's own chipper outlook came from sheer determination, not from any inner sense of optimism.

"At least I finished the book," Merry said. So many book clubs just pretended to read the selection for the month. Some didn't even pretend. But most book clubs weren't led by the town librarian. Merry slung her bulging tote bag over her shoulder and threw the sliding door of the van closed.

"Did you finish your shawl too?" Ruthie asked. In theory each member of the Sweetgum Knit Lit Society was required to complete the book and its accompanying project before the meeting. In reality . . . well, today was one of the rare occasions when Merry had managed to finish both on time.

"I did, thankfully. Jeff agreed to take the kids out for ice cream last night so I could have a little peace and quiet."

"The book and the project? I'm impressed." Ruthie nodded at Merry's knitting bag as they crossed the sidewalk toward the front doors of the church. "So what are you working on now?"

Merry's knees wobbled, but she caught herself in time. "A baby layette. Hat, booties, blanket."

"How sweet!" Ruthie's enthusiasm never seemed to flag. "Are they for anyone we know?"

"No." Merry tightened her cheeks so her smile spread even wider. "Just for a friend who's pregnant."

"Well, you're nice to do such a thoughtful thing for your friend." Ruthie patted her shoulder. They'd reached the heavy mahogany doors, and Merry moved to open one.

"After you," she said, motioning for Ruthie to enter ahead of her. Merry needed a moment, just that brief moment while Ruthie's back was turned, to collect herself.

Late, late, late. She couldn't be. But she was. In more ways than one.

Camille St. Clair had been the first one to arrive at the church that evening. The Sweetgum Knit Lit Society shared space with the "Pairs and Spares" Sunday school class in the education wing. Usually Eugenie, the librarian, got there first. Camille sighed. Like the rest of Sweetgum, Eugenie was quite pre-dictable. In fact, Camille would bet her meager savings account that nothing in her little hometown had changed in her entire twenty-four years. She sighed again and began to unpack her sequined bag, spreading her things on the table in front of her. Her mother's tattered copy of Brontë's *Jane Eyre*. Several skeins of glittery, furry yarn for the halter top she was knitting. The pattern for the top, her scissors, a tape measure to check her gauge for the millionth time. In knitting you had to come out with the right number of stitches per inch if you wanted your garment to fit. You were supposed to knit a sample swatch before you started. Camille hated knitting swatches. She was always too anxious to begin the project itself, and invariably she found herself with a half-done garment that was too big or too small. This time, though, she was determined to do it right, and so she dug into her bag for the size of needles the pattern recommended.

"Hello, Camille!" two cheery voices called. Ruthie and Merry hustled into the room and looked relieved when they saw that Eugenie and Esther, the other members of the Knit Lit Society, had yet to arrive.

"Whew! That was a close one," Ruthie said as she slid into a chair, panting for breath. "I can't believe Eugenie's late. She's never late."

"She's probably finishing up some work stuff," Camille said, waving a hand in the direction of the library.

"Good." Ruthie reached into her bag and pulled out her own copy of Brontë's novel and the soy silk yarn she was using for the shawl project. "That gives me time to read the last few pages. Because clearly I'm not going to finish the shawl before she gets here."

The door opened again, and a small, polished-looking woman a few years older than Ruthie entered the classroom. Despite the warmth of the evening, she was wearing an elegant pale blue suit, opaque pantyhose, and pumps. If she'd had a matching pillbox hat, Camille thought, she would have looked like a blond Jackie O.

"Hello, everyone." The woman moved daintily to her place at the table and set her brown and tan designer bag on top of it.

"Hello, Esther." Camille returned her greeting. "That's a lovely suit." No doubt it was Chanel. Esther flew to New York twice a year to update her wardrobe, an unheard-of extravagance in a town like Sweetgum. Camille would have envied her, except that she knew Esther wasn't nearly as perfect as she liked people to think.

"Oh, I've had this for ages." Esther smoothed the material of the skirt and nodded in receipt of the compliment. She perched on the edge of a chair. "I had a luncheon today and never found a spare minute to change into something more appropriate for this evening."

With Esther, Camille knew, everything was about appearances. She was constantly bringing in photos from her latest Alaskan cruise or her trip to see her perfect grandchildren in Memphis. Sometimes Camille found it hard to believe that Esther and Ruthie were sisters. She wouldn't have believed it if they hadn't both sworn to it the first time she attended the Knit Lit Society.

"Hello, Esther," Ruthie said. "How was the luncheon?"

Tiny lines showed at the corners of Esther's mouth. "You would know, Ruthie, if you'd bothered to attend. We raised a nice amount for the Christian Children's Home." Camille noticed that Esther didn't look at her sister as she spoke. Instead she methodically unpacked items from the Louis Vuitton bag and set them out at precise intervals on the table before her. Luxurious angora yarn for whatever project she'd brought. Some very expensive hand-carved needles. Finally, Esther laid an embossed leather-bound version of *Jane Eyre* on the table—a far cry from Camille's own dog-eared paperback.

Camille looked at Esther and then at Ruthie. She had never wished for a sibling. At least not until after her father left during her senior year in high school . . . and then, well, there'd been barely enough profits from the dress shop her mother had purchased with the divorce settlement to provide basic necessities for the two of them. Camille couldn't imagine stretching their meager resources for a third person. When her father left town after her mother's diagnosis, not only had he taken her future; he'd taken her weekly visits to the tanning salon, her membership to the YMCA fitness center, and her French manicures. College tuition had been out of the question. As had Camille's long-dreamed-of plans to leave Sweetgum.

"I wonder where Eugenie could be?" Merry said, interrupting Camille's thoughts. As usual, the jumbled contents of Merry's bag sprawled across the table in front of her with no particular rhyme or reason. Camille guessed that Merry was part of the group not because of her love of knitting or books but because it was the one place she could escape her minivan-mom existence. Camille herself only came to the meetings at her mother's insistence. Her mother had been an original member of the group, but given how her health had deteriorated in the last few months . . . Well, now she sent Camille in her stead.

A small frown drew out tiny lines of concern on Esther's forehead. "Eugenie's never late." Whatever airs she might put on, Esther seemed to be quite fond of the librarian.

"I'll run down to the library and check on her," Ruthie said, rising from her slouch to move toward the door. At that moment, though, the door opened to admit the librarian in question.

"Good evening, everyone." The gray-haired Eugenie spoke with her usual stiff formality as she walked across the room toward them. "I'm sorry to be late." Eugenie wore a dark skirt, white blouse, and cardigan sweater. A pair of reading glasses hung from her neck by a chain. She was the poster child for librarians everywhere.

And then Camille noticed the smaller figure behind Eugenie. A teenager, and a trashy one at that. Black Goth eye makeup and nail polish and clothes that looked like they'd been fished from a Dumpster. All in all, your basic nightmare.

Eugenie stepped to the side and motioned for the teen to stand beside her. "Everyone, I'd like for you to meet Hannah. She's the newest addition to our group."

Camille felt her mouth drop open. She quickly closed it. Ruthie, however, was not as fast and stood slack-jawed for a long moment. The creases in

Esther's forehead grew more pronounced, and Merry sat frozen, knitting needles in midstitch.

The girl flushed and then scowled, her ghastly makeup and the classroom's fluorescent lighting accentuating the unpleasant expression. Eugenie alone appeared unperturbed by the sudden silence in the room. Of course, for a librarian silence was a natural habitat.

"Hannah, meet the Sweetgum Knit Lit Society." Eugenie took the child by the elbow and pulled her toward the table. "This is Merry McGavin." She paused meaningfully, and Camille watched in astonishment as Merry managed a nod and a garbled hello. "And this is Esther Jackson, and that's her sister Ruthie Allen standing behind her." Both women murmured greetings. "And this is Camille St. Clair."

"Hello, Hannah." Camille couldn't quite bring herself to say anything more. Why had Eugenie brought this girl to the group? From the silence of the other ladies, she knew they were wondering the same thing.

"Hannah would like to learn to knit," Eugenie said, motioning the girl to an empty chair. The teenager set a brown shopping bag with the familiar *Munden's Five-and-Dime* logo on the table.

"Well, learning to knit shouldn't take long," Merry said brightly, not looking at the girl.

"You could probably learn what you need to know tonight," Camille added, relieved. This Hannah wasn't a long-term addition then.

"Hannah, I'm rather thirsty. I suspect you are as well," Eugenie said to the girl. She reached into her pocketbook—Camille doubted Eugenie had ever carried something as current as a handbag—and withdrew some change. "Would you mind going down to the end of the hall for soft drinks?"

The girl looked around the room, then back at Eugenie. "Whatever." She held out her hand, and Eugenie poured the coins into Hannah's palm.

"Thank you, dear." Eugenie waited until Hannah had left the room, the door clicking shut behind her, before she addressed the group. "Actually," Eugenie said, "we're going to be changing the reading list for the next few months for Hannah's benefit."

"Why?" Merry said before Camille could ask the question herself. "We agreed on the list. I've already bought the books."

"Yes, well . . ." Eugenie was rifling through her own knitting bag, one of those stand-up affairs with a wooden frame. The bag sat beside her like an obedient dog. "I discovered that Hannah has never read the girlhood classics."

"Girlhood classics?" Camille echoed. What on earth was Eugenie talking about?

"I've made out a new schedule." Eugenie pulled a sheaf of papers from the knitting bag beside her and one by one passed them to the other members of the group.

"*Little Women*? *Pollyanna*?" Esther's frown was in

danger of becoming permanently affixed to her face. "Surely you're joking, Eugenie."

Lines of tension radiated from the corners of Eugenie's mouth. "I never joke."

Which was true, Camille thought with despair. She pictured the sullen girl again, her greasy hair and dangling skeleton-head earrings. Eugenie would never pull something like this as a prank.

"You want to change the whole list? I already picked out my yarn for the next six months," Camille protested. Each month, their knitting project was supposed to relate to the book selection. At the meeting they went around the circle and showed off their handiwork. Camille had planned six months of knitting with the most furry, glitzy, dazzling yarns available. Something with a little style. Some pizazz. Something you would never see in Sweetgum.

"Yes, well, we'll simply have to select different projects to go with the new list of books," Eugenie said with a sniff. "Next month's assignment will be Louisa May Alcott's *Little Women*." She pulled a second batch of papers from her bag. "I've taken the liberty of assigning a simple project so that Hannah will feel included. It only takes two skeins of worsted weight yarn. A nice wool would be best."

Camille snagged one of the papers from Merry's hand. *A Christmas Gift for Mr. March*, it said. Below was a beginner's pattern for a garter-stitch scarf. Who wanted to knit a boring wool scarf? That's all garter stitch was. Going through the same motions, over and over and over again. Just like Sweetgum.

And then Camille's cell phone rang. Or rather it began to play the latest Gwen Stefani hit in lieu of a ring tone. Suddenly all eyes were on her, not the new reading list, and the other women cast nervous glances at Eugenie. Camille scrambled for her bag and dug through it until she located her pink Razr.

"Sorry!" She glanced at the number on the backlit display and then leaped to her feet. "I'll be right back." She ignored Eugenie's disapproving frown as she slipped out the door and down the hall of the education wing, passing that awful Hannah, who was carrying two cans of Coke. The girl pointedly ignored her. Camille knew Eugenie would fume about her cell phone going off—she was such a pain about stuff like that—but she didn't care. What was Eugenie going to do? Kick her out of the group?

"Hello? Alex?" She pushed open the front door of the church and skipped down the steps.

"Hey, Camille. Am I interrupting something?" His voice, like his kiss, warmed and enticed her.

She leaned against one of the sweetgum trees that surrounded the building. "No. No, not a thing."

"Are you outside?" he asked.

Camille glanced around. "Um, yeah. I was just out for a walk."

"Out for a walk? You?" Alex made it sound as shocking as doing a pole dance in Sunday school class.

"Just getting some exercise."

29

"I guess there's not much else to do in Sweetgum."

"Not when you're not here."

He chuckled, and Camille drank in the sound. If only he were here, next to her, where she could smell the scent of his cologne and put her hand on his arm.

"I'll be back in town in a few days."

"Promise?" Her heart beat faster.

"I promise. By the middle of next week at the latest."

"And then?" The moment she asked the question, she wanted to take it back. She had learned early on that he was not a man to be pressured. He hated expectations.

"Then I'll take you out to dinner. We'll drive up to Nashville."

She was disappointed with his answer but knew better than to let him hear her feelings in her voice. Above her head the sweetgum trees screened out the dwindling September evening light.

"I'll be waiting." He liked it when she said stuff like that. He liked to know she was expecting him. Camille only wished he liked to show up as much as she liked to anticipate his arrival.

"Ciao." Alex made a noise into the phone that sounded like he was blowing a kiss.

"Ciao," Camille echoed.

And then the line went dead. Long before she was ready for it to do so. But at least he was coming back soon. And next time . . .

Well, next time maybe he'd tell her the one thing she needed to hear. Maybe when he came, he'd finally tell her that he was leaving his wife.

Three

Esther stared at her needles in despair. She would not cry. Not in front of Eugenie. Not in front of Merry. And certainly not in front of her sister.

She could feel Ruthie looking at her. With dogged determination, Esther jammed the point of the needle through what she hoped was a stitch. It should have been so simple. She'd been at it for months now but had yet to complete one of the assigned projects herself. None of the other women had problems like this. Even that wretched teenager was aggressively stitching away after a mere fifteen minutes of instruction from Eugenie.

"Mr. Rochester is, of course, the symbol of fallen and broken humanity," Eugenie said, guiding the book discussion as deftly—and dominantly—as she knitted. Eugenie hadn't waited for Camille to return before starting their meeting.

Esther hadn't finished the book—she abhorred the Brontës, all that unnecessary emotion—so she couldn't knit, nor could she contribute to the conversation. How to hide in plain sight? She had never been good at avoiding the spotlight. That was her sister's job. Ruthie, in her oversize sweatshirt and

Lycra pants. Esther could only hope she hadn't worn that getup to work today.

According to her husband, Frank, the potential new minister had dropped by the church to have a look around. *Please, Lord, let the night janitor have vacuumed the sanctuary.* Frank was the chair of the church board. He'd been working diligently to secure a new minister, but it wasn't easy to find an intelligent, accomplished pastor who wanted to live in a small town like Sweetgum. This new man, though, sounded promising. He was a bit too old—over sixty —but he'd grown up in nearby Columbia and had an interest in returning to his roots. At least that was what Frank had reported when she'd called him at his law office earlier. He had given her the update on the search for a minister, and she had told him when she'd booked his appointment with the cardiologist in Nashville.

"Esther, don't you agree?"

Her head popped up. Eugenie's dark brown eyes drilled right through her.

"I'm sorry, Eugenie. I was concentrating on my knitting." She slid the needles into her lap so no one could see the tangled mess. The harder she tried, the more the yarn slid off the needles. She tried to push the loops back on, but she wasn't sure which ones were the actual stitches.

"I asked whether you thought the story represented the eternal human dilemma of obedience to God versus the need for expression of our free will."

Esther clenched her teeth so her jaw wouldn't drop open. "I guess I hadn't thought of it that way," she said, head high and back straight. She never allowed her spine to touch the chair. Legs crossed at the ankles only, never at the knees. She wasn't the first lady of Sweetgum merely by default.

"Why does Mr. Rochester's first wife symbolize evil? After all, he was the one who locked her in the attic," Ruthie said, taking off on a tangent as she always did.

The teenager—what was her name? Hannah?—rolled her eyes but kept knitting away. Esther peered more closely at the girl's work. Her stitches were so tight they were probably waterproof. Esther glanced down at the loose, uneven mass in her lap. Her stitches should have been regular and firm. Where had she gone wrong? She glanced at Ruthie, whose needles flew as if they were motorized. How could someone so sloppy in appearance produce such marvelously even work?

With a sigh, Esther slid her knitting into her lap and picked up her book, pretending to look for a particular passage. She'd perpetrated this charade for months now. Amazing, really, how little people saw of what went on under their very noses. After the meeting, she'd hand off her project to the person she paid to complete them. And the members of the Knit Lit Society—even her own sister—still would not suspect. Fortunately for Esther, Camille came back into the room. Eugenie pursed her lips and carried on pontificating about Charlotte Brontë's use of imagery. Camille slid into the chair on Esther's left, but she offered no apology for the phone call or her disappearance. Esther thought highly of Camille's mother. Nancy St. Clair had worked hard as the owner of Maxine's Dress Shop until her illness had forced her to retire. She had always been able to order what Esther needed when she couldn't get to Nashville or Memphis or New York. But Nancy, unlike her daughter, knew that a small town like Sweetgum thrived on order. On people knowing their purpose. And their place.

As Esther turned to watch Merry effortlessly produce a cable knit baby blanket, she idly wondered if she should pack an overnight bag for tomorrow in case Frank had to have an emergency bypass operation. She would hate to be caught in Nashville without the essentials.

After thirty minutes, Eugenie gave up on the discussion. It was clear that Ruthie and Merry were the only ones who had actually finished the book, and she doubted whether Esther and Camille had even cracked the spine on their copies.

"So shall we display our shawls?" Eugenie asked. They would all have much more to say about their knitting than they ever did about their book selections.

"The silk turned out very well," Esther said, spreading the gorgeous shawl she'd created across the table. All the women made admiring noises, but Eugenie knew their unspoken thoughts almost as if she could read their minds. The yarn for the shawl must have cost in the high hundreds of dollars.

"I made a heavy wrap for Jane Eyre," Merry said, once Esther's work had been sufficiently praised. "When she flees Thornfield, I always feel like she's not warm enough." She withdrew the item from her bag and laid it on the table for the other women to see. The thick eggplant-colored wool formed a large triangle.

"Very nice," Eugenie said, reaching over to finger the piece. "Anyone else?"

Camille spread her work out on the table, a black angora concoction worked in a difficult lace stitch. While Eugenie could admire the intricacy of Camille's work, the shawl was hardly appropriate for a Victorian heroine. "Also very nice," she said though, keeping her judgments to herself. "Ruthie?"

"I'm in love with this soy silk." Ruthie spread out what she'd finished of the cherry red triangle. "I thought Jane could use a little something daring to attract Mr. Rochester's notice. Plus it's organic. They make it out of the by-products from processing tofu."

Eugenie paused before replying. "It's very . . . natural, isn't it?"

"You've got to be kidding."

Eugenie's head snapped up in surprise at Hannah's scornful tone. The teenager slapped her yarn and needles down on the table and leaned back in her chair, crossing her arms over her budding chest. "How lame can you be?"

Eugenie knew a challenge to authority when she saw one. Hannah was most unhappy about the punishment Eugenie had meted out. But learning to knit and reading a few decent books—instead of tearing pages out of them—seemed pretty light as far as sentences went.

The other women looked to Eugenie for her response to Hannah's challenge.

"Hannah, as long as you are a part of the Sweetgum Knit Lit Society, you will conduct yourself with dignity." She shot her a warning look.

The girl rolled her eyes but picked up her yarn and needles, heaved a sigh, and resumed stitching. Eugenie ignored the evil looks the teenager shot her way. Conversion took time, and today was only the first step in what would surely be a long and lively process with Hannah.

"Now," Eugenie said, "does anyone have any questions about next month's assignment?"

Having handled Hannah's rebellion easily, she turned her attention back to the group. She had no intention of letting the Sweetgum Knit Lit Society, the library, or anything else in her life get out of hand.

Ruthie did not want to read *Little Women*, of all things. One sister in this lifetime had been plenty, thank you very much. She couldn't imagine three others, and what's more, she certainly couldn't envision a world where all those sisters turned out to be supportive and caring. There was a reason girls like that only existed in books.

The members of the Knit Lit Society were scattering into the growing darkness as they called good night to one another. The streetlamps had come on, splashing pools of glowing amber along Spring Street. The air was heavy now with the promise of rain and the first hint of fall. She and Esther had studiously ignored one another as they passed through the church doors and went their separate ways. Merry, per usual, made sure to say a proper good night to everyone. Eugenie hustled her latest stray off toward the library, and Ruthie could only speculate about what sin the girl had committed that earned her the Knit Lit Society as penance. Camille had slipped into the darkness too, in that ethereal way she had, studying the display on her cell phone with a frown. Ruthie was the only one who didn't own a car, so she set off for home, her tote bag slung in its customary place over her shoulder. Her worn running shoes slapped against the cracks in the sidewalk where stray tree roots had crumpled the concrete.

In Sweetgum, Ruthie could walk home at night without being afraid. Her snug little clapboard house was only three blocks away, and how much trouble could she possibly encounter between the church and Ragland Street? She should remember to set the ferns out in the yard to catch the rain. They were

38

brown at the edges after a long, hot summer, but they weren't dead yet. It was too dark by now to deadhead the last of the spindly petunias in her front flower bed. They would have to wait until morning. Since she didn't have to be at work until nine o'clock, she had plenty of time to see to her plants and animals before heading off to the church.

Ruthie was sorry that Esther was upset about the luncheon, but if she tried to apologize, it would only make matters worse. Esther would never understand. She saw no reason why Ruthie couldn't pop over to the house on her lunch hour, mingle with the country club set, and then return to typing up the church bulletin for Sunday. They were as different as two sisters could be, and so were their lives. They'd made their choices long ago, and now both lived with the consequences.

If only Ruthie didn't feel quite so alone lying in the proverbial bed she'd made for herself.

She hadn't thought far enough ahead that morning to leave the porch light on for her late return, so her small house lay in darkness. Pecan trees shadowed the front lawn, the little picket fence's disrepair invisible in the gloom. She would have to paint it soon, but her back had been hurting lately and she didn't relish the task. Ruthie had never feared being alone when she was younger. Now she realized how increasingly vulnerable she was becoming. Age would accomplish what her sister's intimidation had never managed. Someday she would have to relinquish her independence and place her life in someone else's control.

Ruthie had one foot on the front porch step before she sensed his presence. The squeak of the porch swing chain confirmed the tingling along her spine. He must have parked around the corner and walked to her house. It had been several years since he'd shown up on her doorstep like this, a specter in the darkness.

"One of these days you're going to scare the life out of me," she said, although she didn't mean it. She didn't look at him.

"I wouldn't come unless it was important."

Ruthie paused, fingers on the handle of her storm door. "Does she know where you are?"

He rose from the porch swing and stepped toward her. "Of course not."

She hadn't expected him to answer any differently, although once upon a time she might have hoped he would. "You can't stay," she said.

"Just five minutes, Ruthie. Please, I need you."

Not enough, though. Never enough. "We made our choices. It's too late to change them now."

"I know. But I still need to talk to you. I need to get something off my chest."

The haunted quality to his words hung in the air, filling up the space between them. She'd loved him for more than thirty years. She certainly wasn't going to turn him away now.

"You'd better step inside before I turn the light on.

I don't want the neighbors to see you here." She opened the front door.

"It's not locked?" She could hear the disapproval in his voice.

"This is Sweetgum, Frank. Who's going to walk into my house that I don't know?"

She waved him inside and then followed behind, closing the door firmly against the night and the outside world.

And she wondered what Jo March would do if she were the one in love with her sister's husband.

Four

Merry knew she shouldn't resent the fact that Jeff was staying at the office after hours to catch up on his backlog of cases. He had always been a hard worker and a good provider. But these days she rarely saw him, and she missed him. Missed the way he came through the door and kissed her, loosened his tie, fixed himself a glass of iced tea and sat down on a bar stool at the kitchen island to tell her about his day and ask about hers.

Merry sighed and continued to chop the onion for the casserole, the hum of the refrigerator and the occasional rumble of the icemaker her only company. She'd been reading the opening chapters of *Little Women*—first in the carpool lane at school and then later curled up in her favorite reading chair while the kids did their homework—and now dinner was behind schedule. But she was determined to finish the book this month and set a good example for the Knit Lit Society's newest member. And so now she was chopping onion double time, trying not to take off the tip of a finger in the process.

The sharp sting of the onion brought tears to her eyes, but she continued on, the knife hitting the butcher block with even, satisfying *thwacks*. The kids would hate this recipe. She didn't know why she bothered.

A scarf. A wool scarf. She couldn't think of anything more boring for the month's knitting project. As for *Little Women*, well, she was determined to at least get an A for effort. She'd read the book once years ago and thrown it away in disgust, just as Jo March had thrown away her chance to marry her wealthy best friend Laurence and instead settled for an old, rumpled German professor and a life of poverty. As a mature adult, Merry still wasn't entirely convinced that the author had made her case for true love over deprivation and hardship. Fortunately for Merry, she hadn't been faced with that choice. Jeff had been her high school sweetheart, and he'd also been smart and ambitious enough to satisfy even Merry's demanding mother.

Courtney appeared in the kitchen doorway and slouched against the frame. "Mom, where did you put my library book?" Like most thirteen-year-olds, Courtney believed that every glitch in her existence was due to her mother's incompetence. Merry remembered feeling that way herself once upon a time, but these days she had newfound sympathy for her own mother.

"I haven't seen your book. It's not in your backpack?"

Courtney rolled her eyes and sighed as if Merry had just uttered the stupidest words ever to fall from the lips of a human being. "No, it's not in my backpack. Would I have asked you where it was if it was in my backpack?!"

She should discipline her daughter for sassing her. Merry knew that. Courtney's attitude had nose-dived in recent months, but Merry was so tired and worried and confused and she'd been letting Court-ney take advantage of her for so long that she didn't know if she had the strength to enforce the rules now.

"Are you sure you brought it home from school?"

"Mom, if you're not going to be helpful, just don't say anything, okay?" Courtney spun away in a twirl of long hair and self-righteousness.

Merry scooped up the onion and dumped it into the bowl with the chicken and rice mixture. She'd clipped the recipe out of *Southern Living* several months ago. The kids would certainly have preferred McDonald's or even frozen chicken nuggets, but every once in a while, she made herself prepare a home-cooked meal and forced her kids to eat it.

"Mom! Where's my uniform? Did you wash it?" Jake came tearing into the kitchen and then slid across the Brazilian slate floor in his stocking feet before coming to a stop with a bang against the custom white pine cabinets. "I've got a game tomorrow."

"I told you to put your uniform in the laundry room if it needed to be washed. Where did you see it last?"

Jake shrugged. "I dunno. You can find it faster than I can anyway."

Merry sniffed and wiped back onion tears. "All right. Let me get the casserole in the oven." Sometimes it was just easier to do it herself.

"Casserole?" He made a gagging sound and clutched his stomach before sinking to the floor in a paroxysm of mock agony. "Don't kill me before the game. My team needs me."

Merry laughed. Jake's sauciness didn't hold the edge of contempt that Courtney's did. He was honest to a fault but rarely judgmental. She wondered if the hormone poisoning that was puberty would turn Jake against her as it had Courtney.

By the time she'd searched the house for Jake's uniform, as well as Courtney's missing library book, she was exhausted. The early stages of pregnancy had always been like that for her. With the older two, she'd been proud of herself if she could stay awake to watch the six o'clock news. When Sarah came along, Courtney and Jake were in school and she'd napped during the day to compensate for her need for extra sleep. Now Sarah was in preschool, but only for a few hours in the morning. Naps were not in Merry's immediate future.

It was after seven o'clock before the casserole finished baking and Merry herded all three children to the table. Guilt pricked at her, sharp and needle-pointed. A better mother would have dinner on the table at six, not seven. A better mother would have served at least two green vegetables (that everyone would eat) along with the hateful casserole. A better mother's children would be devoted to her. That Marmee character in *Little Women* didn't know how good she had it. Sure, her family was poor, cold, and often hungry. But when Marmee came home, the girls vied with one another to plump her cushion, bring her tea, and rub her feet. Clearly Merry had missed the boat somewhere.

"Mom? Where's Dad?" Jake pushed the casserole around on his plate with a fork. He'd wolfed down two dinner rolls in seconds, but he wasn't in any hurry to tackle the main course. Merry sat at one end of the long dining room table, Courtney and Sarah on her left and Jake on her right. The chair opposite Merry's was conspicuously empty.

"He's got a big case right now, Jake, and he's trying to catch up on some things. I know it's hard for you not to have him here, but it won't be forever." That empty chair was the price they all paid for the large Colonial-style house that backed up to the ninth fairway of the Sweetgum Country Club.

"How much less than forever will it be?" Jake looked at her with the wide-eyed innocence of a nine-year-old boy.

Merry chuckled. "A lot less than forever, honey. And Dad will be at your game tomorrow. He promised."

Her reassurance mollified Jake, who decided to risk a bite of the casserole. Merry watched out of the corner of her eye as he placed the tiniest bite imaginable on his fork, transferred it to his tongue, and then swallowed as if ingesting poison.

"Did it kill you?" she teased.

Jake frowned. "I don't know. Depends on if it's fast-acting or not."

Fast-acting? Where had he learned that? Courtney had probably been letting him sneak into her room again to watch the forbidden *CSI: Crime Scene Investigation*.

The rattle and hum of the garage door opening caught everyone's attention.

"Daddy's home!" shrieked Sarah, her blond halo of curls flying as she leaped from the chair and raced out of the room.

"Wait! I get to talk to him first!" Jake yelled, streaking after her. Only Courtney remained at the table with Merry.

"Whatever," she said with a flip of her stick-straight hair over her shoulder. Her darker blond mane would have been as curly as Sarah's if she didn't ruthlessly attack it each morning with her two-hundred-dollar ceramic flat iron.

Merry took the opportunity to wolf down her meal. Rarely did she have the chance to eat her food while it was still warm. Jake and Sarah had Jeff pinned down in the kitchen, and she could hear the two children battling for their father's attention and Jeff's deep-voiced responses. He wasn't the lead bass in the church choir for nothing.

By the time Jeff appeared in the dining room doorway, Merry was finished with her meal. She hopped up, empty plate in hand. "I'll fix yours. Go ahead and sit down."

Jeff smiled his thanks, but he wasn't nearly as chatty with her as he'd been with the kids. He did greet Courtney, who shrugged and responded with a sullen, "Hey."

Merry's eyes met Jeff's across the dining room. They exchanged a mutual grimace at the trials of parenting a teenage girl, and then Merry hustled off to the kitchen for Jeff's dinner. When she returned, Courtney had disappeared, leaving her alone with her husband for the first time in the very long week since the indicator on the little test stick had turned pink.

"You're home earlier than I thought you'd be." She set the plate in front of him. "Do you want some iced tea?"

"That would be great."

Jeff was still as handsome as he'd been the day she married him almost fifteen years ago. How unfair that women battled the aging process with every weapon at their disposal while men simply evolved into a deeper degree of masculinity.

"Mom!" Courtney's shriek traveled down the stairs and into the dining room. "Make Sarah get out of my room!" A high-pitched preschooler wail immediately followed.

Jeff dropped his fork. "Is it too much to hope for a

little peace and quiet when I come home?" Weariness tinged his voice and his expression.

"Mo-om!" Courtney's second wail competed with her sister's sobs.

The dryer buzzed from the laundry room off the kitchen, signaling that Jake's uniform was clean.

"Mom, can you get that?" he called from the family room, where he was no doubt killing an alien life form on his PlayStation 3.

Merry felt the first tear slide down her cheek, quickly followed by the second. Jeff looked at her, and though he tried to hide it, she could see his frustration.

"I quit," she whispered, the words mixed with the salt of tears on her tongue.

"What?" Jeff stood and picked up his empty plate. "What did you say?"

"I quit." More forcefully this time, a bit bolder. The words felt good in her mouth, slipping from her lips.

Jeff did manage a faint smile. "Are you having a midlife crisis?"

Merry laughed, a sharp, short bark that sounded as caustic as she felt. "Hardly."

Now Jeff's brow knitted together in concern. He wasn't a bad man—just an overworked one.

"I'll do better," he said. Merry saw that look of panic edge into his eyes, the look men got when they thought their wife might leave them home alone with the kids.

"I don't know if I can do it anymore, Jeff." She hated that she cried when she was angry or upset. Why couldn't she just rant and rave like her father had? Maybe she should try throwing a few dishes or punching the back door just to see if it helped.

But she couldn't. Of course she couldn't. Not Merry McGavin. Wife of one of Sweetgum's prominent attorneys. One-time president of the PTA. Chair of the Christian education committee at church.

"I'll sort things out with the girls," Jeff said. "Why don't you go take a shower?"

What she really wanted to do was talk to him. Like they used to do, when they were dating. When they could spend hours in each other's company and never run out of conversation.

"Okay. Thanks." A shower would feel good, and she knew it was the best offer she was likely to get.

Jeff stepped toward her and bent down to kiss her forehead. "Sorry for being such a grouch."

"It's okay."

But it wasn't really. Because she was pregnant, and she was afraid to tell her husband. Because the little cracks in her relationship with Jeff—normal, ordinary flaws—now seemed to be multiplying and spreading. And because the life they had built together, which had once seemed to her as strong as an oak, had somehow become as fragile as a house of cards.

Five

Hannah squinted against the darkness to make out the last few words on the page. She ached from sitting on the bare ground outside her mom's bedroom window, but the porch light had burned out again, and only the soft glow from the opening above her head held back the night. She ignored the muffled noises coming from the room above. Gentry Carmichael would leave soon. He never stayed the night. And Hannah wasn't going back in that trailer until he was good and gone.

She frowned as she concentrated on the words that blurred in front of her tired eyes. Something about limes and that stupid Amy wanting money to treat her friends because they had all taken their turn buying limes for the other girls. Hannah rubbed her eyes with her thumb and forefinger, and they came away stained with flakes of dried mascara. She'd probably sleep through class again tomorrow, and Mrs. Windbag (otherwise known was Mrs. Winston) would yell at her.

Limes. What a stupid excuse for a treat. Hannah let out an exasperated sound and closed the book. If the porch light had been on, she would've brought out her yarn and needles from their hiding place underneath the sagging wooden steps. She'd been practicing a lot after school before her mother got home from work, and she thought it looked pretty good. Kind of thick and stiff for a scarf, not soft like she'd imagined, but at least you had something to show for your time when you were done. Not like hanging out at the cemetery with Kristen after school, waiting for the boys to show up with flasks and cigarettes. It hadn't been worth it, just for the chance to borrow Kristen's iPod.

Since her encounter with the librarian, instead of going to the cemetery after school to make out with some loser behind a headstone, she sat in the sun with the yarn and needles in her hands. She'd re-placed the brown paper sack from Munden's with a Ziploc bag she'd scored from the school kitchen. Sealed tight it kept the wet and the bugs away.

A door banged inside the trailer, and footsteps clomped toward the front door. Finally. Midnight had come and gone long ago. Quickly Hannah slid away from the pool of light and around the corner of the trailer into the darkness.

Gentry appeared on the porch, as thick around the middle as he was in the head. He'd never paid much attention to her until last summer when she got her chest. Since then he stared at her—no, at *them*—in a way that made her feel as if she needed a good scrubbing.

She clutched the book in one hand and held her

breath as he thumped down the steps and walked toward his pickup truck. He knew she was out there somewhere in the darkness, waiting for him to leave. Sometimes he came looking for her, and she had to run off into the woods for a good long while. Most of the time though, like tonight, he showed no sign of remembering that she existed. He cranked the truck's ancient engine, stoked the gas pedal a couple of times, and reversed out of the dirt driveway.

Those girls in *Little Women*, those sisters, they didn't have any idea what real life was like. Sure, their father was off fighting a war, but they had a mom who cared if they came home. They had a rich old aunt who would die someday and leave them a ton of money. And they had each other.

Hannah had nobody. She'd learned that lesson a long time ago, and she wasn't about to forget it.

With a sigh, she closed the book and hoisted herself off the ground. If she was lucky, her mom would already be snoring when she sneaked down the hall to her bedroom.

Eugenie turned off the lamp in the living room and walked to the front door to double-check the lock. She was usually in bed by now, but tonight she was restless. She'd long ago fixed her supper and cleaned up the kitchen. Her clothes for the next day were laid out neatly across the other twin bed in her room. Since tomorrow was Tuesday, she would eat lunch at the café rather than bring a sandwich from home. Yes, she'd done everything she always did on a weekday evening, but still her routine felt incomplete, as if she'd forgotten to change her pocketbook to match her shoes or neglected to have the mail stopped the one week a year she visited her college roommate in Louisville.

Incomplete. A nagging feeling that an important task had been left undone. She'd felt that more and more lately since the councilmen had begun to pressure her into retiring. But it wasn't Homer and his ilk, really, that caused the feeling. No, there was some other reason. One Eugenie couldn't put her finger on. And not being able to pin something down was an unusual condition for Eugenie.

Wiggles, her ginger cat, meowed in protest when she slid him from the center of the bed and sat down on the edge of the mattress. The *Sweetgum Courier* lay folded on her nightstand, waiting for her. She would doze off halfway through its pages, waking sometime in the wee hours of the morning to lay the paper aside, turn off the lamp, and truly succumb to slumber. No one who knew her would suspect that Eugenie Pierce couldn't face turning out the light and lying down in the darkness.

The yarn flowed through Camille's fingers like liquid silk. Her mother sat next to her, propped up in the hospital bed that dominated the tiny living room as she read aloud from *Little Women*. Camille might not have been too thrilled with Eugenie's abrupt change of the reading schedule, but Camille's mother was delighted. She'd actually giggled a little bit and said it was her favorite book as a girl.

"We're supposed to reform some terrible teenager by reading what Eugenie calls the 'girlhood classics,'" Camille had told her mother with a frown. "I don't know what Eugenie was thinking."

But Camille's disapproval hadn't dimmed her mother's enthusiasm. Usually Camille was the one to do the reading aloud, so at least her mother's interest in Eugenie's choice meant Camille could make headway on the scarf for next month's meeting. The stitch was fitting. Solid. Unchanging. Boring.

Alex hadn't called, not since the night of the last Knit Lit Society meeting. As each day passed, her anticipation turned to apprehension and then to anxiety. He'd promised to come back to Sweetgum, to take her out to dinner, but then he'd promised before and failed to deliver.

"Camille?" Her mother smiled at her over the top of the book. "Should I stop? I don't think you're enjoying *Little Women* as much as I am."

"No, keep going." She forced a smile to answer the one on her mother's face. "I just spaced out for a minute."

"If you're sure?" Her mother's smile, like Camille's feelings about Alex, turned anxious. "I know you must be bored." Her mother repeated the words that sliced through Camille like a knife. Of course she was bored. She was twenty-four years old, stuck in

Sweetgum with no end in sight, and torn every day between anger at her responsibility and fear of being released from it.

"No, Mama. I'm not bored. Please keep reading."

Amy March, the youngest sister, might have found her happy ending with the wealthy man of her dreams, but Camille knew that only happened in fiction. No one in real life was ever quite that blessed. Yet even that knowledge wasn't enough to kill the hope inside of her.

Esther could hear Frank churning like a buzz saw in his sleep in the bedroom next to hers. She closed her book and set it aside on the pristine white satin comforter. Normally she fell asleep before Frank so she wouldn't be bothered by his snoring. Even with a wall between them, she could hear the cacophony that told her he was lying on his back again without his special mask. Fine. If he wanted to kill himself, he could just keep on going the way he had been. Even the results of the angiogram hadn't been enough to scare him.

Frank had flat-out refused the open-heart surgery the cardiologist wanted to perform. They'd driven home from Nashville in complete silence. Even when they stopped at the mall to pick up his new suit that had been altered, they never spoke. Esther was furious, and Frank didn't care.

Esther's fingers tightened on the covers, and she pulled them up more firmly beneath her armpits. He was throwing his life away. She knew it. He knew it. And they both knew why he was doing it. Only Frank didn't know that she knew. He didn't know that she was well aware he'd paid a visit to her sister. Frank thought she was oblivious, but Esther Jackson was nobody's fool.

She snorted, an unladylike noise she would never have emitted in public. Her gaze fell to the copy of *Little Women* on the bed next to her. She'd always identified with the calm, sensible Meg March. Conduct yourself with dignity. Choose an appropriate man. Raise your children properly, and be an asset to your community. Esther had done all of those things, with one exception. One enormous, life-changing exception. And as a result, here she was sleeping alone, her son and grandchildren hundreds of miles away, her husband even farther, and she was left with only a book for company.

Merry rubbed her eyes, bleary from lack of sleep, and studied the list on the monogrammed pad in front of her. *Blankets, bottles, diapers, onesies, sleepers, crib sheets, burp cloths.* It continued on down the page, an exhaustive recital of all the items a modern-day mother needed before she could bring a child into the world. Merry had given all these things away when Sarah turned three, sure in the knowledge that she would never need them again. The only thing she'd kept was the crib. She'd stored it in the attic, thinking that one day she'd bring it down for her grandchildren to sleep in when they visited.

The clock on the mantel in the living room chimed midnight. Much as Merry hated the inevitable exhaustion tomorrow would bring, she was glad for these few moments to sit and absorb the peace of the house. Her family rested safely and comfortably upstairs. The kitchen was clean, the den picked up, the dining room table wiped clean of dinner debris. She'd made the kids' lunches for the next day, ready to grab in the mad dash out the door to school. The breakfast casserole was assembled and waiting in the fridge, a Tuesday tradition she followed as faithfully as she attended church.

Merry looked at the list again. She would have to hide it. She still wasn't ready to tell Jeff yet and see the discouragement on his face, and she certainly wasn't prepared to break the news to the kids. Courtney would be embarrassed. Jake would think it was weird. Sarah would feel displaced.

Merry sighed, ripped the page from the pad of paper, and folded it neatly. She found her purse on the sideboard and slipped the list into the zipper pocket where she kept her tampons (not much need of those for a while) and Tylenol. Yes, she could predict how everyone in the house would feel about her pregnancy. Everyone, that is, except for herself.

How would Marmee have felt if she'd turned up with child in the middle of *Little Women*? Probably she would have handled it with the same selfless aplomb with which she did everything else.

She wandered into the den, saw her knitting bag by her recliner, and settled in to work for a while. She wanted to finish the scarf for the next meeting so she could get back to work on the layette. She suspected that the next few months would pass as quickly—and as slowly—as any in her life ever had.

Ruthie knew she never should have let Frank in the house that night. With a sigh, she set her book on the end table next to her chair and picked up her knitting needles again. She'd been alternating between the two all evening, too restless to settle into one thing for any length of time. And yet still the time had passed, a great deal of it actually. It must be after midnight.

She didn't believe in television, didn't own one, but tonight she wouldn't have minded the company of a late-night talk show or infomercial. Anything to distract her from a lifetime of regrets.

Ruthie abandoned her favorite chair for the comforts of warm milk in her little kitchen. Ruthie never had trouble sleeping, but since Frank's last visit she'd been as restless as one of those lions at the zoo, wearing out a path in the dirt as it paced back and forth. Caged but not hopeless. Frustrated but not vanquished. An apt description of the last thirty years of her life.

She stirred the milk as it heated in the saucepan

and tried not to remember Frank's words of a few nights before.

"I want to leave Esther." He'd been sitting on the sofa, she in her favorite chair. No part of them but their souls ever touched.

"You can't do that." She'd forced herself to deny him even as her heart thumped so loudly in her chest that she thought she, not Frank, might have a "cardiac event," as folks their age were starting to call it.

"I can leave her. I'm going to." He looked like a petulant little boy, scowling. She could see the fear that had etched new lines around his eyes and at the corners of his mouth.

"I won't do that to my sister." At that point she had leaned over to retrieve her yarn and needles from her bag. Her hands needed something to occupy them so they wouldn't betray her feelings. She couldn't tremble and knit at the same time.

"Our son is grown." Frank shifted restlessly on the worn cushions. "Esther doesn't need me. Just my money. There's no reason for me to stay anymore."

Now Ruthie couldn't look at him. She'd longed to hear these words most of her adult life. True, she could count on her fingers the number of times she'd been alone with Frank since he married Esther. They'd never actually done anything improper. Sitting in her living room late that night had been the most scandalous encounter they'd ever had, but Ruthie knew their propriety didn't make them noble. Doing the right thing was just that—doing the right thing. You didn't get a gold watch or a plaque or the key to the city. No, you just got worn down, year by year, as you watched the person you loved live a life without you.

"We could be together, Ruthie." He had leaned forward when he said the words. "Maybe it's time."

Ruthie didn't know if Esther loved Frank, if her sister had ever truly loved him. But Frank had made a promise to Esther long ago, taken vows right there in the Sweetgum Christian Church, and Ruthie would never be the cause for the betrayal of that promise.

"No." One word, one simple word that cost her more than anything should ever cost a woman.

He stiffened. "Isn't that what you've always wanted? For us to be together?"

"No. I've never wanted that," she lied.

"My heart could be bad, Ruthie. I might not have much more time. Don't say no and then come to regret it."

He didn't understand, of course. He couldn't grasp that to say yes to him would cause her more regret than saying no.

She laid aside her knitting and stood up. "You'd better go."

Frank's face flushed a deep, meaty red. He rose from the couch. "I thought you loved me." He'd spun around at that point and left without saying good-bye. And the next day he called to tell her that he had blockages in three arteries but had refused to have bypass surgery. There was no point, he said. Maybe it was his time.

The milk was starting to stick. Ruthie pulled the pan from the burner and carefully poured it into her favorite ceramic mug, one she'd picked up at some long ago craft fair from some long-forgotten artisan.

Frank thought she'd sent him away because she was noble, and she'd let him believe that, had desperately wanted him to believe it. But the truth was she had turned him down because she was afraid. Afraid to face the truth. The truth that a man who really loved you didn't wait thirty years, until he thought he might die, before he came to claim you.

All the warm milk in the world couldn't help a woman sleep when she'd had that kind of realization.

Six

The leaves on the sweetgum trees outside the church had transformed from green to golden red during the month since the Knit Lit Society's last meeting. Merry hustled toward the doors of the church, late again. By the time she had climbed the stairs to the second floor and made it to the door of the Pairs and Spares Sunday school room, she was gasping for breath. She'd been in much better physical shape when she was pregnant with Sarah. The additional four years of wear and tear on her body wasn't helping matters.

The other ladies occupied almost all the seats around the table, leaving only one chair open—the one next to Hannah. Merry held back a sigh. The teenager didn't look any better than she had the month before. Merry couldn't help but compare Hannah's brittle mop of hair with Courtney's highlighted, straight-ironed tresses. Didn't the girl have anyone to help her with that kind of stuff? Merry vaguely remembered Hannah's mother. Tracy Simmons had been the kind of girl who hung out with the freaks and the heavy-metal headbangers. Merry had been the kind of girl who stayed after school to paint posters for the pep club or wash cars to raise money for student government.

"Sorry I'm late." She slid into the folding chair, thankful for the table that shielded her expanding midriff. She was only three months pregnant, but her body couldn't hold things in like it used to. Fortunately most of her "mommy" wardrobe consisted of stretchy exercise pants and loose tops.

Three months. The cutoff mark. No going back now, no matter how she might feel. The thought made her hands shake, so she clenched them to disguise the tremor.

"We were just getting started," Eugenie said with her usual cross between a smile and a frown that made Merry unsure about the woman's true feelings. "I asked everyone which of the March sisters they most identify with in the story."

Merry's frown was definite, not ambiguous like Eugenie's. She had read the book and completed the knitting project, but in truth, she couldn't identify with any of the sisters. No, she could only dream of being like the mother—pampered and adored by her offspring. No wonder the book was fiction.

"I always wanted to be Amy," Camille said, and with her fair skin and blond hair, it wasn't much of a stretch to see her as the mercurial, artistic youngest sister. "Everyone thought she was so spoiled, but in the end she did better for herself than any of them."

"Material wealth isn't everything," Ruthie said.

"The Bible says, 'Man does not live on bread alone,' and neither can a woman."

"No, no." Camille shook her head. "I didn't mean it like that. Sure, it didn't hurt that Laurie was wealthy and that when she married him, Amy didn't have to worry about being poor anymore. What I meant was that Amy found a way out. She wasn't trapped like the others were in their narrow little lives."

Merry wanted to reprimand Camille for such thoughts, but then she stopped herself. Of course the girl wanted to escape Sweetgum. She'd turned down a college scholarship to stay home and nurse her mother through a long, excruciating illness. Camille never said much about her mother at their meetings, but Merry could guess what their life was like. They lived off of what Camille could make running her mother's dress shop—not an easy proposition since the new Wal-Mart had come to town. Merry tried to shop at Maxine's when she could, and Camille was always helpful and appreciative. But of course it was no kind of life for a twenty-four-year-old girl with dreams of something far more glamorous than a small town in Tennessee.

"I don't think that oldest girl, Meg, was trapped at all," Esther said with a frown. No Chanel suit tonight, but she still looked impeccable in her Chico's separates. "Meg March was sensible. She knew her place and found the right husband for her. A young woman could certainly do much worse."

"I always liked Jo," Ruthie said, a far-off expression in her eyes. "She was determined to live her own life, not the one her bossy aunt wanted her to live."

"Very good," Eugenie said, nodding at all of them. "I picked this novel because the author shows us so many different kinds of heroines. All of the March sisters have something to teach us."

"Except the one that died," Hannah snorted. "The only thing I learned from her was to stay away from your mom when she's been visiting sick people."

Hannah's disdain sent Merry's blood pressure sky-rocketing. What was it with teenage girls these days?

"Did you read the book?" Merry said before she could stop herself. "Beth's death is the most touching part. She's their anchor, and when she dies . . ." She stopped, her throat too tight to continue. Oh for heaven's sake. How in the world could she get so worked up over a book group discussion? It was just this girl, sitting there next to her, disdaining everyone and everything.

"Why don't we show our scarves," Eugenie said, interrupting Merry before she could finish. "I'm interested to see what you all did in the spirit of *Little Women*."

Merry reached down for her bag, cheeks blazing. Thank goodness Eugenie had interrupted. Why in the world had she responded so strongly to the girl's bravado? It was nothing but adolescent posturing. Heaven knew Merry experienced enough of that at home every day.

"I know you said to use worsted," Ruthie said, spreading a beautiful camel-colored scarf out on the table, "but this alpaca just called to me when I saw it online." Like a lot of knitters in small towns, they often had to rely on Internet sites when it came to buying yarn.

"That's very nice, Ruthie," Merry said as she reached out to finger the scarf. The wool was soft and crimpy, a lustrous brown that felt natural, not scratchy and manufactured like less expensive yarn.

"I know it's kind of an unusual texture for a man's scarf," Ruthie said. Her eyes looked sad, and she eyed her knitting wistfully. "But maybe tucked inside an overcoat . . ."

Camille laid her scarf on the table in front of her. "I'm afraid mine's just plain dark gray." She smoothed it with her fingers. "Not very special, but practical." She glanced at Eugenie. "I hope the next project will have a little more flair." She, too, seemed wistful. Merry wondered if something was in the air, the way they were all moping and distracted.

"I chose gray as well," Eugenie said. Her scarf, like Camille's, was strictly utilitarian.

Merry spread hers on the table for the group to see. "I thought I'd give this to Jeff, so I picked the forest green. It'll look nice with his eyes." Although he'd probably never wear it. Winter rarely got cold enough in Sweetgum to require a wool scarf.

"I picked maroon." Esther's scarf was cashmere, Merry noticed.

"What about you, Hannah? Did you have time to finish your scarf?" Eugenie asked with far more patience than Merry would have shown.

The girl looked like she might throw up. Merry watched the teenager's face flush and then turn white as the color drained away. "I . . . I finished." She reached under the table and pulled out a Ziploc bag. The navy scarf was an attractive color, Merry thought, but as she watched Hannah unfold the piece, she bit her lip. What she saw was a classic beginner's mistake.

"Here." Hannah shoved the scarf across the table as if it were a water moccasin she'd found in Sweetgum Creek.

"Good for you, finishing it so quickly," Ruthie said, her soft gray eyes full of kindness. "That's excellent for your first project."

Hannah seemed unimpressed by the praise. Merry could tell without reaching over to touch the scarf that Hannah had knit it far too tightly. The biggest difficulty in learning to knit was getting the yarn tension just right. Too loose and you wound up with a lumpy mess. Too tight, like Hannah's scarf, and you might as well have made a steel wool pad.

"Very nice," Esther added without really looking at the piece. She was refolding her cashmere scarf in some tissue paper.

Hannah rolled her eyes. "Whatever."

"Hannah," Eugenie said in a warning tone.

"I mean thanks. I guess."

68

"What's bothering you, Hannah?" Eugenie asked, and Merry wished that she hadn't. The Knit Lit Society was her peaceful time, the one night a month when she could simply relax, enjoy some good conversation, and not think about anything but books and knitting.

Hannah scowled. "Nothing. I finished the stupid project, okay?"

"You don't seem very happy about it." Eugenie studied the girl over the top of her reading glasses.

The air in the room rippled with tension. Merry laid her needles in her lap, ready for the explosion that seemed sure to follow. She knew this pattern of teenage angst as well as any knitting stitch.

"Nothing's wrong." Hannah slumped back in her chair and crossed her arms over her budding chest.

"Your tension's too tight, honey," Ruthie said. She reached for Hannah's scarf and pulled it in front of her. "But that will come with practice. You just need to relax a little more when you're knitting."

"You never did tell us who you identified with in *Little Women*," Merry heard herself say, even as she told herself not to get involved. She didn't have the capacity to add any more people to the lengthy list of those she cared for and prayed for. Especially not now.

"The book was totally lame. So is this stupid knitting." Hannah hunched her shoulders like a vulture. Or a prisoner about to be beaten.

Eugenie shot Hannah a look that had wilted far

stronger people. Merry was grateful it wasn't directed at her. "Do I need to remind you of our agreement, Hannah?" Eugenie's eyes bored into the girl's. Beside her Merry could feel the tension vibrating off the teenager. Suddenly her irritation with Hannah turned to pity and then to compassion. As overwhelmed as Merry felt, she was an adult—with all the resources and privileges of a grownup at her disposal. Hannah was just a child and an unhappy one at that.

"What's next month's project?" Merry asked. "I'm going to Nashville soon and wanted to pick up my yarn." She was an expert at drawing attention away from conflict. Heaven knows she employed the technique at home on a frequent basis. Bait and switch. Conversational sleight of hand. Her middle name should be Houdini.

Eugenie's eyes brightened. "Excellent. I thought for *A Little Princess* we'd do another shawl. Now that Hannah's mastered a plain garter stitch, we should do a simple triangle so she can learn to increase." She paused, studying Merry with those piercing eyes, and Merry felt the first frisson of apprehension.

"I can pick up yarn for whoever needs it," Merry offered, but she could see from Eugenie's expression that she wasn't going to escape quite that easily. The librarian had a scheme in mind.

"I don't suppose you could take Hannah with you to Nashville?" Eugenie asked. "It would be very helpful for her to see one or two of the yarn stores there. Far more inspiring than the generic selection at Munden's."

Merry would rather eat ground glass, but she kept a smile on her face. "I can't imagine Hannah's mother would let her take off to Nashville with a complete stranger. But I'd be glad to bring her some yarn."

Eugenie was not to be denied, however. "I'm sure I can get Tracy to agree to the trip. When did you say you were going?"

Actually, she hadn't planned to go, not until she'd blurted out the words in hopes of avoiding conflict. "I'm not sure. I need to check the kids' sports sched-ules and see when Jeff can pick them up."

"I'm happy to take care of your flock if you need me," Ruthie offered with a smile. She baby-sat for the kids when Merry and Jeff had a rare night out or an even rarer weekend away. "My schedule's pretty flexible right now." Since the church was without a minister, Ruthie was often at loose ends, Merry knew.

"That would be great," Merry replied without meaning a word of it. Well, for heaven's sake, why not? Why not trap her pregnant self in a van for ninety minutes each way to and from Nashville with a teenage girl even more sullen and miserable than her own?

"I'll speak with Hannah's mother," Eugenie said, effectively silencing any protest the girl might have made. "You can pick her up early on a Saturday and be there when the stores open."

71

As neatly as that, Merry's trip to Nashville was tied up in a package and garnished with a bow. What Jeff would say about this development she couldn't even imagine. He would have to do the soccer run, make sure Courtney made it to cheerleading practice, and keep Sarah entertained. On the other hand, it had been awhile since he'd done any of those things. Maybe it was time he did.

"Okay. I'm sure Jeff can handle the kids, but thanks for the offer, Ruthie. I'll have him call you if he needs backup."

"Since that's settled, let's talk about the book some more," Eugenie said. Merry could feel Hannah shooting her some dirty looks, but she forced herself not to acknowledge them. She knew Eugenie was only trying to help this girl, but Merry was too tired and too stressed not to resent the librarian's well-meant interference. The Knit Lit Society was supposed to ease her stress, not contribute to it.

Seven

Just as Merry was always the last to arrive, Eugenie was the last to leave. She lingered in the room after the others had packed up their knitting and their novels, gathering up the stray bits of yarn and coffee cups that littered the table. Perhaps she should scold the rest of them for not cleaning up after themselves, but in truth Eugenie didn't mind. The scraps and cups were a sign of the health of the group, tangible evidence of their bonds, tenuous as they might be at times.

Eugenie had not been overly burdened in her life with personal bonds. Most people would never guess she hadn't been born or raised in Sweetgum, she seemed so much a part of the fabric of the town. She'd moved there from the nearby city of Columbia when she was twenty-five to become the head librarian of the Sweetgum Public Library. Forty years of overdue books, the demise of the Dewey decimal system, and working six days a week. Forty years of forming the minds and tastes of the reading public.

Forty years of loneliness held back by rigid determination.

Eugenie heard footsteps in the hall outside the

classroom. Napoleon, the church janitor, must be making his rounds prior to locking up. Eugenie appreciated his presence. She preferred not to be in the building alone. Generally she preferred not to be in a church at all, but Esther had arranged for the meeting space when they'd first started the society. Eugenie might have gainsaid a lot of people, but Esther Jackson wasn't one of them.

"Evening, Napoleon," Eugenie called out before she could see him. She dropped the knitting detritus in the trash can and turned toward the classroom door. Only the figure who appeared in the doorway wasn't the custodian at all.

Panic and shock slammed into her. The man framed by the doorway bore no resemblance to the pale, wizened Napoleon. No, this man was tall, a little older than Eugenie, and his face was frighteningly familiar even after all these years.

"Finishing up?" the man asked in polite tones, which meant he hadn't recognized her. Yet. But what on earth was he doing here in the Sweetgum Christian Church on a Friday night? Her blood thrummed in her ears as if her head might explode.

"Yes. Yes, we were just finishing up." She couldn't think of anything to say, could only parrot his words back to him. Her eyes were glued to his face, just as her feet seemed to be frozen to the floor.

The man stepped forward and extended his hand. "I'm Paul Carson. I'm here interviewing to be the new minister."

Eugenie's knees threatened to give way. She gripped the back of the nearest folding chair for support. Sixty-five-year-old women should never be shocked like this.

"Are you all right?" He stepped forward, which only made Eugenie's suddenly dry throat more of a desert.

"Hmm. Hmm. Yes." She drew a deep breath, released the chair, and straightened up. "Sorry. You startled me. I was expecting Napoleon."

"He left early. Something about his granddaughter's science project being due tomorrow and he was needed to help. I wanted to look around the building. He said just to make sure I turned out all the lights and that the door locked behind me on the way out. I apologize if I frightened you."

Eugenie forced herself to breath slowly, in and out, and relax her knees. He hadn't changed, not really, but evidently she'd changed so much that he failed to recognize her even when he was standing less than six feet away.

"You're the new pastor?" She knew she sounded inane, like a feeble-minded old person, but for all her legendary self-discipline, she couldn't make her tongue form the words easily.

"Possibly. My conversations seem to be going well with the search committee." Eugenie vaguely remembered that Esther's husband was chair of the group charged with calling a new minister.

"I didn't realize the church was so close to hiring

someone." She'd given up on religion years ago, right after he . . .

"You look familiar." His hair was white now, but not unattractive. No, not unattractive in the least. Behind the wire-framed glasses, his familiar blue eyes were as clear as they'd ever been. She'd forgotten how tall he was, how standing next to him always made her feel small but not in a good way. He'd been larger than life, and she . . . well, she'd been a silly young woman who knew nothing about anything.

"Familiar?" she croaked. How could he not recognize her? True, she had the wrinkles, liver spots, and graying hair of anyone her age, but had she changed so much as to be completely unrecognizable?

"Well, if you didn't know I was interviewing, then you're definitely not a parishioner. I may need to suggest that the congregation change their name to Grapevine Christian Church." He smiled. "I'm sorry. Speaking of names, I didn't catch yours."

Eugenie clamped her lips together because surely her mouth was opening and closing helplessly, like a fish out of water. "My name?"

His laugh hadn't changed any more than his eyes had. It burned through Eugenie like an open flame. "I really have startled you, haven't I?"

Eugenie had never panicked in her life, but at that moment, with her heart in her throat, anxiety gave wings to her feet.

"I'm sorry. I have to go." She swept up her knitting bag, wrestling the wooden legs together as she moved

76

past him, desperate to hide the tears stinging her eyes. It was only because she hadn't been prepared. Only because she hadn't known she would see him. Hadn't known to expect him. Who could possibly have expected to find him framed in the doorway of the Pairs and Spares Sunday school class?

"Well, good night then," he called after her, bemusement in his voice.

Thank heavens he didn't follow her. As she clambered down the stairs, she could hear him shutting the door to the classroom, and out of the corner of her eye she saw the hallway upstairs go dark. He must have flipped off the lights.

Running away like this would only make it worse. That thought rattled around in her head until her temples throbbed. He would find out who she was sooner or later if he became the pastor. In a town the size of Sweetgum, you couldn't avoid anyone—friend or foe—for very long. But even that thought failed to slow her steps. She would face down her demons later. After she'd had a chance to think. After she'd had a chance to rid herself of these unwanted emotions.

After she figured out why the only man she'd ever loved had to come back into her life when it was far, far too late.

Hannah kicked at the rocks along the side of the road, not an easy feat given the darkness of the October night. She wouldn't have accepted a ride home from Courtney McGavin's mom even if the woman had thought to offer. Not in her stupid minivan. Not to get a lecture about whatever moms like that lectured about. It was easier if your mom just hit you instead of giving off that disappointment and disapproval vibe.

Heroines. What a joke. These people had no idea what real life was like, tucked up in their Sunday school room in their nice little church. And then on top of everything Courtney's mom had criticized her knitting. Well, not criticized exactly. Hannah had to be fair about that. But Courtney's mom had made her feel like she'd done it all wrong.

Hannah was tired of feeling like everything she did was wrong.

She could see the lights of her mom's trailer ahead in the distance, but she couldn't tell if Gentry's truck was there. The darkness would hide her until she could get close enough to see. And if the truck was there, then she'd decide whether she could risk sneaking inside to her bedroom, where she could lock the door behind her. Not that a flimsy doorknob lock would stop a pig like Gentry, but it was better than nothing, and Hannah was tired of sleeping outside half the time.

A hundred yards farther down the road, she breathed a sigh of relief. No truck. She paused beside the front porch—a jumble of redwood decking that sagged dangerously—and stored her plastic bag of knitting in its hiding place. She kept the new book the librarian had given her pressed tightly under her arm, not wanting her mother to see the title if she was still awake. If her mom caught her reading *A Little Princess*, she'd never hear the end of it.

Who do think you are? The princess of the trailer park? That was her mother's favorite question after she'd had a few beers. No need to add fuel to that fire by letting her see the book.

Hannah had lots of practice opening the screen door without letting it squeak. The trick was to move slowly, not to rush. The flimsy wooden door behind it opened noiselessly, and Hannah shut both doors in turn with a soft *click*.

"Where the hell have you been?"

She jumped about a mile. "Jeez, Mom, you scared me." Her mother was sprawled on their Salvation Army couch smoking a cigarette. On the orange crate-turned-end table beside her, the ashtray overflowed with butts.

"It's after nine o'clock. You're grounded."

Hannah forced herself not to roll her eyes. Her mother was always grounding her, but she never enforced it. "I was just hanging out with Kristen and those guys. We lost track of the time."

Her mother snorted. "Yeah, right." She paused. "What's that under your arm?"

The hairs on the back of Hannah's neck stood up. "Nothing. Just a book for school."

"Let me see." Her mother stuck out a bony hand. The men and the drinking and the cigarette smoke made her look twenty years older than the other moms. Hannah was always relieved, at least partly, when her mother didn't show up for school music programs or the class picnic at the end of the year.

Her mother read the title of the book and snorted. "Baby stuff," she said, flipping the book back towards Hannah, who caught it in self-defense.

"It was assigned," Hannah said in the dead tones she'd learned to use with her mother. No hint of emotion whatsoever. Her mom would jump on any whiff of pleasure or pain and stamp it out. Her mother wanted her to be as numb as she was.

"You're still grounded."

"Okay."

She could feel her mom's eyes on her, but she didn't meet them. These kinds of nights were the worst of all, when her mom was spoiling for a fight. Finally, she sighed and waved her hand, cigarette trailing smoke, toward the back of the trailer.

"Go on. Get the hell out of here. Gentry might be here soon, and the sight of you just pisses him off."

"Yes ma'am." She walked away, not too slow and not too fast, swallowing the words she wanted to say. That if Gentry wasn't here by nine, he wasn't coming. That her mother was a fool to take up with a man like that. That someday Hannah would leave this trailer and never, ever come back.

She closed her bedroom door carefully behind her. No use trying to slip into the bathroom to brush her teeth and wash her face. If her mom heard her, it would only give her another excuse to yell at her. Or worse.

Hannah laid the book on the scarred dresser next to the bottle of hand lotion she'd gotten her mother for Christmas. She'd fished it out of the trash can the next day and kept it. She'd saved the money herself to buy it, and she wasn't about to let it go to waste just because her mother thought it wasn't expensive enough, said it smelled like crap.

Hannah pulled on the old T-shirt she slept in and turned out the light. Her bed was a mattress, no box spring, tucked into a corner of the room. She could get up at five, when her mother would be out like a light, and take a shower. Maybe even read some of the new book once the sun came up.

A Little Princess. What could a girl like the one on the cover of the book, a girl in a pink dress with long golden curls, possibly know about her life?

She drifted off to sleep thinking of Courtney McGavin's mom and what it would've been like to ride home in that minivan, glad that no one could see the tears sliding down her cheeks.

"You're going to Nashville with who?" Jeff sat on the edge of their king-size bed clipping his toenails. Merry hated it when he did that. He never picked up the results of his effort, just left them there on the expensive hardwood for her to sweep up. When they'd first been married, she hadn't minded picking up after him. Now she minded a lot.

81

"I'm going with that teenager Eugenie's brought into the Knit Lit Society. I really didn't have much choice in the matter once Eugenie got the idea in her head."

"And so I have to give up my golf day tomorrow for some random girl we don't even know?"

"Just this one Saturday. I'll be back by dinnertime. Maybe before."

He tossed the nail clippers onto his nightstand and rose up off the bed just enough to pull back the covers and climb in. "Some other week, Merry. I know you think golf is for fun, but I'm entertaining some potential clients."

"Jeff—"

"Next Saturday. Or maybe the one after that." He smiled. "I can help out. I just need more notice."

Merry sighed. She was disappointed, but she was also partly relieved. Now she had an excuse to put off the unwanted trip. "You don't have to push so hard, Jeff. We're doing well. I hate to see you work yourself this hard."

"Did you remember to get my dry cleaning?" he asked, changing the subject. "I need my gray Burberry suit for a meeting on Monday."

"It's in the closet."

"What about my shoes? Did you pick them up at the repair shop?"

"Done." In between two trips to the grocery store and a run to the post office. A fairly light day errand-wise, truth be told.

"Thanks, sweetie. You're great." He didn't move but puckered his lips, his signal for Merry to twist around and contort her body until she could lean over and give him a good night kiss. In another couple of months, she wouldn't be able to do that.

"'Night, Jeff."

Some nights, like tonight, she was particularly grateful for the dark because it hid the expression on her face when she kissed him. The one that said she'd rather not be kissing him at all. The one that gave away the secret she was still keeping from him. The one that said she was lonely, even though she'd gotten everything she thought she ever wanted.

Eight

Maxine's Dress Shop was wedged in between two larger storefronts on the downtown square, its more modern design setting it apart from the high Victorian facades of Sweetgum Savings Bank on one side and Hartzler's Insurance on the other. The crisp late October day demanded a sweater, and Esther had left her black cashmere cardigan hanging in the closet at home. To be honest, she had left it there on purpose so she would have a reason to be seen entering Maxine's. And she would definitely need a sweater at Letha Askew's house. The woman had suffered from one long, continuous hot flash for months now. Consequently she kept her thermostat somewhere in the subzero range.

Looking at her, an observer would never guess at Esther's distress over Frank's health problems. At least he hadn't dropped dead of a heart attack in the last month, but he was still stubbornly refusing to schedule the bypass surgery. For the first two weeks she'd nagged. Then she'd cajoled. She'd even asked her son, Alex, to speak to his father, but their rather desultory conversation led nowhere. Finally, she'd resorted to the icy silence that had ruled the house since.

The old-fashioned bell over the door to the shop rang to announce Esther's entrance.

"Esther. Good morning." Camille St. Clair rose from a stool behind the counter near the front. "How are you today?"

Esther would have preferred that Camille address her as Mrs. Jackson as Camille's mother had always done, but she supposed those days were gone. The informality of the Knit Lit Society meant that Camille was free to call her by her first name.

"I'm fine, thank you." She looked around the shop, attractively arranged she must admit, with its stylish mannequins and jewelry displays. "Do you have a plain black cardigan? I'd prefer cashmere, but cotton would do." Perhaps she should have returned Camille's greeting more warmly, but some sense of distinction needed to be preserved in Sweetgum.

Camille's smile didn't waver. "I have a wraparound in cashmere," she said, moving around the counter to stand near Esther. "Or a more traditional style in a cotton-silk blend."

"I need a size 2," Esther said. "Or perhaps a 0. Also I'm in a bit of a hurry." She glanced at her watch to emphasize her words.

"Of course. Follow me," Camille said as pleasant as could be, but Esther could tell from the way the girl's smile dimmed slightly that she'd gotten the message.

"Would you prefer to take them back to the dressing room to try on?" Camille asked. She plucked the sweaters from the freestanding racks as they moved through the shop.

"Here will be fine." Esther paused in front of the three-way mirror outside the dressing room door. Camille hung the sweaters on a nearby rack.

"That's a lovely dress," Camille said. "Is it Diane von Furstenberg?"

Esther was gratified that the girl knew enough to appreciate her designer original. "Yes. I bought it in New York last year." She smoothed the modern black-and-white print of the silk jersey and adjusted the tie at the waist.

Camille frowned. "I'm not sure either of these cardigans will do it justice." She slipped the plainer of the two sweaters from its hanger and held it out for Esther as if she were helping her on with her coat. "But since your dress is a wrap style too, this traditional cut might be better. Belting a sweater on top of that wrap dress might make you look thicker through the middle."

Esther bristled. "I just need something to keep me warm during bridge club," she snapped and slid one arm and then the other into the sweater. She quickly stepped away from Camille and moved toward the three-way mirror.

Hmm. Well, it would have to do, especially since Camille was right about the other style adding too much to her midsection.

"I'll take this one," she said with as much asperity as she could muster. "I'd like to wear it out of the store."

"Of course. I can cut the tags off for you."

Esther followed her to the counter and watched as Camille rang up the sale.

"I brought something for you," Esther said, reaching into her voluminous handbag and withdrawing a plastic sack. "The usual arrangement." She set the sack on the counter.

Camille looked at it, then at Esther. "Are you sure?"

Esther ignored her question and signed the credit card slip. She handed the paper and ballpoint pen back to the girl.

"Thank you." Esther stood still while Camille removed the tags. "You've been very helpful."

"You know, I'd be happy to help you with your knitting sometime if you'd like. With a little extra coaching, I'm sure you'd get the hang of it." She eyed Esther's dress approvingly once more. "I know a wonderful black silk yarn with prestrung beads. It would make an amazing shawl to go with that dress."

"Perhaps. I need to finish the project I'm working on right now first."

Camille gave her a funny look. "Well, I'm happy to help. Anytime."

"I'll keep your offer in mind," she said to Camille. "Thank you for your help." Gracious but distant. Kind but not familiar.

And if she felt a little wistful that she couldn't accept Camille's offer of assistance with her knitting, she neatly tucked the feeling away with all the others that she refused to acknowledge. Just as she had never acknowledged, in their entire encounter, that she was paying Camille to do her knitting for her.

Camille flipped open her cell phone when it rang, not bothering to say hello. "You'll never guess who was just in the store."

"Hello to you too." Alex's soft chuckle felt like one of the new cashmere pashminas against her skin. "And here I thought you were mooning around Sweetgum missing me."

Camille leaned one hip against the counter as she watched Esther walk toward her car, a low-slung forest green Jaguar. The cardigan looked pretty good with the Diane von Furstenberg dress if she did say so herself. For a brief moment, she imagined herself in that kind of dress, walking down a New York street with Alex. Someday.

"I do have a job, you know," she reminded him in a teasing tone. "As do you. What are you doing calling me during the day?" For once she was going to play it cool. Or at least a little more subtly. Last night she'd watched the season finale of a dating show where a man got to take his pick from a group of more than twenty beautiful women. As always, the bachelor in question had picked not only the prettiest girl, but also the one who had made him chase her instead of chasing him. When she had turned off the television, Camille vowed to learn from the mistakes of all those overeager, pushy young women who hadn't landed the man of their dreams.

"It's hard to do my job when all I can think about is you," he said.

Camille forced her knees not to buckle. Sure, it was a cliché. Corny even. But when Alex said something like that, she forgot to be on her guard. Forgot to play it cool.

"You still haven't guessed who was in the shop."

"I don't want to guess. I want to know if you'll come to Memphis this weekend."

Camille's throat went dry. "Really? You want me to come there?" She could picture him in his law office in an old building downtown that overlooked the Mississippi. Of course, she'd never actually been there, so her image was a jumble of what she'd seen in John Grisham movies and memories from her senior class trip, when they stayed at the Peabody Hotel.

"I have the whole weekend free. What do you say?"

Tears stung her eyes. At last. She'd been waiting for this invitation for such a long time. "Does this mean what I think it means?" She would have to find someone to stay with her mother. And find the money to pay that someone. But there was no way she was going to turn down this invitation now that he'd extended it.

"I'm finalizing the lease on an apartment. I'll call you back later in the week to figure out the details," he said.

"But you still didn't guess who was just in the store." She wasn't ready to say good-bye to him.

"Camille, I give up. I grew up in Sweetgum, and I know everybody. And I'm sure they all come into your store at some point."

"Yes, but this was a special somebody."

"Special? As in male special or female special?"

The note of jealousy in his voice sent a thrill through her body. "Female special." She almost laughed. "As in your mother."

She thought he would laugh too. Instead there was dead silence.

"Camille . . ." His voice held that familiar warning note.

"Don't worry. I didn't say anything."

"I'll tell her in my own time."

"I know."

He paused. "So what did she want?"

Camille didn't tell him the truth. Secrecy was part of what Esther was paying her for. "A cardigan. She left hers at home, and I guess she decided she'd rather buy a new one than run home to get the one she forgot."

He sighed. "Sounds like Mom all right."

"She was really nice to me."

"Camille . . ." The warning note again.

"Honestly, Alex, I'm hardly likely to rock her world when she comes into the store to buy a sweater." That sounded good. Especially that little note of sophistication she'd managed to inject into her voice.

"Oops. Gotta go. My next client's here." His voice was brusque again. "Call you later. Ciao."

"Ciao," Camille said brightly, but his scolding had made a little of the glow fade from the day. Still, he'd invited her for the weekend. He was getting an apartment. That had to mean something.

She clicked the button on her phone to end the call and tapped the pink Razr against her chin. Well, at least she had a whole store full of clothes to choose from. And if she was very careful and didn't stain or tear anything, they could go right back on the rack on Monday morning. Customers weren't the only ones adept at the old trick of wearing something and then returning it.

Nine

In the days since the new pastor had arrived in town, Eugenie had avoided the Sweetgum Christian Church like the plague. Of course, since she only went to the church on the one night a month that the Knit Lit Society met, the task wasn't that difficult. The problem, of course, was that the new pastor was bound to venture out of the church sooner or later, and Eugenie could hardly stay holed up in her office in the library simply to avoid an encounter with her past.

So other than avoiding the church, she was determined to stick to her normal routine. After all, no one in Sweetgum knew that there was any connection at all between her and the Reverend Paul Carson. And there was no reason anyone should ever know. As long as matters stayed that way, everything would be just fine.

Except that he'd said she looked familiar. Right before she'd fled as if he were an ax murderer.

So a little before eleven o'clock in the morning, Eugenie walked down the library steps with firmness of purpose, determined not to show any fear or hesitation. This library, this town—they were hers. She would not let his presence take that away from her, not when she'd sacrificed so much to have them in the first place. Not after all these years.

The bright October day was the best kind of Indian summer, warm but not hot and with no humidity to cling to skin or scalp. Eugenie quickly walked the two blocks to Tallulah's Café on the town square. Her only concession to the tension vibrating through her body was the white-knuckled fingers clutching her pocketbook. She had dressed as she did every day—dark skirt, crisp blouse, cardigan. When she crossed Spring Street, she saw Esther driving past, on her way to her bridge club no doubt. She returned Esther's cheerful wave. Once, long ago, the ladies had asked if Eugenie would care to join their group. It hadn't occurred to any of them that she could hardly skip out of the library for three hours every Tuesday. And of course they would never dream of meeting in the evenings when they were home with their husbands and, once upon a time, their children. Bridge club types like Esther had no understanding, really, of what Eugenie's life was like.

Had been like, she corrected herself. Because if Homer and the rest of his cronies had their way and she was forced to retire, everything would change. And she doubted very much it would be for the better for anyone, least of all for her.

Tallulah's Café occupied a corner storefront on the west side of the town square. The square itself, a hodgepodge of buildings of every shape and size, was dominated by the imposing Victorian courthouse in its center, which had been built well before the ravages of the Civil War wracked the town. The café had been serving up fried chicken livers and icebox pie since Eugenie arrived in Sweetgum forty years before. Over the last few years, it had become her regular Tuesday lunch place.

"Morning, Eugenie," Tallulah greeted her when she entered the café. Tallulah Browning was older even than Eugenie, her tanned face lined with wrinkles but wreathed in a smile. No one was forcing Tallulah to retire or telling her that her time had passed. No, those same men who were putting so much pressure on Eugenie, saying she was too old for her job, well, they would squawk like the dickens if anyone suggested Tallulah should hang up her apron.

"Good morning, Tallulah. How are things today?"

"Busy enough to run me ragged but not busy enough to make me rich," she said with a chuckle. "Your table's waiting for you."

"Thank you." Eugenie nodded her gratitude and slid into her usual two-top by the café's large plate glass window. A glass of unsweetened iced tea sat waiting. Tallulah followed her to the table and hovered while Eugenie settled into her chair and carefully unrolled her silverware from its paper napkin.

"The usual, Eugenie? Or do you want to live a little? The special's chicken-fried steak." Tallulah's teasing grin held no malice, and so Eugenie accepted her good-natured ribbing with a smile of her own.

"Just the fruit plate, please."

"All right. If you're sure."

Suddenly Eugenie didn't know if she was sure. For years now she'd been coming to the café every Tuesday and ordering the same lunch—two peach halves and a large scoop of cottage cheese accompanied by a packet of saltine crackers. The fruit plate was by far the healthiest thing on Tallulah's menu, and Eugenie had always prided herself on how well she'd maintained her figure. What's more, since she never gained weight, she never had to worry about buying new clothes every season. Her serviceable skirts and blouses could last for years, a fact that suited her natural frugality.

But now, sitting in the window of Tallulah's with one nervous eye on the square searching for any sign of Paul Carson, Eugenie needed more sustenance—and comfort—than canned fruit and cheese curds could provide.

"Wait." The word fell from her lips before she could talk herself out of it. She looked into Tallulah's kind eyes, blue as robin's eggs. "Maybe I will have the special."

Tallulah was nice enough not to look surprised. "Sure thing, honey. You want your mashed potatoes with or without gravy?"

Why not go whole hog? "Gravy. And some fried okra if you have it." Eugenie couldn't believe what she was saying.

"Coming right up." Tallulah's smile was even wider than usual. Eugenie forced herself to turn her attention back to arranging her silverware on the Formica tabletop. And that was when she heard the familiar baritone voice at the entrance to the café calling out a greeting to the owner.

"Good morning to you too, preacher," she heard Tallulah answer. Eugenie willed herself not to look over her shoulder. Instead she fixed her gaze on the marquee of the art deco movie theater kitty-cornered from the café. She could hardly make sense of what the marquee advertised—something about a new animated children's movie. But as hard as she stared, she couldn't distract herself enough to keep from overhearing the conversation at the door.

"Sit anywhere you like," Tallulah said. Eugenie felt the moment Paul's eyes landed on her.

"Anywhere?" Since the café was empty at this early hour except for Eugenie, he had his choice of tables, booths, or counter seats. She wasn't surprised, though, when she heard his footsteps walking toward her. Didn't all preachers instinctively know how to work a room?

"Morning, ma'am." He appeared at her side and extended his right hand. "We never finished our introductions that night at the church. I'm Paul Carson, in case you don't remember."

Her eyes rose the long, long way up his neatly pressed button-down shirt to rest on his never-forgotten face. She put her own hand out and felt his palm press against hers, his fingers curled around the side of her hand.

"Hello, Paul." She didn't say her name. She couldn't. Her tongue was as thick as a compendium of Shakespeare's plays. The warmth of his hand holding hers sapped the remaining good sense out of her brain.

"Eugenie." His eyes lit with recognition. He didn't so much say her name as breathe it. His face widened in a look of wonder and then one of understanding. "Of course."

"Of course?" she asked, forcing a small smile to her lips. "You were expecting to find me at Tallulah's?" Her wry tone covered the panic that flooded her chest. Every instinct told her to do exactly what she'd done the last time she saw him—flee for her life. Or her sanity. Or both. Anxiety had been banished from her existence for more than forty years. Eugenie refused to entertain, much less tolerate, such a useless state of emotion. But now it was as if every fear she'd ever denied or banished had come flooding back and threatened to swamp her.

"May I?" Paul nodded toward the chair opposite hers. He was still holding her hand, and out of the corner of her eye Eugenie could see Tallulah watching them in fascination.

"Yes," she said, opting for the lesser of two evils. Paul Carson sitting across a table from her had to be far less threatening than Paul Carson standing there holding her hand again after all these years.

"I can't believe it." He sank into the chair and kept his eyes on her face. She could feel the flush rising in her cheeks. She who never blushed. Ever. She wouldn't allow herself to. But now she could do nothing to stop the flood of color or the dizzy feeling that threatened to tip her out of her chair onto the black-and-white tile floor of the café.

He continued to stare at her. She reached for her iced tea and took a sip to calm her nerves. It would take something far stronger than tea to accomplish that task.

"You live in Sweetgum?" he asked, and then he waved a hand as if to dismiss the question. "Sorry. That's obvious. Of course you do. I just can't believe it, after all these years."

"It has been a long time." She kept her words light, refusing to let him see the pain his presence caused. "I'm surprised you remembered me." She didn't mean the self-deprecating words but said them for her own protection.

He frowned. "Remember you? Eugenie, I've never for—"

At that moment, Tallulah walked up to the table with another glass of iced tea in hand. "Here you go, preacher. What can I get you for lunch today?"

"Grilled cheese would be fine, Tallulah. And maybe some onion rings?"

"Sure thing." She turned to Eugenie. "Shall I wait and bring your food out with the preacher's?"

In her wildest imaginings, Eugenie never would have envisioned sitting down to lunch at Tallulah's Café with Paul Carson after forty years of separation.

Or sitting down with Paul Carson *anytime,* for that matter. She'd so neatly and carefully packed away her memories and her feelings. Now they were spilling out of her like a waterfall, and she had no idea how to contain them again.

Before she could answer Tallulah, Paul responded. "The same time would be great. Thanks. Eugenie and I have a lot to talk about."

Tallulah's eyebrows arched like the beams in the church sanctuary, but she simply nodded. "Five minutes or so. Shouldn't be too long." And then she walked away, leaving Eugenie at a loss for words.

"How long have you lived in Sweetgum?" Paul asked. He reached for a packet of sugar, ripped it open, and poured it in his tea.

"Over forty years now," she answered quietly. She was torn between looking into his eyes and avoiding his gaze. "I'm the head librarian." She stopped. "That sounds more important than it is, since the only other staff are two part-time ladies who help me shelve the books and a janitor who splits his days between the library and the courthouse."

Paul smiled. "Knowing you, I expect it's the best-run library in Tennessee. An impeccable collection and nary an overdue book in sight."

Eugenie stopped herself from wincing at the accuracy of his statement. He hadn't meant any insult, she was sure, but somehow his words stung.

"I do my best. It's been a good job."

"Been? You're retired?"

"Not yet, although I'm being pushed in that direction."

Paul chuckled. "I'd like to see the man who's brave enough to try to force your hand." And then his smiled faded. "I'm sorry, Eugenie. I didn't mean—"

"It's okay. I know you didn't."

The whole episode was surreal. Paul. The café. The decades of separation that lay between them on the chipped top of the well-worn table. Eugenie felt like one of those clocks in the Salvador Dali painting, as if she, too, might slide out of her chair and onto the floor. The idea held a certain appeal.

"Is there anyone—" Paul stopped. "I mean—"

"I never married." She looked at him now, bracing herself for the pity she would see in his eyes. That was the worst part, really, of seeing him again. Knowing that he of all people would see the empty spaces around the shape of her life. "Did you? Marry, I mean?" For the first time, she let her gaze drop to his left hand, where it rested on the table. There was no ring on his finger, but she could see the outline where one had been. Her stomach twisted, and she knew she would never be able to choke down even one bite of her chicken-fried steak.

"Yes. After seminary. Helen and I were married for more than thirty years."

"Were?"

"She died two years ago."

"And that's why you're in Sweetgum?"

He laughed, but the sound held no joy. With a sigh

he leaned back in his chair. "You aren't the only one who knows what it's like to be pushed out the door."

"I can't imagine a church asking you to leave." She might have questioned his devotion to her but not to God.

"Really?" He reached for his glass and took a long drink. "Apparently some parishioners prefer that their preacher not engage in anything messy, like a wife fighting a prolonged battle with cancer." He stopped, set the glass down, and took a deep breath. When he looked up again, Eugenie's breath froze in her chest. Rarely had she had the occasion to see that kind of pain in another person's eyes.

"Paul." Instinctively, she reached out to take his hand, but she saw movement out of the corner of her eye and realized Tallulah was only steps away with their plates of food in hand.

"I'm sorry, Eugenie. Didn't mean to be maudlin," he said.

Tallulah slid their plates in front of them. "Here ya go, folks." There was noise and bustle from the doorway as more customers arrived. "Enjoy." And then she was gone, leaving Eugenie at a loss as to how to continue.

What did a woman say to the love of her life when he turned up again after a forty-year absence?

"Pass the salt, please," was all she could think of.

She'd known it would be difficult seeing him again. She just hadn't realized how fresh that long-buried pain would feel now at its resurrection.

Ten

Ruthie stopped to rub her eyes after staring for so long at the computer screen. Sometimes she longed for the old days when she typed up the church newsletter and worship bulletin on an IBM Selectric. True, it hadn't been nearly as flexible as a computer, but a typewriter also wasn't as demanding. Back then all she'd needed to know was how to type and how to do it accurately. Now she was faced with a plethora of choices and decisions. Word processing programs. Publishing programs. Design templates. Uploading the newsletter to the church's Web site. At the end of a long day like today, it made her feel as if her eyes might roll back in her head.

The new preacher had already left. True, he didn't keep overly long office hours, but Ruthie didn't mind. He'd said she could leave as well when her work was done. In his opinion, that's why God made voice mail.

Ruthie heartily agreed.

But Mondays were her long days because the newsletter had to be ready to copy first thing Tuesday morning. The Folding Fiends, as the group of elderly volunteers called themselves, would arrive around nine o'clock tomorrow ready to get to work. By eleven, they would have folded, sealed, and sorted all four hundred newsletters, and Ruthie would take them to the post office on the way to lunch.

No one had experienced true pressure until they'd been under a deadline for the Folding Fiends.

Ruthie's office had two windows—one to the outside and another that was really a glass partition between the church offices and the foyer. Dusk was falling earlier each day. In another hour it would be dark. Ruthie sighed and stretched, arching her back before settling back in to finish the last page of the newsletter. She was typing in the latest additions to the prayer concerns list when she heard the outside door open.

She looked up and saw Esther walking into the church foyer. Ruthie suppressed a sound that vacillated between a sigh and a groan. Why now? Esther had a knack for coming to call at the exact moment Ruthie needed to focus all her attention and energy on something else.

Esther opened the swinging glass door and entered the office area. "Afternoon, Ruthie."

"Hello, Esther." They never called each other "sis" or any easy nickname. No, for as long as she could remember, they'd used their first names and first names only. "What brings you here today?" Normally Esther only came to the church on Sundays for worship or when she had a bee in her bonnet about some church matter. "I'm afraid Rev. Carson has left for the day."

"I'm here to see you, Ruthie." She glanced around. "May I sit down for a minute?"

"Sure." Ruthie got up and went around the desk to pull a chair over from the little sitting area outside the pastor's study. She never kept chairs in front of her desk because she didn't want to give church members a comfortable spot to linger. People liked to talk to the church secretary, and she had difficulty enough managing her time when they had to stand. Imagine how long they'd stay if they got comfortable in one of those chairs.

Esther didn't sit in the chair so much as perch on the edge of it. Ruthie slid behind her desk again. "What's on your mind?"

Esther pursed her La Prairie–coated lips. "I need your help."

Finally. Relief ran through her. She'd been wondering when her sister would come clean about her inability to knit, and watching her subterfuge at the Knit Lit Society meetings had been excruciating. Ruthie often wondered who her sister was paying to complete the projects for her.

"I'd be happy to help you," Ruthie said.

"You don't know what I'm asking yet." Esther's lips pursed more tightly.

"It's not about your knitting?" The moment she'd said the words Ruthie saw that she'd offended her sister.

"My knitting? Why would I need help with that?"

"It just seemed as if . . ." Her voice trailed off.

Few people dared to point out any shortcomings to Esther. The last one who had was the former pastor—emphasis on the word *former.*

"Then what do you need my help with?" *Please, Lord, don't let it be another luncheon.* She'd spent hours crafting the centerpieces for the last one she hadn't attended. Of course she would help if her sister asked, but—

Esther sniffed. "Rev. Carson doesn't keep very long hours, does he?"

"I believe he mentioned stopping by the nursing home to visit Gladys Pippen." That quieted her sister for a moment.

"So we can talk then? Privately?"

Ruthie cast a nervous eye at the screen of her computer monitor and then looked at the clock. Esther couldn't have picked a worse time if she'd tried.

"It's about Frank," Esther said. "I need your help with him."

Ruthie kept her expression carefully bland. Esther had told her about his cardiology appointment, but she knew more than her sister had told her. Far more, obviously.

"What's the matter?"

"You know he's refused the bypass surgery." At Ruthie's nod, she continued. "I need your help to convince him to change his mind."

Ruthie picked up a paper clip from the desktop and twisted it between her fingers. "I don't know how I could persuade him if you can't." She'd spent half her lifetime engaging in this kind of duplicity. No wonder she'd gotten so good at it.

Esther set her designer handbag on the floor and then laid her hands, palm up, in her lap in an expression of supplication. Ruthie couldn't tell if the gesture was intentional or accidental.

"Ruthie, you can change his mind." Esther was looking at her with an uncomfortable degree of intensity. "I know that you can."

What could she say in response to that? Ruthie sat, twisting the paper clip, while the silence grew longer and deeper. Her lack of response was an indictment, but at that moment she couldn't bring herself to mouth any of the false platitudes that had been her life's work when it came to her sister. She suddenly wished for her knitting needles instead of the paper clip she was mangling between her fingers. Their comforting feel, the soothing repetitive motion of stitching, would settle her, guide her.

"Esther, if Frank doesn't want to have the surgery, I doubt there's anything any of us can do to talk him into it."

"I wouldn't have come here if I wasn't sure." Her sister's hands now flexed with anxiety, but Ruthie doubted she was wishing for a pair of knitting needles. Unless, of course, she wanted to stab Ruthie through the heart with one of them.

"Have you asked Alex to talk to him?"

"He said to leave Frank alone because he'd always done as he pleased anyway."

Which wasn't true. Ruthie of all people knew just how false that statement was.

"Then I don't think there's any more you can do."

Esther, to her credit, didn't waver. "Of course there's not. But there's something you don't know, Ruthie. Something that makes a difference."

By now the paper clip held no resemblance whatsoever to any form of office supply. "Esther—"

"Don't." She held up an impeccably manicured hand as if she were a school crossing guard stopping traffic. Then she lowered her hand, but this time her fingers were clenched into a fist. "I need Frank to live," Esther said. Though the statement was obvious, Ruthie could hear the desperation threaded through her sister's words. "We haven't . . . That is, we've always had numerous expenses. The house. Alex's college. And we have a certain standing in the community to maintain."

A cold tremor worked its way up Ruthie's spine. "Are you saying you're in financial trouble?"

"No, of course not," Esther snapped. "However, if Frank's income were suddenly to be lost . . ."

Even after all these years, the depth of her sister's mercenary tendencies could still surprise her. "This is about money?"

"This is about my life!" Esther almost came out of her chair. "Everything I've ever been. Ever done. Of course it's not just about the money. I want my husband to live." She paused, and then the color drained from her face. "Contrary to what you've

107

always thought, I do love him, Ruthie."

Unbidden, the book they'd been reading for the Knit Lit Society came to mind, and Ruthie thought of young Sara Crewe, the little princess of the book's title. She'd borne her demotion from an indulged child of a wealthy man to a servant in the school where she'd been the star pupil with the courage and grace of a classical heroine. Esther, however, was not made of the same stuff as the fictional Sara Crewe. Not when it came to the thing that mattered to her the most—the appearance of perfection.

"What do you want me to do?" Ruthie asked.

"Has he talked to you about this?"

Ruthie's hesitation spoke volumes. Esther pursed her lips. "I thought as much. What did he say?"

Ruthie had been dreading this very conversation for decades, and she had certainly never expected to have it at four o'clock on a Monday afternoon sitting in the church office. She'd imagined different scenarios, of course, most of which involved Frank declaring his love for her and informing her of his decision to leave her sister. But when it had actually happened that night at her house—well, reality was a very different thing from one's imaginings.

"He's just upset. He'll see sense soon," Ruthie said. "I'm sure of it."

"But what did he say to you?"

Ruthie knew now why she never should have let Frank into the house that night. "Whatever he said doesn't make any difference. He's your husband,

Esther. If his mind is to be changed, you'll have to do it."

"Is he going to leave me?" Suddenly, Esther looked every one of her fifty-plus years, something she never, ever did.

"No. He's not going to leave you."

"Because he wants to stay or because you wouldn't give him a reason to?"

The accuracy of her sister's question chilled Ruthie to the bone. "Esther . . ."

"You have to tell me." She leaned forward in the chair, and Ruthie thought she might slip off, her balance was so precarious. "I have a right to know."

All those years, Ruthie thought. Days and weeks and months of living one life while dreaming of another. Guarded words and furtive glances. Loving her nephew as if he were her own, because under different circumstances he might indeed have been hers. All of that was going to end right here in the church office on an ordinary day.

"He said that he'd have the surgery if we could be together," Ruthie said finally.

Her words hung in the air, as fragile and as sharp as glass. Ruthie saw understanding and then acceptance fill her sister's eyes, and it was the most painful sight she'd ever seen. In some ways even more painful than looking at herself in the mirror every day. Because she'd known all this time that she'd been wrong to stay in Sweetgum. She should have left long ago. It would have been the brave thing to

109

do. The Christian thing to do, for that matter. But she'd stayed and suffered and secretly hoped that someday, somehow, this very thing would happen. Even though she'd known that a happy ending for her was no different from a tragic one. The desires of her heart could only come at the price of her sister's broken one.

"You have to go to him," Esther said with a matter-of-fact tone that brooked no argument. "Tell him anything he needs to hear that will get him to agree to the surgery."

"Esther—"

"No." The crossing guard hand again. "You owe me this, Ruthie."

"I owe you this?" A little flame of anger kindled in her chest. "How in the world can you think that?"

"What else am I supposed to think? I've known every day for more than thirty years that my sister is in love with my husband. I've lived with that. Pretended that it didn't matter. Overlooked it with determination."

"And loving Frank puts me in your debt *how* exactly?" Ruthie stood up, and the secretary's chair that had molded to her body over the years rolled to the edge of the protective plastic mat beneath it.

Esther, too, rose to her feet. "It's not your love for Frank that puts you in my debt," she said. "It's his love for you."

"How in the world did you come to that conclusion?" Ruthie moved around her desk to stand a few feet from her sister. "I've never heard anything more ridiculous in my life."

"Because you never told him no, Ruthie. You never did me the honor of killing his hope. Every family dinner, every Christmas, every birthday party for Alex. There you were. A living reminder that his life might be there in our marriage, but his heart wasn't."

"Why didn't you say anything?" Ruthie couldn't believe she needed to defend herself. She had been the one who lost the most. No husband. No children.

Esther scooped up her handbag from the floor and flung it on her shoulder. "It's time, Ruthie. Time to stop all of this pretending. It's not a matter of sibling rivalry anymore. Now it's a matter of life and death. Frank's life and death."

"And your financial well-being." Ruthie knew even as she uttered the words that they were unfair. Life was never that simple. Neither were human beings.

"Do what has to be done, Ruthie. That's what I'm asking of you. Tell him whatever he needs to hear." For the first time, tears appeared in Esther's eyes. "After the surgery, you can tell him that you lied."

"And if I don't?"

"How long do you think it would take for the good people of Sweetgum to run you out of town on a rail when they find out you've been trying to seduce my husband all these years?"

"But that's not true. You wouldn't—"

"What makes you think I wouldn't?"

"I'm your sister."

"And Frank's my husband. Also, you're not in any danger of dying at the moment."

"I won't do it."

"You will. Sooner or later, but it better be sooner, Ruthie. Frank may not have a later."

With that, Esther turned and walked away. She pushed open the glass door and marched across the foyer, and all Ruthie could do was watch her go.

Esther refused to cry in public, so why were tears streaming down her face as she hurried to her car? Anyone might see her, and the last thing she could stand at the moment would be sympathy or concern.

Her fingers trembled, and she struggled to unlock the car door. Cars drove past on Spring Street, but Esther kept her head down. *Hold on,* she ordered herself sternly. *Just a few more seconds . . .*

She slid behind the wheel and pawed through her handbag for her sunglasses. When she had slipped them on, she let out a sigh of relief that sounded more like a choked sob.

He had really done it, the coward. He had told Ruthie he was ready to leave his marriage. The very thing she'd feared for so long had finally happened. Why? Why couldn't he love her, or at least respect her enough to stay away from her sister? And the irony of it? When now was the one time Esther would want her sister to act on her feelings for Frank, Ruthie refused.

She started the engine and checked for traffic before backing out of the parking space. No one who passed by now would ever suspect that Esther Jackson, in her dark green Jaguar, had just sought to bring about the thing she most feared in order to keep her husband alive.

Eleven

Merry never should have agreed to take Hannah to Nashville to the yarn store. She realized that yet again as they drove the long, straight stretch of I-65 north. In fact, after Jeff had been so uncooperative about it, she'd delayed the trip twice until Eugenie had started to pester her about it every time Merry went to the library to return another overdue book for her kids. Then she knew there'd be no escaping her promise. Truth be told, Hannah hadn't seemed any more eager to go than Merry had been to take her.

Merry saw Hannah now and then as she was dropping Courtney off at the middle school, waved to her, and received only a vague nod in return. Hannah rode the bus with the free lunch kids, as Courtney called them despite Merry's scolding. Merry would see Hannah slouching down the long sidewalk from the bus to the school's front door, looking neither left nor right. At first Merry thought she must have headphones in because she seemed so removed from her surroundings. But further observation discounted that theory. No, Hannah simply had the ability to withdraw so far into herself that she almost wasn't there.

Almost.

When Merry had announced her plans the night before at dinner, Courtney had pitched the obligatory fit. "You're doing what?" It had ended with Merry's older daughter stomping out of the dining room. Jake had frowned briefly when she told him she wouldn't be at his soccer game, but he brightened upon hearing that Mrs. Redding was the snack mom for the week. Homemade sugar cookies iced to look like soccer balls could apparently cure any feelings of abandonment. Sarah took the news with the most aplomb, but then she had a play date to spend the day with a friend whose family owned an entire stable of horses.

"You're good to go?" Merry asked Jeff as she stocked her purse with mints and tissues and snagged a bottle of water from the refrigerator. "If you lose track, just call me on my cell phone."

Jeff sighed. "Honey, I manage to run a law office pretty much on my own. I think I can handle the kids for one day."

Merry decided not to correct him. Let him learn for himself why that statement was so laughable.

And now here they were, she and Hannah, having spent most of the last hour in deafening silence. Hannah curled into the passenger seat of the mini-van, her feet propped up on the dash. Merry would never let Courtney get away with that, but she was afraid to say anything to the girl. What if Hannah flat-out defied Merry's authority? It was too late now to threaten to turn around and take her home.

"There are three yarn shops in Nashville. We can visit as many as you want," Merry said as they passed the upscale CoolSprings Galleria. Nashville's newest mall swam in a sea of big-box shopping, the roads packed with cars like schools of fish. "I thought we'd start with the one farthest north and then work our way back this direction."

Hannah grunted what Merry assumed was her assent.

"Sorry it took a couple of weeks to set this up," Merry said and then mentally kicked herself. When it came to teenagers, apologies were the death knell of authority.

They drove for another twenty minutes in the same silence. Merry wished her cell phone would ring. Something, anything to fill the emptiness. Even a wrong number would help.

She exited off the interstate onto White Bridge Road and followed it around toward a commercial area a couple of miles into town. Haus of Yarn was tucked into the bottom level of a brick shopping center across the street from a sprawling Target. The abundance of stores made Merry's mouth water. The shops in Sweetgum could fill most of her family's basic needs, but real selection or novelty required a trip to the city.

"Here we are." She pulled into a parking space and turned off the engine. "Ready to shop?"

Hannah shrugged. "Whatever."

Merry had enough experience with teenage girls

to know that this response could mean one of three things—Hannah was completely indifferent to what was happening, she hated being there with Merry, or she was excited and eager but far too cool to show it.

"This will be my treat, you know," Merry said as they approached the shop. "I insist."

Hannah stopped, clutched her enormous sack of a purse more tightly, and scowled. "I've got my own money."

"But—" Merry knew the girl didn't have any idea of the difference between buying cheap acrylic yarn at Munden's Five-and-Dime and the elegant silks and wools she was about to encounter.

"I said I have my own money."

"Okay." Merry also knew better than to argue with an adolescent when she got that stubborn look on her face. "Then let's shop."

While Camille preferred Angel Hair Yarn in Green Hills and Ruthie was partial to Threaded Bliss in Brentwood, Haus of Yarn was Merry's favorite of the three Nashville shops. A saleswoman greeted them with a cheery hello and an offer of help, but Merry declined. "We just want to look around a bit."

What she really wanted was to give Hannah the chance to explore without someone watching over her shoulder.

"Take your time," she said to the girl, who appeared not to hear her. Merry took a deep breath and plunged in. The shop wasn't large, but it was well laid out with an abundant selection. The bright colors of the yarn stood out against the dark wood of the bins and shelves. Finished pieces—sweaters, shawls, scarves, and more—hung from the ceiling and adorned partial mannequins, a riot of color and texture that both soothed and energized Merry. One of the things she liked best about a yarn shop was the sense of endless possibility. She reached out and fingered some merino wool, silky to the touch but sturdy. Bright pinks and fuchsias contrasted with deep blues and greens. Merry moved from one set of shelves to another, her eyes drinking in the bounty before her. She glanced around the corner of a freestanding set of shelves to see what Hannah was doing, and the sight stopped her in her tracks. The look of joy and wonderment on the perpetually sullen girl's face must've been akin to what Sara Crewe, the heroine of their current novel, looked like the morning she and Becky, the housemaid, awoke to find that "the magic," as they called it, had visited their little attic garret and transformed it into a place just shy of heaven.

Hannah hardly dared breathe. She'd never anticipated something like this. Where did she begin? For a moment she could have sworn she felt someone watching her. She looked over her shoulder, but no one was there. Slowly, she reached out her hand toward a skein of yarn in the bin in front of her. It was as soft to the touch as her only stuffed animal, the one she'd carefully hidden from her mother when she'd gone on that time-for-you-to-grow-up rampage. She'd stashed her ragged teddy bear in the back of the bottom dresser drawer. Since her mom never did laundry, she'd be unlikely to go rooting around in Hannah's meager collection of summer tops and shorts. This yarn, though, felt just like that teddy bear that had comforted her through long, bleak nights when she'd waited for her mother to come home or for Gentry to leave. The yarn was the same color as the bear, too, a warm honey brown. Her mother's hair had been that color once a long time ago, when Hannah was really little. Now her mother's hair was a brassy blond that came from using cheap home-dyeing kits too often.

How much yarn would it take to make the shawl for that librarian's knitting club? She'd have to ask Courtney's mom she realized with dismay. She slid the skein of yarn out of its cubicle and twisted it in her hands, looking for a price tag. When she saw it, she almost dropped the yarn. Fifteen dollars? For one thing of yarn?

"Did you find something you like?"

Hannah whirled around. Thankfully it was the saleslady, not Courtney's mom.

"No. I mean yes. But—"

"What were you thinking of knitting?" The saleslady looked nice enough. She was tall with black-and-white hair, about the age of those sisters in the knitting group.

"A shawl. I'm supposed to make a shawl," was all Hannah could say.

"That would be lovely." The saleslady nodded at the yarn in Hannah's hand.

"How many of these would it take?" Hannah asked, gesturing with the skein.

"Let me check." The saleslady picked up another hank and turned the paper wrapper around the yarn's middle this way and that. "Hmm. I guess it depends if you want something small—more like a wrap—or one that's larger, more for wintertime."

"For the small one—how much?"

"At least four skeins. Maybe five, especially if you want to put fringe on it."

"Oh." Hannah wasn't great at math, but even she could guess at those numbers. Upwards of sixty bucks. More likely seventy-five, plus tax. Her wallet contained exactly twenty-two dollars, most of which she'd earned by picking up aluminum cans along the highway. It took a lot of aluminum cans to equal twenty-two dollars.

"Did you find something?" Mrs. McGavin appeared at her side out of nowhere. She reached out to touch the yarn in Hannah's hand. "That's really pretty."

"It's okay." Hannah shrugged dismissively and crammed the skein back in the bin. She scowled. She had to or else the tears would start flowing. Why had Courtney's mom brought her here in the first place? She had to know that Hannah could never afford this kind of stuff. Sure, she'd offered to pay, but she should know that Hannah couldn't accept a gift like that. Hannah knew all about expensive gifts—she'd seen her mother take enough of them. Gifts like that had strings attached. Especially if you got them from men, but even when they came from a woman like Mrs. McGavin. "It's a stupid color anyway." This store had to have some cheaper yarn somewhere.

"Well, we'll just keep looking." Mrs. McGavin smiled at her kindly. Hannah hated that kind of smile, one step removed from pity. People who smiled at her like that did so because she made them feel better about themselves. Poor, neglected Hannah Simmons. Throw her a few crumbs, and expect her to be grateful. She thought about that book she'd been reading, the one about the princess. If she'd been the scullery maid Becky, she would have led a revolt. At the very least tipped a coal scuttle over that witch of a headmistress.

"Whatever," Hannah said, desperate to escape from the older women. As she moved away, she could tell that the two of them exchanged a look. Honest to God, Hannah was tired of those looks.

Fifteen minutes and dozens of yarns later, she found something she could afford. The sale bins were tucked into a corner in the back of the shop behind a partition. When she saw the fifty-percent off sign, she fell on them like . . . well . . . like a school-lunch kid on his breakfast tray. Ha. She should know about that. Some days it was a long time between lunch and breakfast the next morning. Summers, of course, were

121

the worst, when there was no school lunch or break-fast or anything. She had to fend for herself in the summers. That's what the twenty-two dollars was for. Because her mother was as likely to forget to buy groceries with her Friday check as she was to remember.

The sale bin, though, was a find. The thick wool was clearly a color no one had wanted, a rather putrid green. But it was only five dollars a skein, and they were much larger than the other ones. She could buy three skeins and still have a little bit left after tax. Hannah scooped up the yarn and headed for the cash register.

"You did find something." There was Mrs. McGavin again. She was like the cops or something, prac-tically spying on her. "You can just add it to my bas-ket if you want."

Hannah looked at the large shopping basket hang-ing from Mrs. McGavin's arm. Expensive yarns filled the inside and spilled out over the top. She forced herself to keep her mouth closed so her jaw wouldn't drop in shock. She must have hundreds of dollars worth of yarn in there. Enough to feed Hannah and her mom for months.

"I got it." Hannah turned away and laid her yarn on the high counter. The saleslady stood behind it now.

"Are you sure you don't want an extra hank, just in case?" the saleslady asked. Hannah wanted to reach over that counter and slap her. Did they think she was

122

an idiot? She just looked at the lady without blinking, and the woman got the message. Another minute or two, and her ordeal was over. She clutched the little handles of the clear plastic bag emblazoned with the store's logo as she headed for the door.

"I'll be right out," Mrs. McGavin called after her. Hannah just kept heading for the door, blinking back tears and biting the inside of her cheek to force back the feelings that threatened to overwhelm her. She never should have come. And it was the last time she'd do anything that stupid librarian told her she had to do. Let her call the cops. Fine. She'd go to juvy. Getting slapped around by other girls her age had to be better than this kind of torture. At least against those girls, she could fight back. But Mrs. McGavin and those other ladies? They would take her out with their kindness and move on. Hannah was smart enough to know that other people's charity was about as dependable as Gentry Carmichael.

Twelve

"My mom's new best friend is the biggest freak in the seventh grade." Courtney rolled her eyes as she delivered the verbal blow. Honestly, it was a wonder that the child had any control of her eyeballs the way she was constantly rolling them around in her head. Merry kept chopping the iceberg lettuce with grim determination.

"Hannah's not a freak. She's just . . . different." Even as she said the words, she knew how lame they sounded. Different was the kiss of death at thirteen. Merry wasn't so old that she had forgotten that, even if she didn't have Courtney around every day to remind her of the basic principle.

She'd arrived home late afternoon after dropping Hannah off in front of the saddest looking trailer Merry had ever seen. It was a wonder the redwood deck in the front hadn't collapsed and killed someone. There'd been a black Ford pickup parked in the yard, and Merry couldn't tell for sure, but she thought Hannah grimaced when she saw it. The day had been such a disaster that Merry didn't even ask the girl about the truck. Hannah hadn't said two words since they left Haus of Yarn, just sat sullenly in the passenger seat as Merry made a few more stops. Clearly Hannah had no further interest, or money, to make it worth the bother of stopping at the other yarn stores in Nashville. Merry had managed to get the girl to blurt out a begrudging order when they'd gone through the drive-through at McDonald's, but that had been the extent of their communication.

As Hannah hopped out of the van, Merry had offered to help her start her shawl project. The girl shrugged, paused, and then took off running for her sorry excuse for a house. Merry couldn't stop the tears that stung her eyes as the girl gingerly climbed the steps to the front door and disappeared inside. What must it be like to go home to that every day?

And Merry didn't like the look of that pickup truck. Sure, it was black, which made it automatically menacing. The back window boasted a gun rack and a couple of heavy-metal band stickers. Even at that, it was no different from dozens of other trucks in Sweetgum. Still, it had bothered Merry.

It continued to bother her at home as, having finished the lettuce, she started in on the tomatoes. She'd elected to make tacos for dinner, thinking it would be the simplest thing. She'd forgotten how much chopping was involved.

"Mom, I know you think you have to do this kind of Christian duty stuff, but could you please do it somewhere that my friends won't see you?" Courtney said.

"As far as I'm aware, not a single friend of yours was at the yarn shop in Nashville today."

"Mom . . ." A familiar whine.

"That's enough, Court." She pointed toward the stack of plates on the counter. "Set the table."

Merry tuned out her daughter's mutterings and focused on the tomatoes. She heard Jeff's SUV in the driveway, heralding his return from the soccer field with Jake and half of the boy population of Sweetgum. Their laughter and shrieking as they exited Jeff's car carried through the side door that led in from the garage. A moment later, the door opened and the entire herd stormed into the kitchen like stampeding wildebeests.

"Mom, we won. We won!" Jake raced for the refrigerator, swung it open, and started passing out Gatorade like a seasoned bartender.

"That's great, honey." She would have liked to reach over and kiss his cheek or ruffle his hair, but she couldn't—not in front of his "posse." He'd lectured her sternly about it the last time she'd tried.

"We're gonna go jump on the trampoline," he informed her as he slammed the refrigerator door shut.

"Take off your cleats first!" she called at their departing backs, wondering how soon she'd have to replace the battered trampoline.

"How do you stand it?" Jeff sank into a chair at the table in the breakfast nook, shaking his head. He took off his baseball cap and wiped sweat from his forehead. "It's like *Lord of the Flies* on steroids."

"Only on a good day," Merry teased. "Usually it's straight out of *The Exorcist.*"

Jeff stood up again and opened the refrigerator to swipe his own Gatorade from its depths. "I'm beat. I'm going to shower and sleep in the hammock for a while."

Merry tapped down the flare of irritation that ignited at his words. When she had Saturday soccer duty, she never got to come home and relax. No, she moved straight into dinner preparation or laundry or any of the thousand tasks that never seemed to get done. How did women who worked full-time manage to keep body and soul together? She put a hand to her back and kneaded the sorest spot. Pregnancy made a woman's joints and tendons loose so her body could accommodate childbirth, but all that stretching came at a price.

"I could use some help for a few minutes after you shower," she said.

Jeff scowled. "All I'm asking for is a half-hour nap."

Thwack. She slammed the knife through the tomato so hard that it lodged in the wooden chopping block. "Half-hour nap, my Aunt Fanny," she hissed, careful to keep her voice down. Courtney was still in the dining room setting the table. "All I'm asking for is ten minutes of your time. By the time you shower and sleep, I'll have dinner finished and on the table."

Jeff's face darkened until it reminded her of that pickup truck parked in front of Hannah's trailer. "I

127

do actually work during the week," he said in a low voice. "Not run around with my girlfriends having lunch at Tallulah's and dash up to Nashville to spend our kids' college funds on yarn."

How could this tired argument have become the cornerstone of their marriage? They were supposed to be the golden couple, heir apparent to Esther and Frank—well, maybe not *the* golden couple, but at the very least they were supposed to be special in some way. Boredom, loneliness, bickering—those weren't meant to be the hallmarks of their marriage, much less the pillars of their home.

"Jeff, I'm tired of feeling so alone."

The screen door banged as Jake and three of his buddies streaked back into the house in a blaze of mud and soccer cleats. Merry whirled toward her son. "Jake McGavin! Freeze right there!" But her shout didn't even slow their steps. The boys disappeared upstairs in a thunder of rushing feet pounding against the new hardwood.

Merry turned back to face her husband, who was looking at her as if she'd just announced she intended to join a cult.

"How could you possibly feel alone in this chaos?" he demanded. "The only thing that could make our lives worse would be if we had more kids."

Merry clutched the knife handle. "You don't mean that, Jeff." She still kept her voice low. *Please, Lord, don't let Courtney hear any of this,* she silently prayed.

"This family is out of control, Merry. I spent the whole day driving kids all over Sweetgum. How many activities do they need? Let them have a few friends over and play, for Pete's sake."

"You act like all of this happened while you were out of town on some extended business trip." Merry wrenched the knife free from the chopping block. "You signed Jake up for soccer when he was four years old, not me. You cave in to Courtney's demands every time she asks. And Sarah—" Her voice broke off. Her Sarah. Her own little princess. Jeff never seemed to have any time for her.

"You've had to deal with one day, Jeff. This is what I live every day." She wiped her eyes with the back of her hand to keep from getting tomato juice in them. "I'm one person, Jeff. One. And I'm tired. And I'm lonely. And this just isn't enough anymore."

She hadn't meant to say any of that, but the words tumbled out, spurred on no doubt by the hormones raging through her body.

"What are you saying? That you want a divorce?" Panic etched deep lines in his face.

"No. I don't want a divorce." She reached for a paper towel to wipe up the remains of the tomato. "I want a marriage. And that may be the more difficult of the two options for you to deal with." She wadded the soggy paper towel in her fist and threw it at Jeff's chest. "Cook your own dinner. And the kids' too."

Merry spun around, grabbed her purse and keys from the little desk by the door, and walked out.

* * *

Camille looked out the window of the loft apartment. Over the rooftops of downtown Memphis, she could glimpse the Mississippi River in the distance. The streets below were surprisingly quiet, but then she'd never been in this area of town on a Sunday morning before.

She'd thought when she arrived last night that Alex would take her out for a nice dinner. She'd even surfed the Internet at the Sweetgum Public Library, carefully avoiding Eugenie's shrewd eyes, to discover the names of some of the top restaurants. Instead Alex had produced a couple of steaks, which he'd grilled on the apartment's miniscule balcony, accompanied by a bag of wilted lettuce. He just wanted to be alone with her, he said.

Camille might be only twenty-four, but she wasn't stupid. Except apparently when it came to married men.

"Honey, you want more coffee?" Alex called from the kitchen on the other side of the living room.

"No. I'm fine." She clutched the lapels of her robe closer together. She should have been basking in triumph now that he had left his wife. She should have been standing on the little balcony, trumpeting her success. Instead, she felt hollow inside. She had never anticipated that it would feel like this, that regret would choke her throat so tightly she couldn't swallow the first sip of coffee.

"Be careful what you ask for," her mother had always warned her. *"You just might get it."*

If only she had listened.

"Your cell phone's ringing," Alex called again, unseen. "Do you want me to answer it?"

"No!" She shot across the room and around the partial wall that divided the living area from the kitchen. "It's probably my mom."

Alex was standing in front of the sink filling the coffeepot with water. He chuckled. "You're a grown woman, Camille."

"And Sweetgum is a small town. She might recognize your voice. Besides . . ."

"What?"

She blushed, ashamed of her lack of sophistication. "It would upset her if a man answered my cell phone before eight o'clock in the morning."

Alex reached over to chuck her under the chin. "You're cute." Then he swatted her rear. "Answer your phone."

Camille scooped up her purse and hurried back to the living room. She sank onto the sleek leather sofa—if you could call such a minimalist piece of furniture a sofa—and flipped open her phone.

"Hello?"

"I'm sorry to be a worrywart," her mother said by way of greeting. "Just had to check on you."

"I'm fine, Mom. Is everything okay there? Is Eulene taking good care of you?" Camille had finally found someone suitable to stay with her mother for the weekend, a retired woman who was a friend of Ruthie's.

"Eulene is terrific. She's going to help me with my bath this morning."

Camille covered the phone's mouthpiece to mask her sigh of relief. Her mother must like Eulene if she was letting her help with that particular chore.

"You left your knitting," her mother said. "I thought you were going to take it with you."

"That's okay. I'll be back tonight."

"Are you having a good time?"

A hot rush of shame swamped her. She'd never lied to her mother like this before.

"Your book's still here too. I hope you remembered your toothbrush," her mother teased.

"I did."

"Well, have a good time with Carmen. I'm sure you have a lot of catching up to do."

Another lie. Her best friend from high school lived in Memphis but was conveniently out of town this weekend. It had made for the perfect cover story.

"We stayed up way too late talking," Camille said. How easily the falsehoods slid off her tongue.

And then Alex's deep voice called from the kitchen, "Sure you won't change your mind about the coffee?"

"Who's that?" Camille's mother asked.

"Just Carmen's boyfriend. He came over early to take us out for breakfast."

"Oh. Okay. Well, enjoy yourself, honey. You deserve it."

"I will, Mom. Thanks. I'll see you tonight."

"Drive safe on the way home. Not too fast."

"I won't."

How many times had they had a similar exchange? Camille said good-bye and snapped the phone shut.

Alex appeared around the corner from the kitchen. "Since you don't want coffee . . ." He moved toward her, sliding onto the couch beside her and taking her in his arms. "What do you say we go back to bed?" His kiss was warm, practiced, and effective. Or maybe she just wanted it to be. She just wanted something to stop the pain and the panic and the frustration.

So she said nothing. Just kept kissing Alex, hoping that he really meant it when he said that his marriage was over, that he loved her, that she'd never be alone again.

Thirteen

The cold front arrived the first week of November and stayed well into the second week. As it turned out, Ruthie thought, it wasn't a bad time to be knitting a shawl. She'd been using a lot of her free time at the church office to complete the project. The next meeting of the Knit Lit Society was only a few days away, and she was only halfway done. Perhaps that was because she spent as much time sitting behind her desk lost in thought, the knitting needles motionless in her hands, as she did stitching.

Knitting helped a broken heart to start healing. At least that's what Ruthie's mother had told her when she bought her that first set of needles and skein of yarn thirty-some-odd years ago. Ruthie had just returned from her time in the Peace Corps. She had returned, in fact, to the news that Esther had married Frank. No one had wanted to tell her while she was an ocean away, herding goats or whatever it was she was doing in Africa. Ruthie wasn't sure what they feared—whether it was worry for her mental health or physical safety. Or perhaps her parents and Esther had been more concerned that she might hop on a plane and come home in time for the wedding. In time to stop the wedding.

She would have if she'd known.

But no cable arrived, no telegram, no transatlantic phone call punctuated by static and abruptly disconnected. Instead, Ruthie's parents had been waiting for her at the airport in Nashville on the appointed day. She'd been so excited to be back, although the culture shock proved even more severe than she'd expected despite the warnings of more seasoned Peace Corps veterans. The ease of American life, the bounty at even the smallest convenience store, Cokes in ice-cold bottles—she felt so out of place. How to reconcile the deprivation she'd witnessed in the last two years with the excess of her birthplace? She knew now how much she'd taken for granted. What a tremendous responsibility she bore. And none of her friends or family could even begin to comprehend what had happened to her.

Overwhelmed by the memories, Ruthie set her knitting down and gazed out the window. The sweetgum trees were almost bare. Winter couldn't be far behind. She hadn't spoken to Esther since the afternoon she'd shown up in the church office. She hadn't spoken to Frank either. Every day she'd gotten up, tended to her house and garden, gone to work, come home to a solitary supper, and gone to bed. A mindless routine, although her mind had certainly been busy of its own accord.

Frank kept calling. Thank heavens for caller ID. She

let his calls, and her sister's, go to voice mail. And she knitted, even though she kept ripping out most of what she'd done. She never should have chosen a complicated lacy stitch to begin with. But then she'd never anticipated Esther's request and the havoc it would wreak on her state of mind.

Every day she waited brought Frank one day closer to death. Okay, perhaps that thought was a bit dramatic, but it contained enough of the truth to wake her up in the wee hours of the morning. There wasn't enough warm milk in the world to soothe her back to sleep these days.

Ruthie reached out and fingered the brochure on the desk in front of her. *Namibia*. The word on the cover jumped out at her. She opened it again and reread the contents for the hundredth time. *Two-year commitment*. Her completed application lay underneath the glossy brochure. Beside that a stamped, addressed envelope waited.

Where would she find yarn, she wondered? Or books in English? She'd lived without creature comforts before, but she'd been much younger then. A child, really, in all the ways that counted.

With a sigh, she folded the application, tucked it into the envelope and sealed it, and tossed it into the outgoing mail tray on her desk. Napoleon would pick up the pile of envelopes at the end of the day and take them to the post office.

Ruthie paused. She couldn't sit there all day looking at that envelope, so instead she grabbed her coat

136

from the rack in the corner and scooped up the outgoing mail herself. She needed a break anyway.

She peeked into the pastor's study. "Rev. Carson? I'm going to run to the post office."

"Okay, Ruthie." He didn't look up from the thick Bible commentary he was holding. The man certainly took writing sermons seriously. A refreshing change of pace from the previous pastor, who had downloaded most of his from the Internet. "I'll answer the phone if it rings."

She smiled, but it felt bittersweet on her lips. This trip to the post office might mean he'd have to find a new secretary in a few months.

Outside she pulled the lapels of her coat together at her throat and wished she'd remembered to loop a scarf around her neck before heading out the door that morning. The day was raw, but it was also alive, the stiff breeze challenging her every step as she headed into the wind. She opened the lapels of her coat long enough to tuck the mail into an inside pocket.

The walk to the post office was a good idea. It cleared her head. She passed by familiar landmarks as she made her way around the town square—Kendall's Department Store, the Rexall drugstore, the movie theater, where she'd seen scores of films. Tallulah's Café, with its endless cups of coffee and black-bottom pie. How would she live somewhere that didn't have those places? They were a part of her now. The first time she left home, she hadn't known how dear it was. This time she would know utterly and completely.

* * *

Merry dreaded the November meeting of the Sweet-gum Knit Lit Society with a sense of foreboding she'd rarely felt in her life. Now that she was four months pregnant, more than one person had given her belly a second look. She was still at the stage where her burgeoning middle could be attributed to weight gain, but time was running out on her secret.

And she still hadn't told Jeff.

How could she after the fight they'd had the week before? *The only thing that could make our lives worse would be if we had more kids.* She'd repeated his words over and over so often that they were burned into her brain. And so she kept her silence, even as she tried to keep down her breakfast. She was more nauseated with this pregnancy than with her last. The symptoms were similar to what she'd experienced with Jake, which probably meant another boy.

It was the Friday before Thanksgiving, with all the added pressures of the holidays looming. She parked in her usual spot in front of the church, moving as quickly as her expanding middle would allow through the early evening drizzle. She had to be more careful now about slick spots on the sidewalk. After all, she was walking for two, she thought wryly.

By the time she reached the top of the stairs, she could hear voices coming from the classroom. The ancient radiator system hissed and groaned as it tried to provide a modicum of heat for the old building.

138

"Merry, there you are." Camille met her at the classroom door with a forced, rather brittle-looking smile on her face. "Eugenie wanted to start without you, but I wouldn't let her."

Merry didn't know what to say to this unusual display of attention from Camille.

"Thanks, Camille. I practically had to force-feed Sarah. And then I couldn't find my car keys."

Camille smiled. "You're here now."

Merry followed her into the room. This time she deliberately took the seat next to Hannah, whose hair and clothing showed no marked improvement from two months before. Merry wondered if she should offer to take the girl shopping for clothes, but she doubted Hannah would be any more receptive to that idea than she had been to Merry's offer to buy yarn for her in Nashville.

"Evening, Merry," Ruthie said. "How are you?"

They passed a few minutes in pleasant if inconsequential chitchat. Ruthie said she liked the new pastor pretty well. Eugenie mentioned a few new books that had arrived at the library. When asked, Camille informed them that her mother was about the same. Esther's ten-year-old grandson was evidently about to win a Nobel prize, and Hannah grunted monosyllabic responses to any questions that came her way. *A typical meeting so far,* Merry thought.

"So," Eugenie began, when it was clear that the time for chitchat was over. "Let's talk about the book. I must confess I'd forgotten quite a few details over the years, but one question did keep coming up for me, so I thought I'd ask it of you all." She paused and looked around the circle. "Do you believe there's a princess in every girl?" Eugenie asked.

Hannah snorted.

Merry thought of the Cinderella comforter set she'd just ordered for Sarah's fifth birthday. Ruthie looked militant—she'd no doubt have a great deal to say about antifeminist propaganda—and Esther was practically preening. Not difficult to tell where she would stand on the issue. Esther clearly had no problems whatsoever with cultivating her inner princess.

"I think that's true," Merry said. "Or if it isn't, it ought to be."

"What does that even mean, though?" Ruthie frowned. "I've never understood why we set such unrealistic expectations for little girls."

"Boys have their own superheroes," Esther pointed out. "I'm sure my son spent a lot of time playing Batman or Transformers or those strange turtle creatures. What were they called?"

"Teenage Mutant Ninja Turtles," Hannah muttered.

"Yes. Those things. The idea of being a princess gives a girl something to aspire to, just as boys see their superheroes as models of strength and courage."

"*Princess* seems to have a different definition today than it did when I was little," Merry said. "Back then it was more about looks and being pleasant. Now it's more powerful."

140

Eugenie looked satisfied at the direction of the conversation. "So how is it more powerful?"

Hannah cleared her throat. "You don't need a prince anymore. Nobody needs a prince anymore."

"You're right." Merry nodded. She hadn't thought of it that way before, but Hannah's observation made sense. "All of the stuff I buy for Sarah focuses on the princess. The prince has become an accessory, not a central figure."

Ruthie laughed. "I like it."

Esther pursed her lips. "Feminism." A one-word indictment.

"Reality," Ruthie snapped back. "What did Gloria Steinem say about a woman needing a man? Like a fish needing a bicycle?"

"But we like men," Camille said, frowning. "We're supposed to like them."

"But are they necessary?" Merry heard herself say. "Now that women can get an education and work and fend for themselves?"

"Well, they're certainly necessary in one way." Esther's mouth was tight at the corners. And then she realized she'd said something slightly risqué and fell silent.

Eugenie intervened. "What about the character in this book?" She pointed to her copy of *A Little Princess*. "Did she need a man?"

"In that world she did," Hannah said. "She was just a kid. The grownups were supposed to take care of her."

Merry's throat closed. In her mind's eye, she saw the ramshackle trailer Hannah called home, the sagging redwood deck, the ominous pickup truck.

"So what saved her in the end?" Eugenie asked. "Was it a man, the neighbor who knew her father, or was it her own goodness?"

They fell silent, pondering the question. The radiator in the corner hissed like a kettle letting off steam.

Esther was the first to speak. "The character held her head high even when circumstances were against her. Perhaps that's the mark of a true princess, if that's what you want to call it. I call it being a lady."

"But even she had a breaking point." Ruthie said. "That's the darkest moment in the book. When it seems as if all hope is lost. Even when the 'magic' comes, as she and Becky call it, it's not enough. The headmistress tries to have them arrested for stealing."

"And then she is saved by a man," Esther pointed out.

"So how do you all feel about that?" Eugenie asked. "Do you agree that we can't ultimately save ourselves, as the author seems to say?"

Merry chuckled. "If we can save ourselves, then I've been wasting a lot of years right here in this church."

Hannah snorted. "Ya think?"

"Well, let's move on. What about your shawls? How did they turn out?" Eugenie tactfully brought the discussion to a close and looked at the group

142

with an unusual degree of expectation. Normally she was the most self-contained person in the group. Tonight she seemed almost . . . brittle somehow. Maybe the whole discussion of men bothered her. If you looked up *spinster* in the dictionary, you would most likely find Eugenie's picture.

Merry was happy enough to help Eugenie change the subject. The story of a parentless child left to the mercies of self-absorbed people struck a little close to home, and it couldn't be comfortable for Hannah either. Merry reached into her bag and pulled out the tissue-wrapped shawl she'd brought. This project had been the one bright spot in the past two weeks. She couldn't wait to see Hannah's reaction.

Everyone had something to place on the table. Eugenie's thick, dark green wool looked warm enough to take on a subarctic trip. Camille had worked beads into the lustrous silk of her ruby shawl. Esther's chenille piece shimmered with deep jewel tones. Ruthie's was a vibrant cobalt blue shot through with a silver metallic yarn. And Hannah's dull green wool was once again so tightly knit that Merry had to wonder whether it would give enough to wrap around the girl's shoulders.

"That's very nice, Hannah," Ruthie said with her usual kindness. "You finished that very quickly for a beginner."

Hannah had completed the shawl at an unusually fast pace, Merry realized. The girl must have knit every spare moment to finish on time.

"Here's mine." Merry spread hers out on the table before her, her eyes fixed on Hannah's face to see the girl's reaction. She wondered if Hannah would recognize an apology when she saw it. "It's for you, Hannah." She slid the honey-brown shawl toward the girl. Hannah sat transfixed, showing no emotion. Her expression made Merry even gladder that she'd secretly bought the yarn Hannah had admired. It made those long hours of knitting over the last two weeks well worth the trouble.

"You-shouldn't-have," Hannah said, all the words crammed together in a low monotone. Clearly she was so stunned by Merry's generosity that she couldn't think of anything else to say.

"I enjoyed making it for you," Merry said. "I know you really liked the yarn." And then Merry took a second look at the girl and realized that Hannah wasn't pleased at all. Thin lines radiated out from the girl's mouth. Her slumping shoulders seemed lower than usual, and she wouldn't look Merry in the eye.

"This is lovely, Merry." Ruthie jumped into the awkward silence. "What stitch is it?"

"Fan and feather. Or my version of it anyway." She said the words, but they tasted bitter on her tongue. Half of her understood the girl's response, but the other half struggled with the ingratitude. She was only trying to help. Why couldn't Hannah see that?

"Very nice." Eugenie looked at Hannah. "Merry

went to a lot of trouble to make this for you."

"It's okay, Eugenie. Don't worry about it." The last thing she wanted was to get Hannah in trouble with the librarian. "We just had an unfortunate misunderstanding."

And then Merry saw the tears that were trying to squeeze out of the corners of Hannah's kohl-blackened eyes. "Who else has something to show?" Merry asked brightly, turning their attention from the girl. Merry oohed and ahhed over Camille's project and tried not to look at Hannah anymore.

Once again, by trying to do the right thing, she'd done it all wrong instead.

Fourteen

Eugenie shut her copy of *Pollyanna* and laid it on the tall reference desk in front of her. When the library was quiet, as it had been that morning, she allowed herself to read if all her other tasks had been completed. She reasoned that it never hurt for people to come into the library and see her with a book in hand. She was only setting a good example.

Or so she told herself.

In the last several weeks, she'd struggled to complete her regular duties, turning to the solace of books instead. Hard work had been her motto, her creed, her mantra. Now she struggled to drag herself out of bed each morning, much less reshelve books or help patrons look something up on the Internet.

Paul was to blame, of course. Since that day at the diner, he'd disturbed her daily routine, much less her peace of mind. Once upon a time she had enjoyed her solitary morning walk down Spring Street, past the church and on to the library, where she entered the building at precisely eight o'clock. Now she found herself taking the long way around, through the town square, stopping at Tallulah's for a cup of coffee as an excuse for her detour. Tallulah was always glad to see her, but Eugenie knew that the café owner was nobody's fool.

"You okay, honey?" Tallulah had asked that morning. "You seem out of sorts lately."

"I'm fine." Eugenie was a bad liar. She always had been. Except for that one memorable occasion that involved the very cause of her current distress.

Eugenie was beginning to regret choosing *Pollyanna* for the next meeting of the Knit Lit Society. She'd just gotten to the part in the book where the eponymous heroine explained her personal philosophy. The little orphan girl was a determined optimist. Some people would call it finding the silver lining. Pollyanna called it the glad game. Eugenie's whole life for the past forty years had been a silver lining, a silk purse made from a sow's ear, the living embodiment of the glad game.

I'm glad I've been able to share my love of reading with so many people.

I'm glad I've been independent, able to come and go as I please.

I'm glad I never had to be a preacher's wife. I would have been a disaster at it.

And now Paul was here in Sweetgum, a living, breathing daily reminder of her folly.

How could she be glad about that?

She heard the peculiar sighing sound that the exterior door made when it opened, and she looked up. From her perch, she was a good twenty feet from the library entrance. Late November sunshine backlit the man coming through the door, but Eugenie had no doubt as to his identity. She didn't need to see his face or the color of his eyes. No, she could tell by the shape of his shoulders, the way he carried himself, the line of his jaw. It was Paul, entering her domain for the first time. Eugenie bristled, like a mother wolf called on to defend her cub from a predator.

"Good morning, Eugenie." He greeted her as if they were the oldest and best of friends. As he moved closer, she saw the familiar genial smile on his face. He wore a dark trench coat. Between the lapels she caught a glimpse of a shirt and tie—practically formal dress in a town like Sweetgum. How unfair that he looked even better in business attire.

"Hello, Paul." She was proud of her cool demeanor, her aplomb in handling the situation. Thankfully, the height of the checkout desk hid her wobbly knees. "Have you come to get your library card?" She refused to be thrown off her stride. She would treat him as she did every other new Sweetgum resident who came through the door. She pulled a form from one of the slots built into the checkout desk and set it on the counter. "If you'll fill this out, it should only take a few minutes for me to process it."

His eyes sparkled with amusement. Eugenie clenched her jaw. He had no right to come into her library and sparkle like that. Or be amused. Or, most especially, to treat their past as if it were something that could be easily smoothed over with a lunch at Tallulah's Café and a chat in the library.

"Actually, that's not what I came here for, but it's not a bad idea." He looked around on the countertop. "Do you have a pen?"

Eugenie caught herself in the act of biting her lip. She pursed them instead, took a breath, and laid a pen on the counter next to the application form. "Of course."

And then she waited for him to tell her why he had come to the library if not to establish himself as a patron. Only he didn't say another word. Just picked up the pen, winked at her so that she was helpless against the blush that rose to her cheeks, and began to fill in the blanks in bold, masculine capital letters.

Eugenie picked up her book once more and pretended to read. It was either that or watch Paul's hands —they were awfully tan for a preacher—as he worked.

"Not too busy this morning, huh?" he asked without looking up.

"Monday mornings are usually quiet."

He did look up at her then and smiled. "A librarian's dream come true."

Eugenie bristled but still kept her tongue under control. "We have a tutoring program on Mondays after school. If you had walked in at three o'clock, it wouldn't be quite this peaceful."

"Tutoring? Really?" His face showed genuine interest. "What ages?"

"Older elementary and middle school for the most part." Whenever she could find tutors that was.

Volunteers were pretty thin on the ground these days.

"How many kids do you work with?"

"A dozen or so."

"And they come here?"

"Most of their parents work. They walk over after school lets out and stay until I close up."

"How many do you work with personally?"

She couldn't very well tell him that at the moment she was tutoring all twelve at once. Plus supervising Hannah's hour a day of penance. "I do my share, I suppose."

Paul gave her a knowing look. "I'm sure you do."

What was this newfound penchant for blushing she'd developed? "If you're done, I can type up your card for you."

Paul looked at her in surprise, and then his gaze traveled around the library. "You still have a card catalog?" he asked. "Thank goodness. I'm all thumbs when it comes to computers. Usually have to ask one of my grandkids to bail me out after I crash it."

Eugenie ignored the tightness that seized her chest at his mention of grandchildren. "We have computers for the Internet, but that's as far as we've gotten. The city has been trying to set aside funds to computerize our records, but invariably a water main breaks or some other disaster happens. Then we go back to the bottom of the waiting list." And indeed she wondered if her harping on the need for computerization wasn't one of the reasons Homer Flint and his crew were pushing her out the door. Of course,

she couldn't imagine that any younger, more techno-
logically savvy successor wouldn't push just as hard,
if not harder. But their words wouldn't carry the
same weight in Sweetgum as Eugenie's did.

"Sounds like small-town life to me," Paul said. "But
I guess you must like it to have stayed here so long."

"I forgot to ask you the other day where you've
been living all these years," Eugenie said to divert the
conversation away from herself.

"Nashville for the most part," he answered.

"Oh." She couldn't think of a reply. All that time
he'd been so close. She didn't go to Nashville often,
maybe two or three times a year, but to think that
she might have seen him there. Run into him on the
street. Stranger things had happened. Stranger things,
like his landing right here in Sweetgum.

"I did some volunteering with the literacy council
there," he said. "Maybe I could give you a hand with
tutoring."

Eugenie closed her mouth so she wouldn't blurt
out the "no" that sprang to her lips. She swallowed.
Twice. "We have more need for math help. I'm afraid
I'm not quite as much use to the children when it
comes to algebra."

Paul leaned forward and rested his forearms on the
counter. The pose reminded her of how he used to
stand in that very same way when she'd worked at the
library in Columbia as a lowly assistant all those years
ago. "I helped both my grandsons with that sort of
thing. Maybe you should let me give it a shot."

151

Why was he doing this? Was he that insensitive? Did he honestly think that he could walk back into her life so nonchalantly, as if he'd never broken her heart?

"We like our tutors to make a long-term commitment." *That should deter him,* she thought.

"Not a problem. I plan to be around Sweetgum for a good long while."

His words formed a tight ball of dread in the pit of her stomach. "You're not planning to retire soon?"

"I can't imagine it." A shadow of emotion crossed his face. "It's better to keep busy."

She shouldn't hate that the loss of his late wife still gave him so much pain. Of course he mourned her. Eugenie gave herself a good mental shaking and moved to the small swivel chair behind the counter. Using the ancient typewriter, she carefully pecked out Paul's necessary information onto a small manila card. "Idle hands are the devil's workshop," she blurted out before she could think of anything less trite to say.

"I didn't think you believed in the devil."

She wished he would quit watching her so closely. What was he looking for anyway? "I don't."

"Ruthie, my secretary, says you're not a regular churchgoer."

Eugenie nodded. "Ruthie is correct."

"You were a pretty faithful parishioner once upon a time," he said.

"Yes. I was." Before her heart had been broken by

a man who thought God's call was a justifiable excuse for leaving behind the woman he loved. "Here's your card." She pulled it out of the typewriter and slid it across the counter to him. "You'll need to sign the back."

"Eugenie." He reached out and instead of taking the card he caught her hand in his. "Ruthie says you've never been to church in all the years since you came to Sweetgum."

"I guess it didn't suit me to do so." She said the words in her best buttoned-up librarian voice. "Now was there a particular book you wanted to borrow?"

"Eugenie. It's me you're talking to."

She couldn't look him in the eye because she couldn't afford to let him see what was in hers. "Paul, I know we were . . . close . . . a long time ago. But perhaps we should be honest. We don't really know each other. Not after all this time. I've built a good life for myself. I'm happy. I don't see any reason to look back."

He stiffened. "I see."

"I'm always delighted to have a new library patron, of course. And if you need any books you don't have in your personal collection, for sermon preparation or that sort of thing, I'm here to help."

"That's very kind of you, Eugenie." Tight lines emanated from the corners of his eyes and mouth. "But I won't trouble you any more than necessary." He paused. "There is one book I was looking for. Maybe you can help me with that."

"Certainly." How could such an ordinary conversation cause such extraordinary pain? She wanted to stamp her feet, fling pencils and books and papers at the ceiling, shake him until that concerned facade he wore cracked and shattered. She wanted to reach out for him, grab him, clutch him in her arms. Because it might have been forty years since he belonged to her, but it felt like forty days. Forty hours. Forty minutes. "What book were you looking for?"

"Dante's *Inferno*."

Eugenie locked her spine in place, straight as a ramrod and not nearly as yielding. "We do have a copy of that. Let me see if it's checked out." She reached for the box of patron slips and rifled through them, barely able to remember the alphabet so she could find the right card. "Here it is. I'm afraid it's not due back until Friday. Shall I hold it for you when it comes in?"

He had no right to have that look of pain in his eyes. No right at all. "Please. Should I check back that day?"

"I'll call you when it comes in." Smooth. Professional. Better. "Your number's on your application."

"Right." He hesitated. "Eugenie—"

"There's the mailman." She nodded over Paul's shoulder. The exterior door opened once again with its distinctive sighing sound, and David Gonzalez walked in, his arms piled high with magazines topped by a stack of envelopes. "I'm afraid David gets his daily workout when he delivers here." She stepped around the counter toward the mailman. "Here. Let me take that."

"Morning, Eugenie. Morning, preacher." David had been delivering the library mail as long as Eugenie could remember. He crossed to the checkout counter and plunked down the mail. Once his hands were free, he reached up to rub his right shoulder. "I swear those magazines weigh more than they used to."

"Or maybe there are just more of them," Paul said. Eugenie scooped the mail off the counter and laid it on a table behind her for later sorting.

"Thank you. Mr. Hornbuckle will be in by lunch to see the latest *Bait & Tackle*."

"I know he gets testy when his magazine is late." David lifted a hand. "Gotta be going. Can't stand around chatting with the likes of you all." His wide grin belied the gruffness of his words.

"Go on then. Rascal," Eugenie added under her breath with a bemused smile. They called their good-byes as the mailman headed back into the frosty day.

"I expect I'd better go too," Paul said.

"I'll call you when that book comes in."

"Book?"

"Dante's *Inferno*."

"Oh. Yes. That one." He frowned, paused. As if he were making a decision. And then he lifted a hand, much like the mailman had done, in a farewell gesture. "Thank you, Eugenie."

"You're welcome." He probably didn't hear her quiet words as his dress shoes tapped against the polished tile floor.

Eugenie watched him as he disappeared through the door. Without meaning to, she crossed the lobby and walked to the glass door, her eyes following his tall, lanky figure as he headed up Spring Street toward the church. Yes, she could certainly present him with an indifferent facade. But inside? Well, it was a good thing the Reverend Paul Carson didn't have x-ray vision. Or else he'd see just how much her insides were tied up in knots over his renewed presence in her life.

Fifteen

Everyone else in town had a back porch. Esther had a veranda. She sat there now despite the cold and poured a steaming cup of coffee from the insulated carafe. Frank thought she was out of her head to sit out here on cold mornings, but this wicker rocking chair with its floral cushion and view of the gardens centered her universe. She would no more think of giving it up, no matter what the weather, than she would consider telling anyone about—

Esther sipped her coffee. Any more than she would consider telling anyone about the ashes that had been scattered there, in the far corner of the garden, around the small stone statue of an angel. No one knew about the baby. At least no one who was still living. Her parents had known, of course, but their disappointment over her pregnancy had been mollified by her hasty marriage to Frank. They'd left Sweetgum shortly after their wedding so Frank could attend law school, and before they could even begin to formulate a plan for explaining the baby's early arrival, they'd learned that the infant wouldn't survive for more than a few hours. Esther and Frank didn't come home to Sweetgum until a long time afterward. And she hadn't sprinkled the ashes until they'd bought this, their dream house.

Over her shoulder she heard the sound of the sliding glass door that led from the breakfast room to the veranda.

"I can't believe you're out here." Frank wore his old velour robe over a worn pair of flannel pajama bottoms. On his feet were a pair of even older slippers. "You're going to freeze to death," he said with a frown.

"I have coffee." She raised her cup in a mild salute. "Why don't you join me?"

He looked dubious but moved the rest of the way through the door and closed it behind him. Esther filled the second mug and added a splash of cream and a healthy spoonful of sugar. There was no point in lecturing him about the benefits of skim milk at this late date. He lowered himself into the matching rocker next to her.

"Esther, I need to—"

"I want a divorce, Frank." She handed him the mug but averted her eyes. He accepted it automatically.

"Esther—"

"My mind's made up." She looked at him then because she hadn't been able to when she said the *D* word. He was paler than usual, his lips tinged blue. Was there still enough time? "I want you to move out of the house."

He set his mug on the table between them with a *thunk*. "Have you lost your mind?"

"Not in the least." She'd rehearsed this encounter for weeks now. Ruthie was clearly not going to cooperate, at least not without a little push. And a free Frank would be the final push it would take for her sister to do what she'd never had the nerve to do all these years.

"What are you playing at, Esther?" Frank's eyes narrowed with suspicion.

"I'm most definitely not playing. I've put a divorce lawyer on retainer. You need to do the same. I'm going to Memphis to visit Alex and Melissa and the grandchildren for a few days. When I get back, you should be gone."

"Where in the world am I supposed to go?"

"I took the liberty of renting you a condo at the marina." The new development on Sweetgum Lake had brought a small influx of people from Nashville and Chattanooga who couldn't afford a second home on Center Hill Lake or one of the more popular resort areas.

"I suppose you've furnished it completely."

"Down to bed linens, towels, and a fully stocked kitchen."

"God, Esther, you're a piece of work." His laugh was as bitter as the designer coffee. "You don't even want to talk about this?"

"There's really nothing to say, Frank. You're going to die without the surgery, and I don't plan to sit around and wait for that to happen. If you want to self-destruct, you can do so on your own."

159

"And what about you?" A look of realization crossed his face. "Is there someone else?" She could tell from the surprise in his eyes that he'd never really considered that possibility until this very moment. That thought made Esther bristle. No woman cared to be taken for granted like that, especially not a woman who'd spent her life knowing that her husband loved—

"There's no one else, Frank. Don't be ridiculous."

"When have I ever been anything but ridiculous in your eyes?"

Esther stilled, her coffee mug halfway to her lips. "Is that what you believe? That I think you're ridiculous?"

"I've spent the last thirty years being corrected and chastised by you, Esther Jackson. What else am I supposed to think?"

Hurt clouded her vision. "I was only trying to be a good wife. Help you be successful. We were an excellent team."

Frank twisted his coffee mug in his hands. "Yes. I guess we were."

She hated the sorrow in his tone. "A team's a good thing, Frank."

"But it's not quite the same thing as a marriage, is it?" He paused. "Maybe you're right. Maybe I should move to the marina."

Esther felt her control of the situation slipping away. He wasn't supposed to leave because he actually wanted out of their marriage. He was supposed to move because she was punishing him. For being obstinate. For not looking after her. For loving her sister.

"I'll leave for Memphis in a few hours. Oksana will be in to clean tomorrow." Their Russian immigrant housekeeper came twice a week—more often if Esther was hosting one of her club meetings or one of Frank's office parties.

"Can she help me pack?"

"Just leave her a note. Tell her what you want to take." He'd been right about sitting on the patio. It was cold. Desperately so. Or was it just the atmosphere they'd created that chilled her to the marrow of her bones?

"I never saw this coming," Frank said.

Esther only wished she could say the same. Now it was up to Ruthie to finish the job. If Frank didn't agree to the bypass surgery now, he never would.

"I'll call you when I get to Memphis."

"Are you going to tell Alex?"

"Yes. But not the children. There's plenty of time for that."

Which was a lie. Time was their most precious commodity, thanks to her obstinate husband.

She stood up, cup in hand, and he did the same. "Do you want me to carry your suitcases to the car?" he asked.

Esther looked at his chest, not at his face. "I hardly think so."

A storm gathered on his face. "Esther . . . ," he growled as a warning.

161

"Do you want to shower first or shall I?" she asked.

"Go ahead." He followed her back into the house. "You'll do what you want anyway. You always have."

She couldn't even summon up any anger at his words. She had learned from that first mistake. And her choices had, in the decades since, created a very nice life for all of them. For her. For Frank. For Alex.

Only two things had never responded to her indomitable will—Frank's heart and the child whose ashes mingled with the soil in the corner of the garden.

Camille's mother was the one who suggested they start playing the glad game. She'd never read *Pollyanna*, though they'd watched the movie together when Camille brought home the videocassette from the library. Camille reluctantly agreed to play late one night when she'd been reading the book to her mother and her mother had interrupted to make the request.

The glad game was proving rather difficult for Camille to play.

How could she say that she was glad Alex hadn't called in the weeks that had passed since her trip to Memphis? How could she say she was glad to worry that he might have moved back home with his wife and children? And, most importantly, how was she supposed to find anything in her mother's situation to be glad about? Such naive notions might work fine in children's literature. And maybe that strange teenager could be glad about her tattoos or her horrible makeup or something else. But optimism had no place in Camille's life. Neither did silver linings. The facts were the facts. One day her mother would die. And until then she was chained to Sweetgum as securely as any of the prisoners in the county jail.

"I'm glad you're enjoying running the dress shop," her mother said as Camille plumped her pillows one last time before leaving for the day. For now her mother could manage on her own as long as Camille popped home on her lunch hour to fix her some soup and a sandwich. She hated the thought of her mother being alone all day, but Nancy St. Clair assured Camille that between her romance novels and the television, she was more than entertained. The day would come, though, when her mother would need constant care, and Camille still had no idea how they would pay for it. As a sole proprietor, her mother had never had much health insurance. Now they couldn't afford anything more than major medical, and no company would carry her without charging an exorbitant amount.

Camille gave the pillow one last thump and placed it behind her mother's head. She couldn't think about that right now any more than she could play that silly glad game.

"Can I get you anything else?"

"No, dear. I'm fine." Her mother's pale skin was

almost translucent. Fine blue lines ran across her temples. Her patchy hair could no longer be back-combed over the empty spots.

"All right then. I'll be back at lunch." She leaned over and kissed her mother's cheek. "Behave your-self."

Her mother smiled. "I guess that means I'll have to call Robert Redford and tell him he's uninvited."

Camille forced herself to return her mother's smile. "I guess he can come for lunch. As long as he doesn't object to Campbell's tomato soup."

She blew her mother a kiss and scooped up her mock Kate Spade purse as she headed out the door. Another day at the dress shop. One more day with her mother. One more day apart from Alex.

How in the world could she be glad about anything?

December is the wrong month to read Pollyanna, Eugenie thought as she surveyed her guest bed-room. Plastic tubs and wicker baskets filled the space, each one containing a variety of yarn separated by color or type. Anything that might become moth-eaten—wool, silk, cotton—was stored in a tub and tightly sealed. Acrylics and other less vulnerable fibers could be left in the baskets.

When she'd drawn up the reading list, she thought the story would be a suitable one for the Christmas season. What better time to assign each member the task of knitting something for someone less for-tunate? Pollyanna had learned to play the glad game

164

when the donation barrels arrived for her missionary parents. The Christmas the little girl had wanted a doll, the barrel contained nothing for a child but a small pair of crutches. Her father had taught her the game then, telling her that she should rejoice that she didn't actually need the crutches.

The first time Eugenie read the story as a child, she'd been disgusted with the father. But as she matured, she'd come to see the wisdom he'd been trying to teach Pollyanna. Many things in life were a matter of point of view. Eugenie had applied that lesson diligently for the last forty years—until the day Paul had walked into the Pairs and Spares Sunday school classroom.

The other part of the knitting assignment for the month was to use one's personal stash of leftover, unused yarn for the project. No shopping allowed. And since Hannah had no stash, Eugenie had invited the girl to come to her house and look through hers. Hannah had looked less than thrilled, but she'd agreed. After Merry's unsuccessful trip to Nashville, Eugenie wasn't feeling optimistic about her own chances with the teenager. But she wasn't ready to give up, either. She'd seen far worse cases turned around in her day.

A hat. That's what Hannah should do. A hat for Jimmy Bean, local urchin and Pollyanna's sidekick. She had plenty of yarn that would be suitable for that, and the rescue mission in Nashville was always in need of hats during the winter months.

A knock on the door interrupted her thoughts. Hannah was early. But when she opened the front door, it was not Hannah who stood on the small porch.

"Good morning, Eugenie." Paul wore the same dark trench coat against the cold, but this time she could see a green cable knit sweater peeking out from between the lapels. "I hope I'm not disturbing you."

If she'd had a screen door, she might have at least locked that against the intruder. "I'm beginning to feel a bit stalked," she said instead, before motioning him to come inside. She couldn't leave him standing out in the wintry air, much as he might deserve it. "What are you doing here, Paul?"

"I need your help."

Should she ask him to sit down? No, that would only encourage him. But he looked cold. In need of a cup of coffee, no doubt, which she'd just finished brewing so she'd have something to sip while she waited for Hannah to arrive.

"Would you like some coffee?"

He looked as surprised at her offer as she was at extending it. "Sure. That would be fine."

She motioned toward the wingback chairs in front of the window. "You can sit down. Take off your coat. I'll be back in a moment."

What was she thinking? But at least pulling the cups down from the cabinet and pouring the coffee gave her a moment to collect herself. Automatically she fixed his coffee the way he'd liked it when they were young. What if his preference had changed?

166

With a shrug she picked up the mugs and returned to the living room.

"You have a nice home, Eugenie." Paul's gaze encompassed the small living room and the dining area off to the side. "Very comfortable. Very you."

Again that hated blush rose to her cheeks. "Thank you." She sat down in the chair next to him and resisted the impulse to blow on her coffee to cool it. She set the mug on the table between them. "You needed my help with something?"

The way her pulse was pounding, she might as well be sixteen, not sixty-five. Where was her legendary self-control when she truly needed it?

He paused to sip his coffee. And then he looked at her, really looked at her, and if she thought her heart was thumping before, well, she'd been mistaken. Because that was nothing compared to the drumming that commenced in her chest as he looked into her eyes.

"Why do you think I took the job at the church here, Eugenie?"

No. No. He couldn't do this now. She wasn't prepared, and Hannah would arrive on her doorstep at any moment.

"Paul, I don't see any need to—"

"Because of you, Eugenie. I took the job because of you."

"I find that difficult to believe." There. That was more like it. She sounded cool, in command. "You didn't even recognize me when you first saw me."

167

And then she flushed because she remembered that perhaps the reason he hadn't recognized her was because she'd changed so much, and not for the better.

"I knew it was you. I was just playing it cool."

"Oh," Eugenie said, afraid to make any comment when what she really wanted to say was, "Oh my."

He paused, as if he wanted to say something but then changed his mind. "It took me awhile to find you," he said.

"Really? You make it sound as if I've been in the Witness Protection Program."

"I wondered about you for years. But by the time . . . Well, once your mother passed away, no one knew where you'd gone. You didn't keep in touch with anyone from Columbia."

"No. I didn't."

"Why?"

She shrugged. "The past is the past, Paul. We can't change it. We can only move forward."

"And you've done that. Admirably."

"Thank you." Only she wasn't sure he meant it as a compliment. Not completely anyway.

"So if you don't want to talk about the past, let's talk about the future." His eyes bored into hers.

"The future?"

Stop it, she admonished herself. She wasn't allowed to feel that tiny blossom of hope that sprang up in her chest. And she was a fool if she read anything into his words that he didn't say outright.

Paul looked down at the coffee cup in his hands.

"For a long time after Helen died, I didn't think I had a future." He paused. "I went through the motions. I preached. I made hospital calls, led meetings, tended to my flock. But my life was empty. I was empty." This time, when he lifted his eyes to hers, she caught her breath at the pain there. This was the second time she'd seen that look in his eyes, and it was just as unsettling as the first. "I did a lot of thinking about my life. About what I'd done. What I'd left undone. What I should have done." He reached over and very gently took Eugenie's hand in his. She let him, unresisting, too stunned to do anything but look at her fingers wrapped in his as if they were no longer part of her body at all but belonged to someone else. "I thought a lot about you, Eugenie."

Tears pooled in her eyes, tears she could ill afford to entertain or show. "Paul—" She tugged at her hand, but he kept his hold on it. "Please . . ."

"Not until I've said my piece. I lost you once. Now I have a second chance. Not many people get a second chance in this life."

The knock on the door jolted Eugenie as if she'd been struck by lightning. She jumped, pulling her hand free. *Hannah.* She patted the pocket of her skirt, searching for a tissue. Paul was frowning.

"Don't answer it," he said, but she practically leaped to her feet in her haste to escape the unwanted conversation.

"I have to. It's Hannah."

"Who's Hannah?"

169

She ignored his question and instead used the tissue to dab at her eyes as she stepped to the door. Hand on the knob, she took a deep breath, straightened her shoulders, and opened the door. "Good morning, dear," she said with false brightness.

The girl's eyebrows arched in surprise at her enthusiastic greeting. "Morning," she grunted, then shivered in her thin cardigan. "It's cold out here," she said, clearly annoyed at having to state the obvious.

"Come in. Come in." Eugenie motioned for the girl to move through the doorway.

Hannah took two steps inside and then came to a screeching halt. "What's he doing here?" She looked over her shoulder at Eugenie with anger and hurt mingled in her eyes. "You staging some kind of spiritual intervention?"

Eugenie had to swallow the bark of laughter that rose in her throat. She would be the last person in the world to stage a spiritual anything, but she could hardly say that to Hannah at the moment.

"Not at all. The preacher was just paying a pastoral visit."

"I didn't think you went to church," Hannah said, clearly dubious.

"I don't. That's why he came to call." The lie fell easily off her lips, but it clearly relieved the teenager.

"I guess we got that in common then."

Apparently all it took to raise her in the girl's estimation was a mutual antipathy for organized religion.

"Rev. Carson was just leaving."

Paul wore the look of a man who knew he'd been outmaneuvered but clearly wasn't ready to give up entirely. "I'll come back another time when it's more convenient," he said.

"You do that, preacher." She reached for his coat, which she'd hung over one of the straight-back chairs at the dining table.

"I will," he said, his voice firm, but Eugenie was too relieved at his departure to care. After an exchange of good-byes, he left and she shut the door firmly behind him.

"Now," she said to Hannah, rubbing her hands together to warm them, "let's have a look at that yarn." The teenager looked less than enthusiastic, but she followed Eugenie into the spare bedroom. "I was thinking a hat would be a good project." Eugenie gestured toward the bins and baskets of yarn. "Shall we?"

Again, Hannah grunted, but Eugenie was relieved to see her move toward an open bin and begin to poke through its contents, leaving Eugenie to contemplate what else Paul Carson might have said if Hannah hadn't knocked on the door.

Sixteen

The December meeting of the Sweetgum Knit Lit Society evidenced less Christmas spirit than Ebenezer Scrooge. At least that was Ruthie's assessment as she looked around the table at the glum faces of the women there. So much for Pollyanna and her glad game.

"Is Pollyanna's approach unrealistic?" Eugenie asked, looking at each of them.

No one appeared eager to respond to her question, but Ruthie thought their silence was an answer in itself. She had been pondering that very question for several weeks, and she had yet to come up with a satisfactory answer. Because the thing she'd always believed would make her glad above everything else had happened. Esther had told Frank she wanted a divorce. And still Ruthie couldn't bring herself to play Pollyanna's game.

"It's childlike," Merry said, trying hard to sound upbeat, but the strain showed around her eyes. "Kids are so innocent that they still have hope. Mine do. At least"—she chuckled—"when they're not being rotten."

"Childlike? Don't you mean childish?" Esther

looked tenser than ever, but only Ruthie was in a position to know the cause of her sister's strained expression. "I'm sure this is wonderful fiction for girls, but it hardly provides a way to conduct your life as an adult."

Hannah watched them as if it were a tennis match, their words volleyed back and forth like the ball. Ruthie wondered what the teenager made of all of them. Camille's eyes were red—clearly she'd been crying before coming to the meeting—and Eugenie wasn't on her usual even keel. The librarian's eyes kept darting to the door of the classroom, as if expecting a ghost to appear.

"I mean childlike," Merry insisted. "Maybe we could all use a little dose of looking at our lives through a child's eyes."

Esther snorted, a surefire indication of how over-wrought she was beneath that polished veneer. "Isn't there a Scripture about that? 'When I became a man, I put childish ways behind me'?"

Eugenie stiffened. Despite the fact that they met at a church, she never liked it when one of them brought the Bible into the conversation. Eugenie believed in human reason and human reason alone.

"What do you think, Hannah?" Eugenie asked the girl, diverting the conversation from anything bibli-cal. Ruthie watched the teenager closely, trying to guess her response to the disagreement.

"Perhaps we should try the glad game right now and see if it works," Merry said before Hannah could answer Eugenie's question. "Why don't we go around the table and each say one thing we're glad about?"

Ruthie stifled a groan. Trust Merry to trot out the sunshine and roses. Couldn't she feel the tension in the room? Clearly the younger woman had some sort of death wish. Figuratively speaking.

"For example," Merry continued, "I'm glad that Christmas is just around the corner. We've already put up the tree, and the house smells like evergreen." She paused and looked at Esther. "I bet there's something you're glad about. Won't you see your grandchildren during the holidays?"

Esther's hands stopped moving. She clutched her knitting needles in a death grip.

"Yes. I'll see my grandchildren." Esther piled her knitting on the table in front of her in an uncharacteristically messy clump. "What do you want me to say? I'm glad they'll deign to visit for twenty-four hours, chanting the whole time about how they wish they were at home instead of at my house. I'm glad I'll spend hours cooking a wonderful dinner that no one will want to eat because they're either allergic, too busy watching a ball game, or on the Atkins Diet." Her hands clutched the edge of the table even as her voice rose higher. Ruthie wondered if she should intervene, but something held her back. "Should I say that I'm glad my husband finally agreed to bypass surgery, but only because I asked him for a divorce?" Esther demanded.

An audible gasp rose from the other members of

the group, as much from the shocking news as from the sight of Esther losing control.

"What else shall I be glad about, Merry?" Esther's chin quivered. For the first time in years, Ruthie watched as her sister crumpled before her eyes. Esther had always been such an overwhelming force that the sight was as fascinating to Ruthie as it was frightening.

"I don't think—," Eugenie began, but somehow Esther's tirade had released a surge of emotion in the room. Ruthie watched, powerless and amazed, as one by one the women laid their knitting on the table and took up the chorus.

"I'm glad the holidays only come once a year," Camille said, crossing her arms over her chest. "I spend all day long on my feet in that dress shop. No one wants to wear the same thing anyone else is wearing, but I can't carry only one of each outfit. It's a nightmare."

Ruthie felt herself begin to get in the spirit of this new version of the glad game. "I'll be glad when all the bulletins for the special services are done," she said, "and I don't have to spritz the greenery in the sanctuary with water every day. And I don't have to nag Napoleon to vacuum up all the needles."

"Okay, okay," Merry said with a laugh. "If you want to play it that way, I'll be glad when all the presents are wrapped and the kids quit bugging me for things we can't afford and I don't have to hide the credit card statement from Jeff when it comes in."

Even Eugenie joined in, much to Ruthie's surprise. "I'll be glad when the library closes for the week between Christmas and New Year's. A little peace and quiet wouldn't come amiss right now. Maybe I'll go out of town for a few days." She looked surprised at her own words, but her jaw was set along determined lines.

"Perhaps I'll forget cooking Christmas dinner at all," Esther said. "Perhaps I'll choose instead to be glad that the country club serves a buffet and we can all go there. And my family can complain to the chef instead of me about carbs and soy and all the culinary evils being inflicted on them."

Ruthie didn't think Pollyanna would approve of the twist they'd put on her beloved game, but the energy in the room seemed to have picked them all up and given them a good shaking. All kinds of truth were spilling out.

"What else should we be glad about?" Camille said, chin thrust out like a defiant child. "I might like this game after all."

Merry dropped the next bombshell. "Should I be glad that I'm pregnant and that my husband doesn't want another child?"

Her words were greeted with stunned silence and then a whoosh of air as everyone released the breath they'd been holding. Ruthie looked around the circle, and the expression she saw on each face matched the combination of disbelief and relief she felt in her heart.

"Should I be glad the city council is forcing me to retire?" Eugenie shook her head in disgust. "Forty years and for what?"

"Should I be glad that this might be my mother's last New Year's? That she won't have to be in pain forever?" Camille's voice broke on the last word.

"Oh, honey." Ruthie leaned over and laid a hand on her arm, but the young woman shrank back.

"That's the problem with Pollyanna, isn't it?" Camille snapped. "Sure, in fiction everything turns out okay in the end. But real life's not like that." She dug in her purse, produced a tissue, and blew her nose. The rest of them sat in uncomfortable silence.

"I'm glad school's in session through the end of this week." Hannah's soft voice surprised Ruthie, as it did the other members of the Knit Lit Society. "That way I can get at least two meals a day." She looked around the table, glaring at each of them fiercely in turn. "I'm glad my mom's boyfriend didn't stay over last night because it's too cold now to sleep in the woods, and I'm tired of him looking like he's about to grope me. And I'm glad I only have to come to this stupid meeting two more times before the librarian gets off my back because you people are pathetic." She paused. "Except for her." Hannah jerked her head in Camille's direction. "She's got a right to feel sorry for herself. But the rest of you?" Her kohl-rimmed eyes pinned the ladies to their chairs, and Ruthie felt the truth of the girl's words. "There's nothing wrong with the rest of you that you can't change."

The ancient radiator in the corner clanked and hissed, the only sound in the classroom. Esther had crossed her arms over her chest, and Camille was dabbing at her eyes with her handkerchief. Eugenie and Merry exchanged guilty looks, and Ruthie sat stunned.

"Do you really have to sleep outside?" Ruthie finally managed to say to Hannah and immediately realized it was probably the wrong thing to ask. The girl scooped up her knitting from the tabletop and shoved it in her backpack. She jumped out of her chair and made for the door before any of the others could stop her.

"Hannah, wait!" Ruthie was only a few steps behind her when the girl hit the stairwell, but Hannah was far faster—and younger—than Ruthie. By the time Ruthie made it to the outside door of the church, the only thing she could see beyond the small circle of illumination cast by the church's exterior lighting was Hannah's retreating back.

"Wait! It's too cold for you to walk home." She dashed after the girl, but she hadn't gone twenty yards when she realized she would never catch her. She stood on the sidewalk, panting, and was still trying to get her breathing under control when Camille appeared at her side.

"She's gone?"

"I couldn't stop her."

Camille had her car keys in hand and her purse slung over one shoulder. Her coat was buttoned up tight against the cold. "I'll find her and make sure she gets home safe."

"Thank you." Ruthie had always had a low tolerance for Camille. She thought the girl's mother had indulged her far too much over the years. But tonight she was grateful for her presence and her willingness to help.

"Any idea where she likes to hang out?" Camille asked.

"No. None." Ruthie paused. "I guess I don't really know her all that well."

"I think that's what we all figured out tonight." Camille stepped toward her small silver convertible, bought for her on her sixteenth birthday and now beginning to show its age. "Don't worry. I'll find her."

"Okay."

Camille hopped behind the wheel and took off after Hannah. Ruthie could only envy her that youthful energy. She hadn't moved like that in at least a decade, maybe more. And yet inside she still felt no older than Camille.

Was she glad or sorry that her youth was gone? The thought nipped at her heels as she reentered the church and climbed the stairs back to the Sunday school classroom. Pollyanna might always be able to see the silver lining, but Ruthie had been wrapped in a cocoon for so long that she wasn't sure what was lining and what was the outer layer anymore.

Camille spotted Hannah two blocks from the church.

179

Her headlights caught the girl's neon lime green jacket, which was much too thin for the wintry weather. She swerved to the curb and came to an abrupt halt. Throwing open the passenger side door, she barked at Hannah. "Get in." Camille wasn't feeling particularly pleasant at the moment, but she'd taken the excuse of going after the girl to get away from the meeting.

"I can walk."

Camille was young enough to remember how it felt to be thirteen but old enough to be impatient with it. Besides, it was freezing. "Of course you can," she snapped. "But why would you want to when I'm willing to drive you home?"

Hannah stopped. After a long moment, she turned toward the car. "All right." She said the words as if she were doing Camille a huge favor. Maybe she was. Camille had revealed far more than she meant to back in that meeting. She'd learned long ago, when she wasn't much older than Hannah, how important it was to keep your private life close to the vest.

Hannah slid into the car, slumped down in the seat, and scowled.

"Put on your seat belt," Camille said as she shifted the car into gear.

"Yes, Mrs. McGavin."

Camille ignored her sarcasm. Merry had clearly gotten under the girl's skin, and Camille knew from experience that when something got up next to someone like that, it meant a nerve had been struck. Maybe hammered. Or, as it appeared in Hannah's case, blasted to smithereens.

"Which way?" Camille would have felt more indignant at the girl's lack of gratitude, but she was just too tired. Her mother hadn't slept well the night before, and then Camille had spent the day waiting, yet again, for her cell phone to ring. For weeks now her phone had been silent. Alex had moved back home for the holidays. Just for the children, or so he'd told her, and she'd chosen to believe him. She had called him last Saturday night, and they'd had a whispered conversation. Well, she hadn't whispered, but he'd been at a party, standing in the walk-in closet of his host's master bedroom, so he kept his voice low. He and his wife were attending a Christmas party at the senior partner's home. The place was crawling with people from his firm, he'd said. He'd call her soon when he could really talk. It had been almost a week since that conversation.

"I'm sorry about your mother." Hannah blurted out the words, as close as she was going to come to an act of contrition. Camille could feel Hannah's eyes on her. "What's she sick with?"

Camille thought about the question for a good long while. The answer wasn't as easy as most people might think. In the end, she answered Hannah's question with a question. "Does it matter?"

The teenager shrugged and turned back to stare out the front windshield. "Guess not."

"I'm sorry about *your* mother," Camille said in return. She knew better than to reach over and pat Hannah's hand or use some other lame gesture to try and comfort her. And despite her own pain, she could still feel for the girl. People thought abuse meant hitting a kid or screaming at her. But neglect could do just as much damage. Camille's mother had never done anything but indulge her. Still, that had never made up for her father's departure. He was out there somewhere, and he didn't care enough to check to see if she and her mother were alive or dead. And pretty soon there would be a permanent answer to that question. Pretty soon it would be too late.

"Turn up there." Hannah pointed toward a dirt road that connected with the main highway. Camille followed her directions, wincing at the potholes as her convertible shimmied and bumped on the gravel surface. Out here beyond the town lights, the pitch-black night closed in with a vengeance.

In the distance, Camille saw a solitary light. As she drove closer, she could make out the outline of a dilapidated mobile home. The only car in front of the house was a battered old Ford Escort.

"Will you be okay?" Camille asked. The sight of that trailer in the cold, dark night scared her. It was so different from her mother's neat little bungalow, tucked in its row of similar houses on a quiet, tree-lined street.

Hannah shrugged in response.

"Is he here? Is that his car?" Camille had been pursued by enough creeps to understand the girl's fear of her mother's boyfriend.

Hannah froze.

"What is it?" Camille could feel the anxiety radiating from the girl. "Is something wrong?"

"He's not here." But there was no relief in Hannah's voice.

"Do you want to come home with me?" The moment Camille asked the question, she wished she could take it back. Only a few people, mostly the nurses from the hospice and the chaplain, came into their home these days. Why had she invited Hannah?

"Nah. I'll be okay."

"What about yarn for the *Heidi* project? Do you have what you need?" Eugenie had assigned them to make a felted lunch bag for Peter, the goatherd.

Again the girl shrugged, her matted hair falling across her face to shield her expression.

Camille started to reach out to lay a hand on Hannah's arm, but she stopped herself. "I'll pick you up one day after school if you want and take you to Munden's to look for yarn. You'll probably need help with the felting part of the project. We can do that at my house if you don't have a washing machine."

This time Hannah's shoulders slumped instead of her spine. The curvature of a teenager's body could express a huge difference in emotion, depending on where the bend occurred. Camille had used her own spine and shoulders in a similar way not so long ago.

"Why do you want to help me?" Hannah looked her in the eye again, and Camille had to steel herself not to flinch.

"Because I can't help myself right now, so I might as well be of use to somebody," Camille answered honestly.

Hannah nodded, solemn as a judge. "Okay. I get out of school at three."

"I remember." Eleven years ago she'd been Hannah's age. It seemed more like a hundred. "I'll see you soon."

Hannah bolted out of the car, slammed the door shut, and took off for the trailer. Camille watched as she paused by the rickety deck that did duty as the front porch. Then she was in motion again, scrambling up the steps and disappearing inside.

Camille put her car in reverse, turned around, and headed for home, both grateful for and tormented by the prospect of what waited for her there.

Seventeen

Christmas had, thankfully, come and gone.

Ruthie walked home from her job at the church more quickly now that it was January. Head down to protect her from the icy sting of the wind and longing for a hot cup of tea, she made a beeline from the church to her own front door. Only today instead of pausing at the mailbox on the street to retrieve the daily deposit of circulars and unwanted solicitations, she stopped suddenly in the middle of the sidewalk. Stopped and stared at the familiar figure once again seated on her porch swing.

She hurried toward the house, fumbling in her bag for her keys. Since the last time he'd appeared, she'd been locking her front door. "Frank—"

"Don't scold me, Ruthie. Just let me inside. I'm close enough to frostbite as it is."

She complied with his request, her heart in her throat. Other than at the Knit Lit Society meeting, Esther hadn't spoken to Ruthie since the day she'd come to the church office. Well, perhaps that wasn't quite true. Esther had spoken to her at Christmas lunch, when Alex and his family came to town and they'd all gone to the buffet at the country club.

185

Esther had greeted Ruthie the times she'd come to speak with the new pastor and Ruthie had been behind her desk, hard at work. But as to any meaningful conversation between sisters, well . . . No. Radio silence had ruled. Ruthie knew full well what her sister wanted her to do, but she couldn't. Not like this.

"Get in here before you catch your death," she said to Frank. She unlocked the door and shooed him inside like a naughty child, but her palms were sweating and she almost tripped over the welcome mat. Since she turned her thermostat way back when she left for work each day, the small living room wasn't much warmer than the outdoors.

"Keep your coat on for a minute," she instructed him. She dropped her bag on the coffee table and moved to the fireplace to light the gas logs. "It'll warm up pretty quickly."

"Ruthie." His voice was low and serious. "Stop."

She paused, kneeling there on the hearth with her back to him. He came toward her, and she straightened so abruptly that she hit her head on the corner of the mantel.

"Ow!" Tears filled her eyes, and she clasped her hand to her head. "Shoot."

"Are you okay?"

He was next to her then, one hand on her shoulder and the other gently moving her fingers away to assess the damage. "No blood," he said, his voice as soothing as his presence was unnerving. "Do you want some ice?"

186

"No. I'll be okay." The tears receded and she stepped away from him. "Clumsy of me." The fire had begun to warm the room, and she reached to unbutton her coat. "Do you want some tea? Or soup?" Sitting out in the cold couldn't be good for his heart.

"I don't want tea or anything else. I just want to talk to you. Sit down. Please."

She did as he asked, perching on one end of the couch while he took the other end. With a start, she realized that she was still wearing her coat, but her hands shook too badly to take it off.

"Frank—"

"No, Ruthie. I'm going to do the talking now."

She nodded. How many more times would she have to do this? Escape was still weeks away. The thick registration packet had arrived yesterday, and she'd worked late into the night filling out all the necessary forms that she could. Others, like a health screening from her doctor, would require a little more time.

"You said you couldn't find your own happiness at Esther's expense, and I admire that about you." He inched closer on the sofa and reached for her hand. She let him take it and bit her lip against the sorrow rising in her chest. "But things are different now. You know that," he said. "Esther's the one who kicked me to the curb." He squeezed her fingers. "I'm a free man, Ruthie. No encumbrances. No guilt. And now the holidays are past—Esther and I didn't want to upset the grandchildren—but now that's over and you and I can be together."

Once again, her sister had manipulated her so neatly that Ruthie had to admire her for it at some level. Hadn't Frank figured that out by now, that Esther always got what she wanted in the end? But no. He'd never seen that side of his wife, or never allowed himself to see it. Either way, Frank had no idea how self-serving his wife's request for a divorce really was.

"Frank—" Her hand, wrapped in his, felt warm and safe, something she hadn't felt in a very long time.

"No, Ruthie." Now he laid a finger to her lips. Shame on her for the thrill that raced through her. She was too old, too principled, but mostly too scared. She didn't want this to happen, but it was going to, no matter what she did. Esther had seen to that. "It's our time. Finally. Or at least it will be once the divorce goes through. But I have a favor to ask."

She knew what it was, could see it coming as clear as day.

"I'm going to have the heart surgery after all. Next week, in Nashville. I want you to be with me."

"What about Esther?" she asked past the sudden dryness in her throat.

"I think she's made her position in all of this pretty clear."

If only she could tell him the truth. But if she did, he would change his mind about the surgery. And right now, like her sister, she needed him to be alive more than she needed to be truthful.

He put his other hand on top of hers, trapping her as securely as her sister had. "Please, Ruthie. For years I've felt dead inside anyway. Now I have a chance at a new life. With you by my side." His voice choked with emotion. "We've denied our feelings for a long time. Don't you think it's time we were honest for a change?"

"Yes. Yes, I do." What else could she say? The lie almost stuck in her throat, but she'd learned long ago to hide her feelings from the world. Even Frank would never guess what was truly going on in her head and heart.

"Good. Then you'll come with me to Nashville for the surgery?"

"We can't be anything more than friends as long as you're still married to Esther," she warned him. On that count, at least, she was determined to prevail.

His smile took root slowly and then blossomed. "All right, but just remember that I'm a very determined man. And soon I'll be a free one."

She wanted to feel the happiness that was trying to bloom in her body just as the smile had bloomed on his face. But how could she when she knew that this new turn of events was just as false as the last three decades of their lives? Not only could appearances be deceiving; they could be devastating as well to the people who had to maintain them at all costs.

* * *

Merry sat alone in the dining room, waiting for Jeff to come home. She'd dropped the kids off at her mother's house an hour before with plans to pick them up again later in the evening after dinner. She hadn't told her mother why she needed emergency baby-sitting, and for once her mother hadn't asked. And so now she sat at her beautiful Ethan Allen teakwood dining table with the walnut inlay, admiring the handsome matching china cabinet and its treasure trove of contents. Waterford crystal. Wedgwood china. Twenty-four place settings of sterling silver. Linen tablecloths and napkins for every occasion. Yes, the china cabinet had everything a successful lawyer's wife could possibly need to ensure that her guests dined in comfort.

Why then did the room feel so empty?

Without the usual clattering and banging the kids created, she could fully appreciate the silence, punctuated only by the sound of the furnace clicking on or off as the thermostat dictated.

She'd spent the day wrestling the crib down from the attic and assembling it in the guest bedroom—not the easiest task for a woman who was as pregnant as she was. Through the kitchen doorway, she could hear the hum of the washing machine in the combination laundry/mud room that led to the garage. The occasional *bang* told her that the tennis balls she'd put in the water with her knitting project were doing their job. After another cycle or two, her felting would be complete, and she'd have a sturdy lunch bag worthy of any self-respecting Alpine goatherd. At least the project for *Heidi* had helped keep her hands, if not her mind, occupied over the last few days. Time had run out. She had no choice but to tell Jeff about the baby. She was scheduled for an ultrasound tomorrow. Jeff had been with her for that particular test with each of the children, and she didn't want this baby to be any different. So she had to tell him tonight. And tomorrow she'd find out whether she was going to have a boy or a girl. Tonight she was going to find out if she still had a marriage.

If she thought about it, though, she'd cry, so she stood up and walked back through the kitchen to check on the washing machine. Before she could get there, the louder hum of the garage door opening overrode the sound of the washing machine. Jeff was home.

Merry froze. He was early, or at least he was early for Jeff. She double-checked her watch. It was barely after five. She thought she'd have more time to figure out what to say. Of course, she knew what she had to say. She just hadn't figured out yet quite how to say it.

The door to the garage opened and there he was, framed in the opening, as devastatingly handsome as ever. He took one look at her and frowned. "Merry? Are you okay?" He shut the door behind him and put a hand on her shoulder. "Honey?"

She hadn't meant to scare him. At least not by standing in the laundry room like a zombie.

"Hi. You're home early."

"What's wrong? Is it one of the kids?" His eyes darkened with worry.

"No. No. Everything's fine."

He looked over her shoulder and then cocked his head as if listening. "Where are they?"

"They're at my mom's. She invited them for dinner."

"Oh." Disappointment lined his face. "I took off early so I could spend some time with them this evening."

Normally she would have been over the moon with joy at his words, but tonight they were like a knife in her heart.

"I'm sorry. If you had let me know—"

And then the lines of disappointment in his face turned to sadness. "Sorry. I didn't know I'd be throwing a major kink in the works."

This wasn't going at all the way she'd planned. "Jeff—"

"It's okay, Merry. Sorry. Don't know what I was thinking."

No, no, no. This conversation was not supposed to play out like this. Even if she hadn't prepared down to the last detail, she did have a general idea of what should happen, and this definitely wasn't it.

"Jeff." She caught the sleeve of his navy blazer as he moved past her. "Wait."

Heavens above, she'd never planned to tell him about the baby while standing in the middle of the laundry room, but apparently there was never going to be a better time.

"What?" He wasn't rude, but he wasn't very cooperative either. His arm was stiff as a board beneath her hand.

"Actually, I asked Mom to take the kids tonight. I wanted us to have some time together. I need to tell you something."

She had his full attention now. "That sounds pretty ominous."

"It's not. I mean, I don't think it is. I hope you won't."

He looked more confused than ever, his face mirroring the exhaustion she was feeling these days.

"What is it, Merry? If the kids aren't here, I'm going to go take a nap before dinner." He looked toward the kitchen.

"I'm pregnant." She felt like she might vomit. Bile stung her throat. "That's what I needed to tell you. I'm pregnant."

She'd read in books where folks talked about time standing still, but she'd never actually experienced it before. Jeff's mouth hung open, and she resisted the urge to reach out and push his chin up to close it.

Relief and fear raced through her veins in a potent mixture with the regret and panic already residing there. "I didn't mean to tell you like this. I was going to fix a nice dinner. We were going to eat by candlelight. And then I was going to tell you."

"How did this happen?" He looked as astonished

as he had the first time she'd communicated this kind of information over thirteen years ago.

Merry laughed. How could she not? "The usual way, Jeff. I would think you'd be up to speed on that part by now."

"But we—"

"Nothing's a hundred percent effective."

And then his shoulders sank. There it was, the response she'd been dreading, the reason she'd put this off as long as she possibly could. Now instead of handsome and strong, he looked defeated and about a decade older than when he'd walked through the door.

"I thought you were just gaining some weight. Merry, we can't—"

"We don't have any choice, Jeff. It's too late. And we wouldn't have done anything about it anyway."

He nodded, but he didn't look at her. "You're right. It's just that . . ."

"What?" she asked softly. She reminded herself that she'd had several months to get used to the idea. Jeff was just beginning that journey.

"Merry—" He pressed his palm to his forehead and rubbed his hand across his brow and down the side of his face. "Oh God, Merry. I don't know how to tell you this."

Now her pulse was racing, and she could feel her knees quaking beneath her. His new paralegal. What was her name? Mitzi? Missy? A new kind of panic swamped her. Sure, she worried about that quite a bit. Jeff was so handsome and charismatic. But deep down she'd never really thought it might happen, that he might—

"Jeff?"

She couldn't believe her marriage was going to end in the laundry room. The bedroom she could understand. The dining room, or even the kitchen. But here? With piles of dirty clothes strewn around their feet and the smell of bleach and Mr. Clean permeating the air?

"Just say it, Jeff."

He heaved a sigh. "Okay." Then he looked at her, and she wished he hadn't. She'd never seen that look of total defeat in his eyes before, not even when he lost some very important, vital cases.

"You're not saying it."

"I will. Just give me a minute."

"Jeff . . ."

"It's not what you're thinking."

"What am I thinking?"

"It's not another woman. Nothing like that."

"Then what is it?"

He took a deep breath and then let it out in one long whoosh. "I came home early because I had to file for bankruptcy today."

Eighteen

Camille couldn't believe she had to spend a month reading *Heidi* and knitting a lunch bag. She'd never had any interest in felting—the process where you knit a wool item oversize and then shrink it in the washing machine. The end product was quite literally felt—like the stuff her mom used to cut up to make Christmas tree ornaments. Well, not exactly like that but the same texture and toughness with the little bits of fuzz attached. Felted knitting looked rustic, exactly like something the fictional Heidi would use to tote around bread and cheese to sustain her through a long day of scrambling up and down mountains.

Camille was not a fan of *Heidi*. The outdoors held no allure for her, and the one time she'd watched a movie version of the book she'd been disgusted with the whole plot. Heidi seemed to her to be a needy wimp who would attach herself to anyone who threw her the smallest crumb of affection. Camille couldn't relate to that at all.

But here she was, once again reading to her mother in hopes of keeping her suffering at bay for a few precious hours. Her mother had given up on reading aloud after *Little Women*. She didn't have the stamina. So Camille read, watching for the moment when her mother fell asleep and she could set the book aside and pick up her knitting until it was time to leave for work and open the dress shop.

She had promised to pick up Hannah after school and help her buy yarn for the felting project. Munden's would have some cheap wool that would work, but Camille had her doubts about how well it would felt. No two yarns shrank in the same way or at the same rate. She'd help Hannah get the yarn, and then maybe Merry or Ruthie could take over for the felting part. If nothing else, Camille knew her limits. Well, sometimes she did.

As her mother snored peacefully and the clock in the corner of the room ticked on, Camille kept her eyes on her knitting and her ears cocked in hopes that her cell phone would ring.

Lunch was the worst time of the day for Hannah. Thirty-five minutes of torment, and she could only spend so much time standing in the cafeteria line or dawdling in the bathroom. The worst part was at the cash register. She was a check mark girl, had been since her mother dropped her off that first day at kindergarten.

"Burrito or chicken patty?" Luellen, the ancient cafeteria lady, asked the question in her usual monotone.

Hannah paused to consider which option would

keep her stomach full longer. "Burrito, please."

Luella picked up one of the prefab burritos and plunked it on a plastic tray, which she pushed down the line to the next worn-looking cafeteria worker. Sometimes Hannah felt as old as the ladies looked. One by one, they slapped her green beans, fruit cocktail, and peanut butter cookie on the tray. She grabbed a carton of milk, accepted her tray from the last worker, and approached the cashier, Mrs. O'Brien. The cashier looked at her expectantly and then heaved a big sigh when Hannah didn't flash any cash. Mrs. O'Brien lifted the clipboard from the counter beside her.

"Name?"

You'd think after all these years the old bat would acknowledge that she knew every kid in Sweetgum like the back of her hand, but the routine never varied. It was designed for maximum humiliation each and every day. Mrs. O'Brien didn't approve of the free lunch kids.

"Hannah Simmons."

Ogre O'Brien, as Hannah liked to call her, scanned the list four or five times before heaving yet another enormous sigh and making a check mark by Hannah's name.

"Next?" She looked right past Hannah, as if she were as transparent as glass. Ogre O'Brien didn't need to perform her elaborate ritual every single day. Hannah had gotten the message long ago.

The second worst part of lunch was emerging from

the cafeteria line. There she was faced with long rows of tables filled with her peers. Also known as her tormentors. Except for Kristen, but she wasn't speaking to Hannah these days. Not since Hannah had refused to make out with Jimmy Clausen in the cemetery on a regular basis. Or on any basis at all.

Today she was lucky. She spotted an empty table near the door at the far end of the room. She could wolf down her food and make a break for the bathroom.

Hannah plopped her tray on the empty table and herself in the ancient folding chair. She'd brought her book too, carefully covered. She'd used a sack from Munden's, turned inside out, to make a plain brown wrapper for *Heidi*. All she needed was for someone to spot her carrying around a kid's book. She'd be more of an outcast than she already was, if that was even possible.

Five minute later Hannah was lost in the book, mindlessly chomping on her burrito, when a lunch tray thumped down next to hers. She jumped, looked up, and felt like the burrito might reappear. Courtney McGavin stood next to her, the world's fakest smile planted on her face. "Mind if we join you?"

Crap. Double crap. She shrugged, playing it cool even while her heart climbed up in her throat. "Whatever." She shut the book and put it in her lap. Instinct told her to pick up her tray and run for the door, but she couldn't back down. Courtney had two other girls with her, Heather Brown and Lindsey

Myers. Hannah studied them out of the corner of her eye. Heather was a barracuda, but Lindsey had always seemed okay. In fact, she looked uncomfortable as she sat down across from Hannah and shot Courtney a worried look.

"So what are you guys wearing to the winter dance at the club?" Courtney asked, including Hannah in the question. "There's nothing decent in that lame dress shop on the square." She paused to pick at the dressing-free salad on her tray. "Of course, if my mom weren't so involved in her *charity work,*" she cast a meaningful glance at Hannah, "she might have had time to take *me* to Nashville to shop."

This was going to be bad. Hannah clutched the book in her lap.

"Yeah, your mom must really be into helping poor people," Heather said. She was going to enjoy this just as much as Courtney. Hannah kept her silence. Either they'd get tired of goading her and leave, or it would get so bad that she'd have to be the one to flee. But she wasn't going to concede the field of battle without putting up some sort of fight.

"Maybe Hannah has something I can borrow?" Courtney turned to face her, and Hannah could feel the gaze from Courtney's MAC-heavy eyes boring into her. "Maybe you could knit me a dress?" She snickered and Heather joined in.

"Guys . . ." Lindsey looked around and leaned forward to speak in a low voice. "Come on. Let's go back to our table."

"You don't think Hannah's enjoying our company?" Courtney flicked that hair like it was Zorro's blade. "What do you say, Hannah? Want to knit me a Dolce & Gabbana cocktail dress? Or maybe a Vera Wang?" Her snicker turned to a full on laugh. "God, how lame can you be?"

Hannah bit her tongue until she tasted blood. If she said anything, did anything, she knew what would happen. The free lunch girl versus the prepsters. She'd never stand a chance in the kangaroo court known as the principal's office.

"You're so pathetic," Heather said to Hannah, all pretense of politeness gone, claws fully extended. "If you really want to be Courtney's clone, you're going to have to get some decent highlights. And lose a lot of weight." She exchanged a look of triumph with Courtney, and they both burst out laughing. Obviously they'd been rehearsing this for a while. But Hannah refused to give them the satisfaction of so much as a wince.

"Not my problem if your mom would rather hang out with a slacker than a wannabe princess." Hannah kept her voice low and didn't look at any of them when she said the words.

"What did you just say?" Courtney's voice rose to a squeaky pitch. "Tell me you did not just say what I think you said."

"I didn't just say what you thought I said," Hannah replied, sarcasm dripping from her words like poison.

"OMG," Heather said, her jaw hanging open. "Do you have, like, a death wish?"

"Y'all, that's enough," Lindsey said quietly. "Let's go."

"No." Courtney's cheeks were flushed beneath her expensive blusher. She looked like a clown Hannah had seen once at a low-rent circus her mother dragged her to. Of course, her mother had been more interested in entertaining one of the roadies than her daughter. "No," Courtney repeated, her tone edging toward hysterical. "I don't think Hannah here has quite gotten the message yet."

Before Hannah could do or say anything, Courtney slapped her hand down on the inside edge of Hannah's cafeteria tray, flipping it. Quick as lightning, the contents—burrito stub, green beans, fruit cocktail—hit Hannah's chest before falling into her lap, covering the book that lay there.

For a moment Hannah was so stunned that she couldn't move. Courtney and Heather laughed, high-fived, and scampered off as quickly as they'd materialized in the first place. Lindsey started to get up, shot a longing look at the departing queen bees, and then sank back into her chair.

"I'm sorry." She pulled her napkin from underneath her silverware and thrust it toward Hannah. "I swear I didn't know they were going to do that."

"Whatever." It seemed to be the only word she could say, might be the only word she'd ever say again. She knew Courtney McGavin was going to make her pay for that whole trip-to-the-yarn-store disaster sooner or later. "Just leave me alone."

"Come on. Let's go to the rest room." Lindsey stood up and came around the end of the table. She grabbed Hannah's backpack off the floor and motioned for her to stand.

Hannah hesitated. Was Lindsey sincere, or was this just a setup for another humiliation compliments of Courtney McGavin?

"The longer we stand here, the more people will gawk." Lindsey jerked her head toward the door. "Let's go."

Hannah scraped the jumbled mess of food from her book and shirt back onto the tray. She stood up on legs so shaky she thought they might collapse underneath her, but she refused to give Courtney and Heather that satisfaction.

"You're committing social suicide," she hissed at Lindsey, reaching out to snag her backpack off the other girl's shoulder. "Just go back with your pack of she-wolves. You've done your good deed for the day."

"Quit being stupid." Lindsey turned and headed toward the exit closest to their table. The girls' rest room was just across the hall. Left with no choice, Hannah started after her—scared, confused, and biting her lip hard so she wouldn't cry. She refused to give Courtney McGavin the satisfaction of making her cry.

* * *

Hannah looked at herself in the bathroom mirror and took a deep breath to remain calm. The juice from the fruit cocktail had soaked through her T-shirt, leaving it practically see-through in critical spots. Her coat was in her locker, two hallways away, and she had nothing else to wear. The bathroom didn't have an air-dry machine, so she dabbed at the stains with a paper towel. The bell was going to ring any minute, and she couldn't go to class like this. But she couldn't stay in the bathroom either. One more screwup and she'd be spending a whole lot of quality time in detention with Mr. Wharton. She could get a lot of reading done there, but he wouldn't let her knit. She'd tried to last time, and he'd almost confiscated her yarn and needles.

"I've got another shirt in my locker." Lindsey was standing in the corner watching Hannah dab at the stains. The other girl looked at her cell phone, checking the time. "We have six minutes before the bell rings and every girl in Sweetgum Middle School comes in here to reapply lip gloss."

Hannah's hand stopped midswipe. "Why are you doing this?" She was looking in the mirror, but she could see Lindsey's reflection next to her own. "Being someone's *charity* case is what got me into this. Go back to your pack and leave me alone."

"Bite the hand that feeds you much?" Lindsey smiled, but not in a mean way. "Just because Courtney's my friend doesn't mean I approve of everything she does. She's lashing out at you because she's mad at her mom. It's not fair, just fact. I'm trying to minimize the collateral damage." She stuck her cell phone back in her purse. "And now I'm about to risk detention on your behalf by sneaking to my locker to get you something to wear."

"You don't have to."

Lindsey gestured toward Hannah's now see-through T-shirt. "Oh yeah, I do." She paused. "Look, I really am sorry about Courtney. I'll try to keep her away from you."

Hannah didn't get it. Since when did any of the popular posse care about the feelings of a free lunch kid? But before she could say anything else, Lindsey slipped out of the rest room. Hannah took one last swipe at her shirt and finally, now that she was alone, allowed the tears that had been threatening to fall freely. No good ever came of other people's kindness. She ought to have learned that lesson by now.

Nineteen

Munden's Five-and-Dime hadn't changed since Camille was a child. While the elderly Mr. Munden had been replaced behind the cash register by his daughter Maria, the all-purpose store continued to offer the same array of goods that couldn't be found at the Rexall drugstore or Callahan's Hardware. Munden's was where you went if you needed office supplies, craft items, toys, or holiday decorations.

Camille and Hannah moved across the brown tile floor underneath the fluorescent lights, passing shelves of picture frames, candles, and plastic flowers for decorating graves. Camille averted her eyes when they passed the flowers. Death haunted her enough without having to be reminded of its consequences in aisle three.

"What colors do you want?" Camille asked when they reached the back wall. Shelves of yarn stretched six feet high and ten feet across. Hannah had a pattern clutched in her hand. It looked like a freebie she'd downloaded off the Internet.

Hannah shrugged in response. If they had developed any closeness during their ride home from the last meeting of the Knit Lit Society, it had evaporated. Camille wanted to brush off the disappointment she felt, but the girl's cold shoulder bothered her. Hannah hadn't spoken more than three words to her since she'd picked her up at school.

"Can I see the pattern?" Camille tried a different tack. Honestly, she didn't have the time or energy to put up with Hannah's sullenness. But the continued silence of her cell phone had her acting strangely, more like her mother than herself.

"Here." Hannah thrust the paper at her. Camille unfolded it, smoothed out the wrinkles, and studied the design for a simple bag. Two identical squares, which were sewn together, and then a long strap for the handle. Well within Hannah's capabilities as a beginner.

"Looks good. Are you going to keep it or give it away? Knowing who it's for can help with picking colors."

Again the girl shrugged.

"Look, Hannah, you've got to cooperate a little here." Camille tried to keep the impatience from her voice. Besides Sunday, Monday was her one day off. In her fantasies, she would be getting a manicure at Mademoiselle Salon or a facial at the new day spa on the outskirts of town. In reality, she needed to catch up on the laundry or the grocery shopping that never seemed to end.

"Whatever." The girl snagged a few skeins of dark brown yarn from the nearest rack. She whirled around toward the front of the store, but Camille put a hand on her arm to stop her.

"Wait a second. That won't felt. It's acrylic, not wool." If Camille was going to give up her time off, then Hannah was at least going to have to pick the right yarn.

The teenager stuffed the brown hanks back where she'd found them. "Then you pick," she said with a scowl.

"Fine." Camille pulled out several skeins of Pepto-Bismol pink wool. "Here you go." She bit back a smile when she saw Hannah's look of revulsion.

"But—"

"You said you didn't care." Even as Hannah frustrated her, Camille understood where she was coming from. A caged animal has only a limited number of ways to maintain the illusion of control.

"I don't care," Hannah repeated for emphasis.

"But you wouldn't tell me even if you did."

Their eyes locked, a silent battle of wills right there in the back of Munden's Five-and-Dime.

"Come on," Camille said finally, breaking the deadlock. "There's someone I think you should meet."

Camille had never been a selfless person by nature. She wasn't vicious like some of the girls she'd gone to high school with. It just simply didn't occur to her most of the time to look out for other people. She had enough to handle looking out for her mom and herself. But the sight of that run-down trailer and

Hannah's palpable fear at being left there had made an indelible impression. Maybe it was just the common theme of abandonment running through both of their lives. Or maybe Camille was trying to salve a guilty conscience by doing a good deed. But at that moment, she knew beyond a shadow of a doubt that she needed to take Hannah home and introduce the girl to her mother.

The unflappable Maria Munden didn't bat an eyelash when Camille St. Clair bought three skeins of hot pink yarn for Hannah Simmons. Hannah said a begrudging thank-you but held the brown paper sack containing the yarn as if it were a dead skunk. They walked to the car in silence, the same way they drove from the town square to the little bungalow on Carruthers Street. Camille turned off the engine and then swiveled in her seat to face Hannah.

"Just one thing before we go inside," she said.

"What?"

"Be nice to my mother, or I'll make your mom look like a pushover."

Hannah blanched, but Camille could also see a light of respect in the girl's eyes.

"Come on." Camille climbed from the car and headed for the house, Hannah right behind her. She wasn't sure she was doing the right thing, but her mother always enjoyed visitors now that she was bedridden. Camille would get Hannah started on the felting project, let the girl visit with her mom for a while, and then take her home.

And then her good deed for the day would be done and she could get back to wallowing in her own misery.

The surgical waiting room at St. Thomas Hospital in Nashville contained the usual assortment of exhausted relatives, fast-food wrappers, and desperation. Frank had been admitted to the hospital the night before. Ruthie and Esther had arrived very early that morning after spending the night in the upscale Loews Vanderbilt Hotel. Ruthie had wanted to stay at the more economical Hampton Inn, but Esther insisted. And since Esther was footing the bill, Ruthie complied just as she usually did. Still, she resented both the enforced luxury and the reminder that no matter what Frank might believe, Esther was still calling the shots.

"Do you want more coffee?" Ruthie clutched her empty cup. "I can go get some." The Starbucks cart was conveniently located just outside the waiting room so that anxious friends and family could further caffeinate their agitation even as they told one another how soothing they found it.

"No. I'm fine." Esther reached into the designer bag beside her and pulled out her confounded knitting. The whole charade struck Ruthie like a punch to the midsection, leaving her breathless and aching. Her sister might think that merely by willing something to be fact she could make it so, that by passing off someone else's work as her own, she could be a bona fide member of the Knit Lit Society. Maybe that approach worked for Esther much of the time. But knitting, unlike so many other things in life, couldn't be faked.

"I can go to the cafeteria if you're hungry." Ruthie would rather not sit in the waiting room, there amongst the soothing teals and sea foam greens. Every time the phone at the information desk rang, she jumped as if a shot had rung out.

"I'm not hungry." Esther was as calm and poised as always. You'd never know to look at her that her estranged husband was upstairs being cracked open and his chest splayed out. Ruthie both resented and envied Esther's calm, but then she'd felt like that about her sister most of her life, so today was nothing unusual.

"The new minister said he'd come by today." Esther had a habit of sticking her tongue out the tiniest bit when she was concentrating on something difficult, like trying to knit. Ruthie's nerve endings felt raw and exposed. How could she possibly sit here for hours on end, acting as if nothing was wrong? Frank didn't even know that Esther was there, for heaven's sake. He'd made Ruthie promise she wouldn't let her come, but how on earth was Ruthie supposed to do that? So she lied to Frank the night before, telling him she was off to spend the night alone at the hotel when she knew full well that Esther was there waiting to have dinner with her. They'd gone downstairs to the confusingly named Ruth's Chris Steak

House. In other circumstances, Ruthie would have enjoyed a nice meal out. But under these conditions, she could only choke down a few bites of filet mignon before setting her fork aside.

Esther had eaten her entire steak and then asked to look at the dessert menu.

Unable to come up with a good excuse to leave the waiting room, Ruthie sat down in the chair next to her sister. Although they'd arrived very early, they had to settle for plain chairs instead of the more luxurious reclining ones. But they were near the information desk and could easily hear when the volunteer called for "the Jackson family."

Esther continued to stab away at her knitting. Ruthie finally gave in to the inevitable and took her own yarn and needles out of the bag. She'd finished *Heidi* the night before in the hotel room, leaving the book on the nightstand for Esther in case she wanted to read it later, although Ruthie was pretty sure Esther hadn't read any of the books that had been assigned since Eugenie changed the reading list.

Ruthie picked up her needles, threaded the yarn through her left hand, and began to stitch, but she could hardly concentrate she was so distracted by Esther's stabbing motions. The would-be piece had more holes than Swiss cheese. Did Esther not know that anybody who was any sort of knitter could tell what a tangled mess she was making? Yet she sat there, calm as you please, as if she were the most capable knitter anyone would ever run across. Finally, Ruthie couldn't take it anymore.

"If you'd thread the yarn through your left hand, you could get enough tension so it wouldn't be so lumpy." She couldn't help it. The words jumped from her mouth of their own accord.

Esther looked up from her knitting and frowned.

"I know you don't want my help," Ruthie continued before Esther could say anything. "But maybe you want to do this right more than you hate having to ask me for something."

Ruthie bit her lip. She should have been more diplomatic, and for heaven's sake, now was certainly not the time to try and change the way she and her sister had interacted for the last fifty years.

Esther looked at her, then down at her knitting. Ruthie could almost see her weighing her decision, like a butcher piling meat onto his scales. "All right," she said after several long moments. "Show me then."

Ruthie looked at her in surprise. "It's really not so difficult. You just need to—" Ruthie sighed. It was too hard to explain and much easier to demonstrate. "Here." She reached toward Esther and took the yarn that hung from near the tip of the needle. "Lift up your forefinger and pinkie." Esther did as suggested. "Okay, then slide your middle finger and ring finger underneath." Esther followed her instructions. "Now when you turn your hand up like this," she rotated her sister's wrist so that her thumb pointed to the ceiling, "you have better tension on the yarn. Almost like threading a sewing machine." Although Ruthie doubted Esther had ever threaded a sewing machine in her life.

Ruthie watched as her sister started to knit, slowly at first and then gradually beginning to get the hang of running the yarn through the fingers of her left hand. Most people knitted what was called English style, with the loose yarn trailing off to the right, but that required a large wrapping motion for each stitch. If Esther could manage with the thread through her left hand, she would be knitting Continental style. Not so common, but faster and often with better results.

Esther continued haltingly for the rest of the row, the yarn slipping off her fingers several times and Ruthie patiently helping her to thread it again.

"I think that's working," Ruthie said, a strange feeling of triumph welling in her chest. When was the last time Esther had ever let her be the expert on anything? True they were in a mess right now with Esther's machinations to get Frank to have the surgery. But perhaps this could be a turning point. Ruthie didn't want to leave without—

"Oh, honestly, this is ridiculous." Esther's fingers tangled in the yarn and she threw the needles in her lap in disgust. "Your method's supposed to be easier?" She shot Ruthie a dark look. "Or are you just trying to sabotage me?"

Ruthie bit her tongue. What use was there in pointing out that Esther's approach hadn't been working to begin with?

"Why on earth would I want to sabotage your knitting?" The moment Ruthie asked the question, she wished she hadn't.

"Because—" And then Esther stopped. Suddenly, she looked defeated and far older than her years.

The phone at the information desk rang. "Will the Jackson family please come to the desk?" the volunteer in the pink jacket called out. Ruthie's pulse skyrocketed. She scooped up her own knitting, shoved it back in her bag, and wasn't more than a step behind Esther when she made it to the information desk.

"The doctor's on his way down," the volunteer said.

Ruthie had meant to spend the morning praying, not trying to teach her sister to knit. Esther reached over and gripped Ruthie's hand. Hard.

"It'll be okay," Ruthie heard herself say. Not because she believed it, but because she thought it needed to be said.

"Of course it will," Esther snapped, but Ruthie knew her sister's bravado for exactly what it was.

Fear. Fear that her whole life might collapse. Fear that her plan hadn't worked, that it had been too late to save Frank. Ruthie knew what Esther was feeling because she felt exactly the same.

Because even with everything that had happened, they were still sisters.

Twenty

Since the moment Merry hung up the phone with the middle school principal, she'd been dreading the inevitable confrontation with Courtney. Now, hours later, they sat on opposite sides of the dining room table, Merry rubbing her belly and Courtney with her arms crossed over her chest. The table felt as wide as the Mississippi.

She'd been rehearsing her speech all afternoon. She hadn't even mentioned the phone call until after she'd dropped off Heather and Lindsey. She'd kept her silence until they'd arrived home and she'd installed Sarah in front of the television set with an hour's worth of *The Wiggles* playing on TiVo.

"I'm really disappointed in you, Courtney." She'd been so weepy the past couple of weeks, mostly due to hormones, but knowing that didn't help Merry control her emotions in the long run. "Hannah's done nothing to you, and you deliberately embarrassed her. You've never done anything like that before. I don't understand, so I need you to explain it to me." She'd gotten that last sentence verbatim out of one of her "parenting your teen" books.

Courtney gave her obligatory rolling of the eyes.

"It's not that big of a deal. You wouldn't have even known about it if Lindsey hadn't gotten caught in the hall by Mr. Wharton. Jake gets in fights all the time, and you don't go all commando on him."

"First of all, Jake is nine and you're not. Second, we're not discussing your brother. We're talking about you."

"Wouldn't that be a refreshing change of pace?" Courtney snapped.

No one could infuse a question with sarcasm quite like a thirteen-year-old. "That attitude's not going to help us solve this problem."

"What problem is that, Mother?" Courtney only called her *mother* when she needed to put Merry in her place. "If you want to hang out with the dregs of society, that's entirely your business."

Ah, so that was the problem after all. Merry had thought of it as soon as the principal related the story of Courtney's misbehavior, but she hadn't wanted to believe it was true.

"Just because I spent some time trying to help Hannah doesn't take anything away from you, honey. Can't you feel a little compassion for the poor girl?" She reached her hand across the table, hoping Courtney might meet her halfway, but her daughter's hands remained firmly tucked in her armpits.

"I get it, Mom. I get how not important I am to you."

"Courtney! What in the world are you talking

about?" Her lower back felt like it might snap, and the baby was doing somersaults worthy of an Olympic gymnast in her stomach. "Can you please try not to be so dramatic? Just this once?"

The flash of hurt in her daughter's eyes was as uncomfortable for Merry as her swollen belly or feet, but honestly, couldn't Courtney think about someone besides herself for a change?

Courtney's face screwed up with the effort of trying not to cry. "I begged you to take me to Nashville to shop for a dress for the winter dance. And you took that scummy Hannah instead. You've been nagging me for two years to let you knit me something, and I finally see a pattern I like in that magazine you had. The one for that cute pink shrug. And then you spend two weeks making an ugly brown shawl for *her*. Okay, Mom. I get it. You're disappointed. I'm an embarrassment to you. Whatever. Message received, loud and clear. Courtney McGavin, oldest daughter, Not Important!"

With each word out of Courtney's mouth, Merry felt her heart thump faster. She was short of breath anyway since the baby was pushing against her ribs, but as the truth of her daughter's words washed over her, she was a drowning woman with no access to oxygen. Dear, sweet heaven, it was true. Every word out of the child's mouth. She'd been so busy being frustrated with Courtney, being mad at her, fuming at everything her daughter hadn't done, that she'd ignored what Courtney was actually trying to say to her. And what Courtney was trying to say was no different than what she'd said to Merry when she was Sarah's age, poised at the top of the playground slide. *Watch me, Mommy. Watch me.* Only now, at thirteen, Courtney wanted far more than her passive attention. Despite her push-me-pull-you act, what she'd wanted all along was her mother's presence in her life. Here she was on kid number four, and she still hadn't gotten the hang of being a mother. Not in the most important ways. Not in the ways that counted.

"Oh, Courtney." She tried to lever herself out of the chair, but such a task was easier said than done. "Sweetie, it's not like that."

Courtney's sobs grew until she was in full-blown weeping mode. "It feels that way to me." She wiped her nose with the back of her hand like a little child.

With a final push, Merry made it out of the chair. She maneuvered her way around the table to stand beside her daughter. "I'm sorry, honey. I didn't mean to hurt your feelings." How in the world did parents ever survive having teenagers? In so many ways they were like toddlers—only more articulate and with more expensive tastes.

"Look, you'll have the spring dance in a few months, and we'll definitely go to Nashville then." Of course, they wouldn't be able to afford to shop at their usual haunts, not with the bankruptcy looming so large, but Merry would figure something out. She would have to.

Courtney shot an angry look at her belly. "No, we can't. You'll have just had the baby."

Merry smiled and stroked her daughter's hair. "Well, you're too young to remember, but when you were little, I took you everywhere. Just you and me and the stroller. Your dad was finishing law school. We didn't have much money, but you and I had a lot of fun taking long walks and feeding the ducks in the city park." She leaned over and hugged her daughter as best she could. "You'll always be my first baby, sweetie."

Courtney didn't say anything, didn't get up from the chair. But she did reach up and put her arms around Merry. And that, at least, was a start.

Frank's face looked whiter than the sheet beneath his head. A large teddy bear lay improbably by his side, there for him to clutch to his chest and cushion his torso when he coughed. The night sounds of the hospital crept around the partially closed door—muffled footsteps, the nurse typing at the computer station outside Frank's door, the rattle of a cart as the meal trays were finally taken away by some unseen hand.

He's alive, Ruthie reminded herself. That was what mattered. If only Ruthie's heart was in half as good a shape as his was now. She kept the small light over the bed burning so she could see to knit, although truth be told, she could probably stitch in the dark if she needed to.

"You still here?" Frank mumbled from the bed. His speech was slurred, the effect of the pain medication in his system.

"Guilty as charged," Ruthie said. "Do you want some ice chips?"

They'd kept him in the intensive care unit for two days and moved him into this regular room earlier in the evening. Step-down unit, they called it. Ruthie thought "step-up" would have been a more inspiring name.

"You don't have to stay," Frank whispered. "Go and get some rest."

"I wouldn't be going anywhere but to the hotel." She set down her knitting so she could reach over and place her hand on top of his. "That cot over there's as comfortable as anything at the Hampton Inn." She was still maintaining the fiction that Esther wasn't in Nashville, still covering up the fact that they spent their nights at the Loews Vanderbilt Hotel. Tonight, though, she simply couldn't deal with her sister anymore, so she'd elected to stay at the hospital. Ruthie looked at Frank and ignored the moisture that gathered in the corner of his eyes. "Besides, someone has to be here to make sure you don't yell at the nurses."

He looked away. "It hurts, Ruthie. Hurts pretty bad."

"Here's your button." She handed him the contraption that looked like the buzzer contestants used on *Jeopardy*. "That's your morphine drip. Just keep pushing it." She couldn't tell him that the timer on the machine showed he wasn't due for another dose for twenty minutes. She'd have to distract him until then. "We can buzz your nurse if you'd like some broth or something else to drink."

"No. Ice is fine."

She was surprised to feel so awkward with him, but this was an intimate situation, and they didn't have decades of marriage to rely on for familiar routines and habits.

"You should go to the hotel," Frank said again.

"Am I making you uncomfortable?" No sense beating around the bush. "You're not used to having me around when you don't feel well."

He spread his fingers so that hers fell between them, interlocking. He squeezed her hand. "No, you don't make me uncomfortable. And there's no one else I'd rather have around."

His eyelids slid down, and soon he was snoring lightly. Ruthie remained where she was, her hand in his, treasuring the contact. So little after all these years. But somehow, for just this moment, it was enough.

The scrape of the door to Frank's room woke Ruthie early the next morning. She'd fallen asleep in the chair beside the bed. Rubbing her bleary eyes, she tried to focus on the person entering the room. To her surprise, Esther walked in like the Queen of England making an entrance at a state dinner. Her outfit was as impeccable as her makeup, not a hair out of place.

"You can go now," Esther said calmly and without preamble.

Ruthie glanced at the clock on Frank's bedside table. It was a few minutes past five o'clock in the morning. "What are you talking about?" Bleary-eyed, she struggled to sit up straighter in the chair.

Esther set her bag on the counter next to the sink, but her eyes wouldn't meet Ruthie's. "Frank's going to be fine. The doctor told us last night that he's officially out of danger. I appreciate your help in this matter, but now that the surgery's over I'll take it from here."

"Esther—" If only she weren't so tired and could form a coherent response.

"Yes?" She was checking her lipstick in the mirror above the sink.

All her life Ruthie had wanted to have the ability to arch one eyebrow as Esther was doing now, but apparently it was a gift. You were either born with it or you weren't. Esther had been born with it. Ruthie hadn't.

"I can't just leave. Frank will worry—"

"I'll explain everything to him when he wakes up."

Even though Ruthie had known this might happen, she still wasn't prepared for it. "Don't you care about his feelings at all?"

Ruthie could count on one hand the number of

times in her life she'd truly seen into her sister's soul. Esther had always kept everyone—including her only sister—at arm's length. Today was no different.

"Of course I care about his feelings." Esther turned to face her. She looked genuinely wounded, but Ruthie wondered whether it was because she was questioning her sister's integrity or because Ruthie was putting up an argument. "How could you even suggest such a thing?"

"Because—"

"Midlife crisis." Esther waved a dismissive hand in the air. "That's all this has been, brought on by his heart problem. Whenever men are faced with their own mortality, they try to jump back into the past. But," she said, giving Ruthie a pointed look, "they always come to their senses and return home, where they belong."

Could you claim to have been played if you knew the score all along? Ruthie wondered as she got up from the chair, collecting her purse and tote bag. "Please don't upset him when he wakes up," she begged her sister. "The doctor said no excitement."

"I'll tell him you were too exhausted to stay."

"But he won't be expecting you. He thinks you're in Sweetgum."

Esther shooed Ruthie toward the door with a wave of her hand. "If you want to take my car and drive back to Sweetgum, Alex can bring us home in a couple of days when Frank's released."

Dissed and dismissed. Ruthie had no idea how she

knew that slang phrase, but it popped into her mind. Rather appropriate.

"Esther . . ." But really, what was there to say? After all they'd been through, she should know by now that her sister would never really change.

"I'll call you when we get home to let you know everything's all right." Esther smiled as if they were exchanging the cheeriest of farewells. "Get some rest." Her sister would never acknowledge everything that had happened in the last few weeks. Not unless Ruthie forced the issue, and as Esther well knew, Ruthie never forced the issue.

"Okay then. Good-bye."

There would be no tearful farewells, no emotional explanations for Frank to struggle to comprehend. Esther would deliver the news of Ruthie's departure with all the precision and impersonal skill of his heart surgeon. Only not even Esther knew how final this good-bye would be.

Ruthie would go home and pack. That's what she would do. Her visa should arrive soon, and once that came through there was nothing tying her to Sweetgum. She tightened her grip on her tote bag, slipped out of the hospital room, and made her way toward the elevators.

She had known it would have to end. She just thought she'd be more prepared when it did.

By the time Frank awoke, Esther had set the hospital room to rights. She'd introduced herself to the nurse on duty, organized Frank's toiletries, and read the morning paper. So she was more than prepared when her husband finally opened his eyes.

"What are you doing here?"

Esther smiled. True, his words hurt, but she refused to let him see how his question pained her. "I'm here to take care of you, obviously."

"Where's Ruthie?"

"She's gone, Frank."

"Where?"

"Home. To Sweetgum."

If possible he suddenly looked paler against the snowy sheets. "What about the divorce?"

"Divorce?" Esther looked at Frank and frowned. He didn't understand. "I've changed my mind."

His face turned purple then, but now the harsh color didn't frighten Esther. It was an indication of his emotional state, not his physical one. She had known he would be angry, had prepared for how she would handle it, so she kept moving around the room, straightening a bouquet on the windowsill, throwing away the straw wrappers that had accumulated on the bedside tray.

"You tricked me."

"Yes."

The fight went out of him then. He closed his eyes for a long moment. "God, you're good."

The contempt in his voice almost cracked her resolve. She dug her nails into her palm to keep from showing any emotion. "It's not a matter of being good, Frank. It's a matter of doing what's right."

"What's right for whom?" he barked. "For me? For your sister? Or for you?"

Something inside Esther snapped. "Ruthie can play the pure in heart all she wants, but she's the one who chose to go to Africa rather than stay home and marry you. I'm not the villainess of this piece. You didn't wait twenty-four hours after she left before you asked me out. And I agreed to the date because I'm not a fool like my sister. I know to grab on to a good thing when it comes along." She stopped, took a deep breath, and looked him in the eye. "I wasn't looking to ensnare you, Frank, but you made it pretty clear that you wanted me." She paused. "You made that more than clear."

"I was just a kid. I was angry with Ruthie. I didn't know what I wanted."

"And now you do?" Esther laughed. "Please. You've always prized your own comfort above everything. And in all these years, I've never given you anything to complain about. I've been a good wife. And now that your heart is healed, we can continue to be just as successful as we've always been."

She saw the mist in his eyes but hardened her heart against it. Men like Frank were made to be managed. Otherwise they were lost little boys. If he and Ruthie had truly wanted to be together, they'd have found a way long ago. Esther refused to have her life ruined because other people didn't have the courage she possessed or her determination to do the right thing.

"Now, here's the lunch and dinner menu." She picked up the pencil lying next to the piece of paper. "What would you rather have? Grilled chicken or a turkey sandwich?"

He took his time answering, which made Esther a little nervous. But at length he mumbled, "Turkey sandwich." Then he closed his eyes, sighed, and went back to sleep.

And that moment of capitulation was the moment Esther knew she didn't have to worry ever again about her sister stealing her husband.

Twenty-One

The January meeting of the Sweetgum Knit Lit Society began on a slightly more congenial note than the previous month's gathering. This lighter atmosphere was due in large part, Eugenie thought, to Frank's successful surgery and even more remarkable recovery. Esther was practically glowing, and Ruthie looked pleased, if a bit weary, at the mention of her brother-in-law's improved health.

"Yes, we're all relieved and glad to have him back home," Ruthie said. "Something went wrong with my felting though, Eugenie." She spread the bag she'd made out on the table between them. "It shrank in height, but not in width. I've never had that happen before."

Eugenie peered at Ruthie more closely, surprised at how quickly she changed the subject from her brother-in-law's health. And Ruthie's comment meant that they ended up sharing their projects before discussing the book. For once, Eugenie decided to go with the flow.

"Hannah's came out very well," Camille said. She nodded to the teenager to pass the hot pink bag around. "If you wanted, you might sew some different colored buttons on it. Or maybe decorate it with glitter."

Hannah sat quietly, but she looked pleased as her bag was handed around and admired. Eugenie watched the two of them, Camille and Hannah, exchange a smile of satisfaction. Hmm. She'd been wondering what the next step was for the teenager. The girl had been showing up at the library faithfully for almost four months now, and Eugenie was running out of tasks for her to perform. But she needed to be kept occupied. No reason for her to go home after school every day to sit in an empty trailer. Eugenie had, for a brief moment, considered taking Hannah in. She had dismissed the thought as quickly as it came. A teenage girl needed a family, not an aging spinster who hadn't lived with another human being for the last forty years. She'd never considered taking in any of her previous strays. It was better not to start now.

Eugenie's and Ruthie's felted bags were sturdy and functional, despite Ruthie's difficulties with the felting process. Merry's bag was a misty green. Camille's bag was turquoise and tangerine wool in a randomly striped pattern. Esther's was a dark gold and looked more like a chic tote bag than something suited for a goatherd.

"You all did very well," Eugenie said. "Now, what did you think of *Heidi*?" As much as she valued her knitting, she loved books even more, and the discussion was always her favorite part of the meeting.

"It wasn't at all as I remembered it," Ruthie said.

"How so?" Eugenie asked.

"I guess I've seen the movie so many times that I'd forgotten what was in the book. All of that information about the grandfather and his tortured past. A great deal of it was his own fault, but still. You certainly have more empathy for him when you know why he has retreated to a hermit's life on the mountain."

"It's natural though, isn't it, to turn away from the world when you've been hurt?" Esther said, her glow dissipating somewhat. "Some people aren't equipped to deal with the imperfections of life."

Eugenie bristled. She doubted Esther knew very much at all about the imperfections of life. And she certainly wasn't having them thrown at her on a regular basis, as Eugenie was every time she saw Paul Carson.

"What would you say was the book's theme?" Eugenie knew this question always prompted good discussion. Plus it had the added benefit of changing the subject.

"Home?" Merry suggested. "Maybe family?"

"What's that old saying?" Ruthie said. "That home is where they have to take you in?" She smiled wryly. "Although I don't guess that's always true."

"Home isn't a place." Camille looked at all of them with a strange light in her eyes. Her animation troubled Eugenie. Something was going on with that girl, something she hadn't told anyone in the group.

231

"Home is the people, not the house." Of course Camille would understand that important distinction, given her mother's condition.

"Maybe the book is about being needed," Hannah said quietly. Her words surprised Eugenie, but she nodded in understanding.

"Can you say a little bit more about that?"

"Heidi was just a little kid, and she needed somebody to take care of her, but the grandfather—well, he needed her too. He needed someone to love him again after all that bad stuff he'd done."

A long moment of silence hung suspended over the group, like a raindrop on the edge of a leaf. No one seemed to want to break the stillness in the wake of Hannah's observation. Finally, Eugenie said, "I'd never thought of it that way before. I guess the grandfather did need Heidi."

"She brought him back to life," Camille said, her expression less guarded and now looking more earnest. "He was grouchy enough about it, but she made him care again."

"So what you're saying is that home isn't where you're loved. It's where you're needed?" Eugenie wasn't sure she agreed, but she threw the question out there to see what the others would say.

"It's both." Merry spoke emphatically. "You have to be loved and needed, or there's no point." She shifted in her chair. "Although I guess it's always a continuum. Sometimes the folks around you swing more one way than the other."

232

"The problem comes when the pendulum's always stuck on one side," Ruthie added. "It should even out over time. Love and need have to strike a balance in the long run."

Eugenie looked at Esther, who was sitting still with her arms crossed over her chest. Yes, the glow was definitely gone. "I think this book is about the sister sloughing off her responsibilities on the grandfather. She was young and able. She could have married someone from the village and provided Heidi with a home."

"But then the grandfather never would have been redeemed," Ruthie snapped. The air between the two of them fairly crackled with tension now. *Oh dear,* Eugenie thought. What a sad lot they were. She with her discomfort over Paul's presence in Sweetgum, Merry pregnant when she obviously didn't want to be, Camille troubled over her mother, if not something else, and Ruthie and Esther clearly engaged in some sort of sisterly spat. At the moment, Hannah seemed to be in the best shape of any of them. A sad commentary on the current condition of the Sweetgum Knit Lit Society.

"So the theme is redemption?" Eugenie intervened before the sisters' disagreement could devolve into a full-fledged tussle.

"I think so." Ruthie shot her sister a glance that Eugenie couldn't interpret. "But then I actually read the book."

Esther snapped her mouth closed and sniffed.

"Wouldn't you like to visit Switzerland?" Merry interjected with false brightness. "I've always wanted to climb the Alps, maybe with a pack of goats at my heels." She patted the felted bag on the table in front of her. "And now I have my lunch bag, so I'm ready to go." Ever the peacemaker, Merry smoothed the rough edges off the group with her smile.

"And I've always wanted to toast cheese over an open fire," Ruthie said, picking up on Merry's example and evidently willing to avoid further conflict with her sister. *Perhaps Frank's surgery took more of a toll on Esther and Ruthie than any of us know,* Eugenie thought.

"I'd go to Paris first," Camille said with a dreamy expression on her face. "The shopping would be amazing." Eugenie was reminded once again just how many dreams Camille had set aside to care for her mother. Because of Camille's history, folks in Sweetgum sometimes still thought of her as a pampered princess, but that was no longer true. In a small town, though, perceptions took a long time to change. Almost as long, Eugenie thought, as they sometimes took to build.

Eugenie lingered at the end of the meeting so she could catch Camille on the way out. Not just because she didn't want to risk running into Paul alone again, but because a plan had been brewing in her mind since the beginning of the evening. Camille and

Hannah appeared to get along very well. Perhaps Camille was the next logical step in Hannah's journey.

"I know you need to get home to your mother, but could I speak to you for just a moment?" Eugenie asked as they walked down the stairs.

Camille looked up, surprised. "Um, sure."

"It's about Hannah. I wanted to say thank you for helping her with the bag. The two of you seem to have really hit it off."

Camille shrugged. "We did fine, but I don't know if I'd say we 'hit it off.'"

"Well, I was wondering . . ." Eugenie found herself at a loss for words. She prided herself in speaking straightforwardly and without hesitation. But a sudden tightness gripped her chest. She'd grown used to having Hannah around the library, sullen expression and all. But she wasn't always that way, Eugenie admitted. And something about the sight of the girl when she would forget to dust and would plop down on the floor between the stacks with her nose in a book, something about that sight, touched Eugenie in a way that nothing had in a very long time.

"I've run out of things for her to do at the library," Eugenie said. She and Camille had reached the bottom of the stairs and exited the church building. "She needs a new challenge. I'd like to continue to keep her occupied with positive activities." Eugenie had heard through the Sweetgum grapevine about the middle school kids who were now hanging out in the cemetery. Hannah had occasionally been seen among them according to Eugenie's sources. "Why don't you ask Hannah to come in and work for you in the dress shop after school?" Eugenie asked. "I'm sure she could be a great help."

"I couldn't. She's too young." Camille's frown showed that she was clearly not taken with the idea. "There's no way I could pay her anything, even under the table," she admitted. "Things are pretty tight."

"Why not let her work for some clothing," Eugenie suggested. "Heaven knows she needs it, and then there would be no question of payroll. She'd simply be helping out in exchange for a few pairs of jeans and some shirts."

Camille shook her head. "I don't think my mother would—"

"I'm sure she would be supportive of anything that helped you." Eugenie knew she was pushing too hard, but the conversation about *Heidi* had unsettled her. Was she like the grandfather? And if she was, did she truly want to be redeemed, to be resurrected so that she had to risk hurt and betrayal all over again? Her soul had barely withstood it the first time. She didn't think she could survive that again.

"But—"

"Please, Camille. She needs you." Eugenie decided to appeal to the young woman's better nature, the part of her that had set aside her own dreams to care for her mother.

"I'm not sure that I—"

"If not you, then who?"

Camille's face grew troubled, as if she saw a distressing image in her mind's eye. Eugenie waited, poised next to her on the church steps, ignoring the cold that nipped at their noses and ears.

"I guess we could try it. For a week or two. See if it works out."

"Excellent."

"But not immediately. I need some time to think about how to handle this. And to make sure I'm not doing anything illegal."

Eugenie thought of all the sons and daughters, nieces and nephews, who pitched in at almost every business in Sweetgum. When it came to employment, a small town tended to turn a blind eye to children under the age of fifteen putting in a good day's work.

"Perhaps in a couple weeks. I'll keep her busy at the library until then."

"All right."

Eugenie wasn't sure why Camille had agreed to her proposal, but she was glad and, to be honest, a bit relieved that the younger woman would be taking Hannah off her hands. She'd begun to care too much about the teenager. Always before that had been her signal that it was time to back out of the situation. It was the reason she'd been so successful rescuing all her strays. She never allowed them to become too dependent on her. She always focused on giving them wings.

For the first time, though, she admitted that handing off her protégés served another purpose as well. It kept her heart protected, wrapped in the layers that had ensured its safety all these years. Detaching was the smart thing to do. It ensured survival.

It was also incredibly lonely. She'd managed to ignore that truth for a long time. Until Paul Carson had reappeared and threatened to capture her heart all over again.

Twenty-Two

Homer Flint, city councilman, visited the library about as often as Santa Claus came around, so when he showed up in front of the circulation desk right before closing time in early February, Eugenie knew enough to be worried. Thursday was her late night, so Homer was out past his suppertime. Clearly this was no social call.

"Good afternoon, Homer." Eugenie set the books she was about to shelve on the cart at her side. "What can I help you with today?" He was wringing his hat between both hands, a clear sign of his nervousness. Well then. Her six months were up. The council must have finally decided to force her hand.

"Could we talk in your office?" he asked with a nervous look over his shoulder.

"Of course." Heavens, it felt like a Mafia hit the way that Homer wanted to get her out of sight of any potential witnesses—not that there were any witnesses since the library was empty at this late hour. "This way." She waved him in the right direction, as if he didn't know where her office was, right behind the circulation desk.

Eugenie held her head high, kept her spine

straight, but inside she felt beaten down, defeated. All those years of faithful service to the citizens of Sweetgum, and for what? To be dismissed merely because she had gray hair and a few wrinkles?

"Eugenie, we've talked about this before," he began, closing the office door behind him. She took her seat behind her desk, grateful for its scarred bulk. She fought not to reach out and grip it as if it were a life raft. "The council believes it's time to make a change here. You've been diligent and faithful, and we all appreciate it. In fact, after all these years, you deserve a little time off. Time to do the things you've always wanted to do." His smile was as oily as his hair. "Don't think of this as retirement. Think of it as your reward for a job well done."

She had thought she was prepared for this. Thought she could handle the feel of the chopping block on her throat, the ax on the back of her neck. But she wasn't. She hated the fact that Homer Flint could make her cry. His words of appreciation for her years of work and loyalty were as false as his semi-successful hair plugs.

"Who do you have in mind to take my place?" she managed to choke out as she reached in her skirt pocket for a tissue. *Breathe, Eugenie. Just keep breathing,* she reminded herself. How unfair that men who had done nothing for the library all these years unless she shamed them into it were now preaching to her about their deep passion for the institution.

"Well, Ed Cantrell has a niece who just graduated

240

from Middle Tennessee State with a degree in library science, so we thought we'd bring her on and see how it goes."

Of course. She should have known that her retirement had been motivated by more than pure cost-cutting measures. Cronyism was alive and well in Sweetgum.

The admission made Homer shift nervously from one foot to the other. "You weren't much older than she is when you came to Sweetgum." The words were part defense, part justification, and all hooey. After she and Paul had parted ways, she never thought she'd feel this kind of betrayal again. In fact, she'd gone to great lengths to make sure she wouldn't have an opportunity to. But here she was, once again at the mercy of a man who wanted to decide her future for her. Forty years later was she any smarter, any savvier, than she'd been the first time around?

She opened her mouth to speak, but Homer stopped her. He held up one hand, both to silence her and perhaps to ward off any potential blows. "Now, Eugenie, don't be difficult about this. We've made no secret of the way the wind was blowing for a good while now."

That was true. But that didn't make it right.

"When do you want me gone?"

"Aw, don't put it like that, Eugenie. We believe in positive transitions. We thought we'd do a big reception for you in a couple of weeks, but definitely by the end of the month."

241

Long before the spring came, then. She would miss watching the robins that built a nest in the tree outside her office window. Would Ed's niece see that the stray black cat that loitered outside the library was fed so that he didn't feast on the robins?

"It's not right, Homer. You know that."

He had the good grace to nod slightly at her words. "I understand your feelings, Eugenie, but nothing stays the same forever."

Why did people always speak in platitudes and clichés when they had to say something unpleasant? Couldn't they find their own words to deal with the situation? Obviously not.

"Will you want me to stay until Ed's niece can get a handle on running things?" She couldn't imagine anyone walking into the library cold and trying to pick up the reins. Especially not someone straight out of school. "If she doesn't have much experience—"

"The budget won't allow for that, I'm afraid. Besides, clean breaks are always better," he said. "Less messy. She'll figure it out as she goes along."

Eugenie put a hand over her mouth to muffle the bitter laugh that threatened. Like most people, Homer assumed that a relatively intelligent ape could do her job. After all, how hard could it be putting books back in their place and sending out overdue notices? It was almost funny. Emphasis on *almost*.

"I appreciate you taking it so well, Eugenie." He reached in his pocket for a handkerchief and wiped the beads of sweat that had accumulated on his forehead. "It's really for the best."

"Pardon me, Homer, if I don't agree with you on that." She stood up and gathered her purse from the desk drawer and her coat from the hook on the wall behind her. "Now, if you'll excuse me, it's time to close up for the day."

To her chagrin, Homer lingered while she double-checked the back door and flipped out the lights in the children's area and then in the main part of the library. Homer followed her out and waited as she locked the door. "Would you like a ride home, Eugenie?"

She kept herself from saying the first thing that sprang to mind, something having to do with a very warm clime freezing over.

"No, thank you, Homer."

"It's dark."

"Yes. It is." She wrapped her scarf more securely around her neck. "Good night, Homer."

"Eugenie . . ."

She didn't wait to see what else he had to say. Just whirled on the heel of one of her sensible shoes and started walking. Quickly.

Perhaps if she walked fast enough, she could outrun what had happened to her. A nice thought if a fanciful one. For some reason she thought of Dorothy desperately clinging to the belief that the yellow brick road was the one sure way to return home. Now she too was in exile, but the sidewalk beneath her feet was the usual slate gray. No helpful color-coding to tell her how to find her way back to what she'd lost.

Eugenie kept going, one foot in front of another, and as she crossed the street and approached the church, she saw that the light was on in the pastor's study.

She pulled her coat tighter around her. She wouldn't go in, of course. Even if the light was on. Probably just Napoleon emptying the wastebaskets and vacuuming because Paul had surely gone home for the evening. Still, she moved closer to the front of the church, and when she reached the steps, she grasped the rail and climbed them. The door was still open. Perhaps she'd just sit in the quiet, darkened sanctuary for a few moments. She needed a little time for reflection.

Hah! Her cynical side could only be squashed for so long. She hadn't set foot in a sanctuary in forty years, so she'd hardly be seeking one out now. No, she had come here, consciously or unconsciously, because *he* was here. She shook her head, ashamed of her weakness. Strange how the past could suddenly come alive again, even after years of entombing it beneath thick layers of denial.

She turned left in the narthex just inside the door, avoiding the sanctuary altogether and slipping into the foyer outside the offices. The fluorescent lights in this part of the church were so bright you could perform surgery under them. She blinked against their harshness and then moved toward the door that separated Ruthie's office from the foyer. She opened it and stepped inside. Beyond Ruthie's work area, she could see through the doorway into the pastor's study. He was there, his back to her, typing away on his computer. She froze, afraid he'd heard the sound the door made when it closed behind her. What was she thinking? Clearly she'd lost her mind. Or rather Homer Flint had taken possession of it. Afraid to move too suddenly lest she catch Paul's attention, she slowly turned to leave.

Please don't let him—

"Eugenie."

Her feet turned to lead. What on earth had possessed her to—

"Eugenie."

She turned around. There was nothing else she could do. The flush on her cheeks was no doubt as bright as the fluorescent lighting.

"Good evening, Paul."

He stood up, rounded the corner of his desk, and came out of his office. "You look like you've seen a ghost." Lines of concern etched his face. "Are you all right?"

"I'm fine." But she wasn't. "I thought that . . . I mean, I hoped maybe Ruthie . . ."

"She left a couple hours ago." Why did he have to look at her like that, with compassion and warmth and that hint of understanding that made her want to sink to the floor?

"I wanted to talk to Ruthie."

Was that disappointment in his eyes? "Oh. Can I help you with something?"

"Yes . . . I mean, no. I'll just call her when I get home."

"Would you like to sit down?" He gestured toward the chairs in his office.

"Yes." What? What was she saying? "Yes, I would."

From the look in Paul's eyes, her answer astonished him as much as it did her. "Come in then."

She preceded him into the study, hoping he'd have the good sense to leave the door open but not wanting to mention it in case he might think . . . well, that there was anything of a personal nature to this visit. She was just upset, that was all.

"Why don't you tell me what's wrong," he said. "Because clearly something's upset you."

She sat down in one of the visitor's chairs in front of his desk, and he lowered himself into the chair beside hers. She would have much preferred that he take his proper place behind his desk, as she had with Homer.

"It's nothing really. The proverbial ax finally fell. Homer Flint informed me that my services at the library are no longer required now that I've reached retirement age." She knotted her fingers together in her lap.

Paul said a word that ministers probably weren't supposed to say. "Clearly they've lost their minds."

"Ed Cantrell's niece will be taking over."

246

"The one that just graduated from college?"

Thank heavens, Eugenie thought. He looked as incredulous as she felt. She nodded her answer, not trusting herself to speak.

"How much longer will you work?"

"A couple of weeks. They want to throw me a retirement party."

"And you'd rather be boiled in oil." He smiled a little, very softly, and the humor in his face eased the ache in her heart just a touch.

"Yes. Not to put too fine a point on it."

And then he was reaching out to take her hand in his. She let him, watched him do it, and made no move to resist. Like those out-of-body experiences she'd read about in books, she observed the scene impartially. Or at least she did so for several long moments. And then the warmth of his hand, the pure sensation, burst through, shattering any pretense of detachment. Oh heavens, she'd missed that so. A simple touch. The most basic of gestures. How could she have forgotten how magnificent it felt?

"So they think Ed's niece can do your job?"

"Apparently I could be replaced by any well-trained monkey."

"Ouch." This time his smile was conspiratorial. "I've experienced the same phenomenon. You'd be surprised how many people think a minister only works on Sunday. Church members are always saying, 'I'd like a job where I get paid to work one day a week.' If I had a quarter for every time I'd heard that one, well, let's just say that my pension would be a lot fatter than it is."

Eugenie chuckled.

"There. That's better." With his other hand, he reached over and brushed her nose with one finger. "I've got a bone to pick with anyone who wipes that smile off your face."

At his words, cold panic seized her. This was exactly why she never should have come here. She pulled her hand free from his. "I have to go."

"Eugenie . . ." Exasperation and tenderness warred for the upper hand in his expression.

"I'm sorry." She stood up too quickly, and blood rushed to her head. She reached back to grab the arm of the chair for support, but Paul was there first, his hands on her shoulders holding her upright and steady.

Eugenie hadn't been this close to a man in a very long time. Longing seized her in its grip, like some pathetic heroine in a trite romance. Only what she felt wasn't trite at all. It was amazing and terrifying and scared her to her very core.

"I think you'd better sit back down."

"No. I'm all right. I just need to eat something."

"Okay."

"What?" She didn't like the way he said that one word. It sounded both agreeable and full of portent.

"We're going to get you something to eat."

"I just need to get home—"

His hands cupped her shoulders, and his face was

so close to hers. She remembered, through the fog that seemed to shroud her brain, how they had stood this close every night when he walked her to her door all those years ago. Her mother would be right inside, hand on the light switch, ready to flick the front porch light off and on if Paul got too fresh.

"I'm taking you to Tallulah's."

"She's about to close."

"I bet she'll feed us if we go right now."

Before she could muster a stronger protest, he had grabbed his coat from the rack behind the door and was ushering her into the outer office. He locked the door behind him, flicked off the lights as they went, and before Eugenie could extricate herself from the situation, they were out the door of the church and walking toward Paul's sensible four-door sedan.

Twenty-Three

Eugenie had been right about Tallulah closing up the café. As they approached the front door, the owner was just about to flip the sign to Closed, but when she saw Paul and Eugenie, she motioned them inside.

"Come on, stragglers," she said as they entered. "As long as you'll settle for something easy. My cook's gone home for the night, but I've got some soup left and I can make you"—she nodded at Paul—"a grilled cheese."

Paul had certainly charmed his way into Tallulah's heart in a short time. Eugenie tried to tamp down the feelings of jealousy that threatened to work their way to the surface. "Thanks, Tallulah. We appreciate it," she said. And then she wanted to bite her tongue when she saw Tallulah's face light up at her use of the word *we*.

"Pick any table you want," Tallulah said with an expansive grin that lit up her tired eyes. "I'll have your food in a few minutes." Then she turned and walked into the kitchen, leaving Eugenie alone with Paul.

"Here you go." Paul pulled out a chair at a table for two and gestured for her to take a seat.

"Thank you." She felt like a teenager on a first date, which was entirely ridiculous. She was far too mature and sensible to entertain, much less tolerate, the giddiness in her limbs and stomach.

"Eugenie—"

She held up a hand to forestall him. "I appreciate your listening ear, but I don't want you to worry about me. I'll work this out. I'm sure everything will be fine."

"I'm sure it will be. That wasn't what I was going to say."

"Oh."

"It looks like you'll be making a few changes in your life pretty soon," he began, but his leading tone made her nervous. She glanced toward the kitchen, willing Tallulah to reappear, but force of will alone was clearly not enough to make her friend materialize at their table.

"Eugenie, I want to be a part of those changes." He reached across the table and took her hand in his. She flinched at the contact. As nice as it had felt in his office, now it overwhelmed her. She wasn't used to being touched. He saw her response, but he didn't let go.

"Paul, I—"

"Let me finish. I think I've made it pretty clear what my intentions are here. I never thought, after Helen died, that I'd want to share my life with anyone else again. I didn't think I'd be capable of it."

A part of her hated that he'd had such a happy

251

marriage. She knew it was small and petty, but his years of fulfillment had come at a pretty dear price for her.

"It's too late—," she began, but he interrupted her.

"If I've learned anything in the last few years, it's that it's never too late."

"I'm set in my ways, Paul—"

"Aren't we all?"

"I've never learned how to share my life with anyone."

"We'll both have some learning to do."

But her objections weren't really the heart of the matter. Or they weren't what troubled her heart so deeply. He might want to wave a magic wand and resurrect a love that was four decades old, but that love hadn't been enough the first time around. What made him think it would be sufficient now?

"I don't think—"

"Yes, you do." He smiled, a dimpled grin that tugged at her heartstrings. "You think all the time. You think too much."

His last words stung. Of course she analyzed everything. She'd had to be careful, a woman on her own all these years. Her brain was her only ally, and she'd cultivated it with every breath in her body, every fiber of her being, every—

"I'm sorry," he said. "I didn't mean to offend you." Now he looked contrite, which was just as appealing as his affable smile. "Forgive me."

Forgive me. Two words she'd waited years to hear.

He said them now so easily, with such nonchalance.

"I can't," she whispered past the sudden constriction in her throat.

"What?" Confusion darkened his eyes. "I'm sorry, Eugenie, I was just being—"

"I can't forgive you." And then she saw the moment when he understood what she meant.

"Because I asked you to wait for me when I went to seminary?" He grimaced. "Eugenie, that was years ago."

"Would you have come back?" The question had gnawed at her all this time, despite her every effort not to think of him.

Paul's face was somber now, frown lines etching the corners of his mouth. "We'll never know. Because you didn't trust me enough to give me the chance."

"Trust is a pretty easy proposition when it's all on one side," she pointed out.

"You don't think I had to trust in you to leave you behind?" The first signs of anger—the clenching of his jaw, the way he released her hand so abruptly—told her his feelings on the matter weren't any more dead and buried than hers had been.

"I think you were going to do what you wanted to do no matter what I said."

"I would have waited for you," he shot back.

"Would you?" Now it was her turn to pin him with her questions. "Then why didn't you ask me to marry you and take me with you? If you'd been a hundred percent sure, you never would have gone to Memphis without me."

His shoulders slumped. "I had nothing to offer you, Eugenie. And I wasn't about to let you support me through seminary."

She laughed, but there was no humor in it. Only years of bitterness and rancor that she thought she'd shed long ago. Now they resurfaced in her voice, weighing down her limbs, sharpening her tongue to a razor's edge.

"You wanted to be the one to make the decision." Her voice caught in her throat, and she hated the little sobbing sound that accompanied it. She would not show weakness now. She simply refused to do it. "The irony is, if you'd asked me to go, I would have turned you down. I would have waited for you to finish school if I'd been sure of you." She paused to breathe, to remind herself of the necessity. "I understood you completely. You, on the other hand, had no clue about me."

"I was supposed to read your mind?" His eyes clouded with emotion. "Or pass some sort of secret test? Every day was a struggle to win your heart all over again. You were a moving target from the moment I met you. I'm just a man, Eugenie. A broken, flawed man who loved you. Or tried to anyway. You made it so difficult. You made it so d—" He broke off.

She didn't want to let his words hurt her, but even her iron will couldn't deflect the pain. "In my experi-

254

ence, people always do exactly what they want to do in the end."

"I came back, you know." He was gripping the edge of the table with both hands now.

"What do you mean?"

"Two months into my first semester. I came back to town looking for you, and no one knew where you had gone." Funny how suffering that was so old could find a fresh expression on his face. Eugenie winced. "Nowadays I would have just Googled you and found you in an instant. But back then . . ." He broke off. "And then my pride took over. I admit that. I was too young to know any better."

She wouldn't let him off with such a weak excuse. "I was young too, and I knew the score."

"The only score was the one you kept."

"What do you mean by that?"

He sank back in his chair, defeated. "You were always sizing me up, judging me, testing me, only I never knew what subject matter you were going to cover on any given day." He paused, took off his glasses, and folded them neatly. Then he slipped them into his shirt pocket. He took her hands in his, and though she tried to jerk them away, he held them firmly. "You never surrendered, Eugenie. To your feelings for me, I mean. They were there, but you couldn't trust them. Maybe that's why I didn't ask you to go with me."

"You proved me right, Paul. I wasn't going to sit and wait to be abandoned. I found a new life here in

Sweetgum. I have friends. And I have the library. It's been my life. My one true love."

He squeezed her hands. "An institution can't love you back, Eugenie."

"Neither could you, apparently."

He was quiet for a long moment. The cold air seeped into her bones despite her thick cardigan. Where was Tallulah with that soup?

"Love and control are two different things." Paul's gaze held hers, and as much as Eugenie wanted to look away, she couldn't. "I don't think you've ever learned the difference."

"That's a typical response from a man. If a woman wants commitment or security, she's being controlling. Well, the Sweetgum Public Library may not have loved me back, but its patrons have. We've had a long and healthy relationship."

"But now they're done with you, and where are all those patrons? Do you think there will be a rally to save your job?"

She would not cry. No matter what he said. If she did, she would only prove his point.

"I wasn't the only one who thought an institution was more important than people. You left me for the church."

"I left you to go to school. And I told you I was coming back. But you didn't trust me."

"You didn't give me a reason to."

He sighed, rubbed his eyes. "The thing about people, Eugenie, is that they're not books. They're living, breathing beings who make mistakes."

The first tears threatened to overwhelm her control. "I have to go." She searched blindly for her purse at her feet.

"Eugenie." He reached for her arm, laid his hand there, curled his fingers around her wrist. "Don't run away. Please. Not this time."

"I was never the one who ran away." She had to harden her heart—right here, right now—if she was going to survive this. If there was a God, He had a very cruel sense of humor. To taunt her like this with Paul, after all these years, after all the work she'd done to forget him. Her mother hadn't helped—she'd been under strict orders not to reveal Eugenie's whereabouts, but she continued to send clippings from the Columbia paper about his ordination and eventual marriage. Eugenie had known exactly what she was missing but had convinced herself it was never what she wanted. Eugenie Pierce as a pastor's wife—it never would have worked.

She rose from her chair and he did the same, but he kept his grip on her arm. Why did he have to look at her like that, with warmth and sadness and something else she couldn't name in his eyes? It was that indefinable something that scared her the most.

"I know about the string of strays you've rescued at the library," he said. "And I'm not talking about the black cat you feed every day."

"I just don't want that creature to eat my robins."

"So think of me as one of your strays."

"What?"

"The lonely widower who's new to town. Forget the past. Forget that we knew each other a long time ago. Let's start over." He released her arm and then offered his hand, as if meeting her for the first time. "Hello, Miz Pierce. I'm Paul Carson, the new pastor at Sweetgum Christian Church."

"Paul . . ."

"Meet me halfway, Eugenie. That's all I'm asking."

She ought to be long past any hint or hope of romantic entanglements. For heaven's sake, within two weeks she'd be retired. She should be ready for a rocking chair, not—

"I can't. I'm sorry." Panic seized her. Out of the corner of her eye, she saw Tallulah emerging from the kitchen. "I have to go."

Eugenie turned and fled. For the first fifty yards beyond the door of the café, she expected to feel his hand on her arm again, stopping her, trying to persuade her to stay. But the only thing that grabbed at her limbs was the icy February wind that swirled around her in the darkness.

Camille was certain that winter had never lasted so long. Her trip to Memphis seemed a lifetime ago, and nothing had changed in the intervening weeks. Alex never called unless he was desperate to see her. And once he'd seen her, it was a good long time before he got desperate again.

She couldn't let things continue like this. Each day another scale fell from her eyes. And each day she watched her mother's condition worsen. Camille had awoken that morning, Valentine's Day, to two realizations. One was that Alex was never going to deliver her from her life in Sweetgum. And two was that in all likelihood, it was the last Valentine's Day she would spend with her mother.

So when her cell phone rang just as she was closing up the store and she heard his voice, she was at last prepared to be firm in refusing to see him. Prepared but not determined enough, as it happened.

She'd driven to their meeting spot, let him greet her with a peck on the cheek, and settled nervously into a chair.

"I'm really not comfortable here, Alex." The last place she'd expected to find herself on Valentine's Day was Esther Jackson's veranda. Even though the weather was warm for February, a chill tinged the evening air.

"My parents are still at their condo at the lake." Alex's expression bordered on a sneer, which made her almost as uncomfortable as sitting on his mother's veranda while he drank his father's scotch. "It's Valentine's Day. I thought you'd want to see me."

"Someone might see *us*," she pointed out.

"See what? Two grownups having a conversation?"

"It's not quite that simple, Alex."

"Only because you're complicating it."

When had the difficulties in their relationship

become all her fault? When had the tide shifted, bringing in blame instead of romance?

"You can't have it both ways, Alex. Either you're married or you're not."

He tossed back the rest of the scotch. "Easy to say when you're twenty-three."

"I'm twenty-four."

On the street a car passed by. Camille thought it was driving awfully slowly. Was someone looking at them on the veranda? Was it anyone who might recognize her?

"I can't stay here." She rose from the wicker rocking chair, unable to figure out where it had all gone wrong. She thought he loved her. She'd been so sure of it. But—

"If you leave, don't bother coming back."

"Alex—"

"I mean it. We can't all live in your perfect little world, Camille."

Perfect little world? Had he even been listening during all the conversations they'd had over the last few months?

"My world is hardly perfect."

"Yeah, yeah. I know. *My mother is dying, so you have to do what I say,*" he mimicked in a cruel tone.

Hot sobs choked her throat. How dare he? But he'd been drinking. He didn't mean it.

Oh yes, he does mean it. Unbidden, Hannah's voice spoke in her head. *Just because they're drunk doesn't mean they're not saying what they think.*

"I'm leaving." She pulled her knockoff designer purse tighter against her body and walked toward the steps.

"Don't make the mistake of thinking I'll come after you," he called.

She hunched her shoulders, hoping none of the neighbors were outside. Humiliation was not something folks in Sweetgum associated with Camille St. Clair, and she'd like to keep it that way.

She slid into her car and slammed the door loud enough so he couldn't avoid hearing the sound of her anger and frustration. She'd known it was wrong. She'd prayed for forgiveness every night. She'd spent hours trying to determine when he would finally leave his marriage for good and their new life together could begin. She'd employed every kind of justification and rationalization she could think of. But there was one question she couldn't answer, despite the hours she'd spent obsessing over her relationship with Alex.

At what point had she failed to notice that her Prince Charming had turned into a horrible, horrible toad?

Twenty-Four

By the following morning, Camille's frame of mind hadn't improved. Unfortunately for Camille, Hannah showed up to work her first after-school shift at the dress shop right as Alex pulled up in the alley behind the store. By now Camille could recognize the sound of his car's engine. She motioned for Hannah to stay in the main part of the shop, but the girl ignored her command and followed her to the back, hot on Camille's heels.

Alex's black BMW was far too conspicuous for him to park it in the front of the shop on the town square. Camille met him at the back entrance but stood in the doorway, blocking his way into the shop.

"Come on, Camille. It's cold out here." He wore a navy blue blazer, no overcoat, and his hands were tucked into his armpits. The warm spell had given way during the night to much colder temperatures.

"There's no reason for you to be here." She could feel Hannah's curious stare digging into her back, right between her shoulder blades.

"We have to talk."

"I don't think there's anything left to say, Alex."

"It's now or never, Camille. If you send me away—"

The threat was enough to push her over the edge. "I'm not sending you anywhere. I'm just shutting the door and going back into my store." She started to push the door closed, but he stuck his foot in the opening.

"Camille! I'm warning you—"

"What are you going to do, Alex? Tell your mother on me? Or maybe I should tell her myself at the next meeting of the Knit Lit Society."

"Don't make empty threats, Camille."

"Believe me, there's nothing empty about it. Maybe next time we're all gathered up in that Sunday school room at the church—"

"You wouldn't." His words were strong, but the worry in his eyes showed that he wasn't as certain as he wanted to be.

"Try me," she warned him. "We'll see what happens."

From behind her, she heard a muffled noise. She stifled a groan at the thought of Hannah witnessing their exchange. Well, the cat was out of the bag now. Those girls in the novels the Knit Lit Society had been reading made being a heroine look so easy. Sure, they had struggles, but the reader always knew that everything would turn out all right in the end. Camille had long ago given up on any assurances, or even any hopes, that her life would come close to resembling her dreams. Not since the day she'd written the letter relinquishing her scholarship to Vanderbilt. Or, more to the point, not since the day her father had left Sweetgum.

"If you tell my mother, you'll be the one who suffers." Alex's features twisted with rage.

"That may be true. I may suffer, but I won't be the only one." The tightness in her throat made it hard to say the words. It didn't seem so long ago that it had been September and she'd been head over heels in love, convinced that he felt the same way about her. That once she was free to leave Sweetgum— But no doubt that had been a large part of her attraction for him. She couldn't leave, even if he'd begged her to do so.

"Fine." Alex's full upper lip turned skyward, and he looked more like a petulant child than a successful attorney. "Don't call me anymore." He took his foot out of the door.

Camille bit her own lip to keep it from curling in the same way. "I was never the one who called you, Alex. I was always the one waiting for you to call." Well, she was done with waiting. Waiting on a man, at least. She had enough waiting to do at home with her mother. The last thing she needed was more of it.

He opened his mouth as if to say something else but then closed it, spun on his heel, and strode back to his BMW. In a matter of moments, he roared off down the alley, gone for good.

Camille kept her face away from Hannah long enough to compose herself. She straightened her spine before turning around to face the girl. What a way to start her new job at the dress shop.

"Why would you waste yourself on him?" Hannah de-manded before Camille could say anything. The girl's crossed arms and cocked head showed her own distaste for Alex, although Camille couldn't see any judgment in Hannah's eyes—just simple curiosity mixed with revulsion.

"I thought he was worth it," Camille replied. "I thought he loved me." The words didn't sound any more convincing than they felt.

"No man's worth that."

Camille looked at her, confused. "Worth what?"

"That piece of your soul that it costs you to have him. How do you think my mama ended up like she is?"

Camille had always thought of herself as mature for her age. She'd taken over the dress shop before she was twenty and had been the primary caretaker of her bedridden mother. But Hannah was the true old soul, Camille realized with a start. Nobody should have to be that ancient at thirteen.

"Did you read the book for the meeting yet? I've always liked *The Wonderful Wizard of Oz*," Camille said, desperate to change the subject.

"Nah. I've seen the movie on TBS."

"You know they're not exactly the same, right?"

Hannah made a face. "Great."

"If you need a copy of the book, I can lend you mine."

She expected her offer to be refused—at least a dismissive shrug. Instead Hannah said, "Okay. Thanks."

They moved back into the main part of the shop. "The first thing you can do is dust," Camille said, retrieving a large feather duster from behind the counter where the cash register sat. "I have no idea how this place gets so coated, but I have to use this all the time." She could tell Hannah wasn't exactly thrilled with her first assignment, but the girl accepted the feather duster without comment. "Eugenie said you'd been dusting the shelves for her at the library."

"Yeah." Hannah's soft answer made Camille look at the girl more closely.

"Not big on dusting?"

Hannah shrugged.

"I'll let you pick out your clothes at the end of the week," Camille said, changing the subject yet again.

"At least I'm getting something for this job," Hannah muttered. Her sarcasm irritated Camille. Eugenie had done the girl a favor not turning her over to the authorities for vandalizing a library book. What did Hannah expect? Fabulous cash and prizes?

"You're lucky Miss Pierce let you dust those shelves. Things could have been a whole lot worse."

"Yeah. Right."

Camille knew she should just shrug off Hannah's attitude, but she was too raw from the breakup with

Alex. "Ungrateful much?" she snapped. "None of us have to be doing this, you know."

"Doing what?" It was a good thing that the feather duster wasn't a weapon the way Hannah was wielding it. Camille might have been concerned for her safety.

"Helping you."

Hannah rolled her eyes. "A regular bunch of saints. Such good *Christians*." She emphasized the last word with a sneer.

"What's your problem?" Camille felt heat rising along the back of her neck. She did not need this kind of attitude right now, not from a girl who was so far from the wrong side of the tracks that she couldn't even hear the train whistle when it blew.

"I don't have a problem. None. Zero. So you do-gooders can leave me alone."

"Lucky you, with no problems." Camille picked up a pen from the counter and twisted it between her fingers. "You know, we could've just turned a blind eye."

Hannah laughed, which irritated Camille even more than the eye rolling. "I'm so glad I could help you all feel good about yourselves."

And that's when Camille realized the problem. Hannah was angry that Eugenie had sent her to work at the dress shop. Camille recognized the symptoms of abandonment and betrayal. Goodness knew she ought to considering what had happened in her own life in the past twenty-four hours—never mind the past twenty-four years.

"Just because Eugenie asked me to take you on here doesn't mean she's not interested in you anymore," Camille said.

Hannah blanched, and her entire body stiffened. "I don't care what that old biddy thinks. As long as she doesn't call the cops. I've got one more meeting of that stupid knitting group to go, and then she can't boss me around anymore."

"Hannah? What's really going on?" Camille's stomach knotted, thick and hard. She recognized so much of her own struggle in this girl. Fear for the future. A present full of pain. And not old enough to have a past to take comfort in.

"Nothing's going on."

Camille almost smiled because she remembered when she used to answer her mother with those same words and in that same tone. Nothing was never nothing. It was always something.

"Did something happen at home? With that guy?"

"No." Hannah crossed her arms over her chest. "I'm sorry I ever said anything to you. I didn't know you were gonna throw it in my face all the time."

Camille decided not to point out that asking her about her mother's boyfriend one time was not exactly throwing anything in her face. But Hannah's answer told her all she needed to know. She had started to change over the last few months, change for the better. What had happened to bring the old Hannah back to the forefront?

"If you need an adult to help, Hannah, all you

268

have to do is ask. There are five of us who would be happy to do so."

"Why do you think you can help me when you can't even help yourselves?" Hannah's eyes widened as she realized what she'd said, but she didn't look away.

For a long moment Camille couldn't respond to the stinging question. "I don't need help," she finally said, but even she knew how defensive she sounded.

"How long do you think those ladies would let you stay in their club if they knew you were sleeping with that old witch Esther's son?" Hannah's eyes were lit with triumph. "Want to place a bet on that? 'Cause anything over ten seconds would be money in my pocket."

"Don't turn on me just because your life stinks," Camille shot back. She couldn't believe she was arguing like this with a thirteen-year-old.

"Stinks?" Hannah's laugh was as bitter as any medicine Camille had to give her mother. "You have no idea. You with your fancy dress shop and your mother who would do anything for you. Don't tell me what I do or don't need."

"You're a kid. There's a lot you don't know."

"I haven't been a kid in a long time, only no one else wants to admit it. Adults only tell me I'm a kid when they want something or when I tell the truth."

Camille had the grace to blush. Hannah was right. It hadn't been that long since people had done the same thing to her. Still did, to some extent, if she ever said more than the bare minimum about her mother's health. People only wanted to hear what they wanted to hear. That fact probably didn't change whether you were thirteen or a hundred and three.

"I'm sorry." Camille doubted the words would make much difference, but they needed to be said. "I didn't mean to sound so awful. It's just been a really bad day."

The unexpected apology seemed to drain the tension out of Hannah's body. Her shoulders sagged. "No big deal."

"Hannah, do you want me to try and talk to your mom? About her boyfriend, I mean?"

Fear widened Hannah's eyes and pinched her mouth. "No. There's no problem."

"Hannah, you said—"

"I made it up."

"You did not."

"I did so!" Hannah balled her fists so tightly that Camille thought the girl might snap the handle of the feather duster she held.

"If he's done anything to you—"

"He hasn't. I wouldn't let him."

"It's not always a matter of 'letting' a guy do anything," Camille warned. "Your mother should be protecting you." She paused. "Does she even know about the library stuff? Or the Knit Lit Society? Or your coming here after school?"

Camille hadn't asked the questions to hurt Han-

270

nah, but she could see past the heavy makeup to the pain in the girl's eyes.

"It wouldn't make a difference if she did. She doesn't care."

Camille could hardly argue with that. "Will you promise to tell me if you need my help?"

"I promise to think about it."

Camille knew that was as good an agreement as she was likely to get. "I hope you'll do more than that." Pursuing the matter anymore, though, was unlikely to improve the results. "Now, you'd better get started with the dusting. We close up at six."

Hannah's eyes widened. "You think it will take me two hours to dust this place?"

"To my satisfaction?" Camille asked. "Probably."

"I should have stayed at the library," Hannah grumbled, but she did as she'd been asked, and for the next two hours Camille could take comfort in the fact that at least for that amount of time, no one would hurt or bother the girl.

What happened after they left the shop at closing time was another matter entirely.

Twenty-Five

The phone rang next to Merry's head, waking her as it sent her pulse skittering and shortened her breath. She looked to the other side of the bed and saw Jeff there, snoring contentedly. A ringing phone wasn't enough to blast him out of his slumber.

She groped for the receiver and hit the button to answer the call, her eyes too bleary to read the caller ID. "Hello?"

"Mrs. McGavin?" The voice was small, scared, and familiar.

"Hannah?"

"Mrs. McGavin, could you come get me?"

Merry glanced at the clock. Two in the morning. "Where are you?" She could call 911 and have the sheriff pick Hannah up. He'd probably get there faster than she could anyway. "Are you okay?" A small part of her had been expecting this kind of call for a while now.

"I'm at the Rest-A-While Truck Stop on I-65."

"What?" That truck stop was a good forty-five minutes away on the two-lane state highway that led from Sweetgum to the Interstate. "Hannah, you need to call the police. Right now."

"No." She was sobbing. "They'll take me to juvy as a runaway. Please, Mrs. McGavin."

Courtney was going to go ballistic. The thought popped into Merry's head, and she shoved it away. Too bad. Courtney would have to deal. But that meant Merry would have to put up with more tantrums and recriminations.

"All right. I'll get there as quick as I can." She pulled back the covers and levered herself out of bed, not an easy feat now that pregnancy had shifted her center of balance. "Do you have any money? Is there anybody there who looks trustworthy?"

Hannah's bark of laughter was more fear than humor. "At a truck stop in the middle of the night?"

"Okay. Okay." She poked around in the darkness for a pair of maternity jeans and a sweater. "Sit at the counter, and order something to eat. Surely there's a waitress or something."

"Yeah."

"Fine. I'll be there in less than an hour."

"Okay." The word ended on a sob.

"Hannah, it'll be all right." She was afraid to ask how Hannah had wound up in such a place. She was afraid she already knew the answer.

"Mrs. McGavin?"

"Yes?"

"Hurry."

Jeff wasn't going to be any happier than Courtney. "I will, honey. Just sit tight." She pushed the

273

button on the phone to end the call and set the receiver back in its cradle.

"Jeff?" She nudged her husband as she sank down on the bed to slip on her shoes.

"Hmm?" He rolled over and opened one eye.

"Emergency. I've got to go out."

Both eyes popped open. "What?"

"It's Hannah Simmons. She's at a truck stop on I-65. I have to go get her."

He sat upright so fast the momentum almost knocked Merry off the bed. "Hold on a second."

"I can't. I have to go. Now." She tried to remember where she'd left her purse. On the sideboard in the dining room maybe? "I've got my cell phone. I'll call you when I get there."

"Merry?" He rubbed an eye with the palm of his hand. "This is ridiculous. Just call the state troopers, and tell them to pick her up."

"So they can put her in a holding cell at the county juvenile center for the rest of the night?"

"Where else is she going to go?"

Merry didn't answer, and then the light of understanding dawned in his eyes. "Oh no, Merry. Not here."

"Where else?"

"What about some of those knitter friends of yours? Let one of them take her. Like Miss Pierce, the librarian. She's probably got a spare bedroom. Where are we going to put her?"

Merry hadn't considered that until Jeff raised the

274

question. "I guess there's only one place." She thought of the canopied twin beds in Courtney's room. Courtney had been after her for months to get rid of them, had denounced them as being for babies like Sarah, which had sent Sarah off into wails of humiliation.

"You're seriously going to stick that girl in the other twin bed in our daughter's room?"

Merry took a deep breath. "Looks that way."

"What if her mother charges you with kidnapping or something?"

"I doubt Tracy Simmons will even notice that Hannah's gone if she hasn't already." She headed for the door. "Plus I know a really good attorney." She paused. "I'll be back in a couple of hours."

"Merry—"

She didn't wait to hear any further objections. Just took the stairs gingerly in deference to her burgeoning midsection and located her purse on the kitchen cabinet next to the refrigerator. Keys in one hand, she grabbed Jeff's shearling coat off the rack in the utility room as she passed. Then, on impulse, she grabbed a second coat—Courtney's North Face jacket. Given Hannah's lack of outerwear, the girl was probably freezing.

A few months ago, Merry never could've imagined setting off for a truck stop in the middle of the night, pregnant and alone, to rescue a stranded teenager. Now she couldn't imagine not doing that very thing. *Welcome to Oz, Dorothy,* she thought as she opened the door to the driver's side of the mini-van and tossed Courtney's jacket onto the passenger seat.

Thankfully not much traffic flowed along the two-lane highway in the middle of the night. Merry had no trouble staying awake. Adrenaline pounded through her veins, which in turn supercharged the baby. By the time she hit I-65, her insides would be black-and-blue from all the kicking and shoving.

Forty-five minutes later she pulled into the parking area of the Rest-A-While Truck Stop. A few cars littered the lot, and she could see a number of eighteen-wheelers parked in the huge open area beyond the main building. *Please, Lord,* she prayed, *don't let anyone have hurt Hannah.*

The truck stop's twenty-four-hour diner looked like it was straight out of a movie set, a long chrome counter dividing the kitchen from the dining area of red vinyl booths under a bank of windows. Merry spotted Hannah immediately. The girl was slumped on a stool at the counter, her hands curled around a coffee mug as if she were holding on for dear life.

"Hannah." Merry kept her voice low, not wanting to draw attention to the girl. A waitress at the far end of the diner looked up and then went back to gossiping with a cook. "Thank heavens." Merry slid onto the stool next to her and reached out to put an arm around her. But Hannah shrank back.

"It's no big deal. I just need a ride." Despite her

brave words, her eyes were red from crying, her thick mascara streaked down her cheeks.

"Okay." Merry at least knew enough about thirteen-year-old girls not to push. Not now. Later, when she got Hannah home and they'd both had some sleep, well, that would be another matter entirely. "Have you paid for your hot chocolate?"

"It's coffee," Hannah said in a challenging tone.

"Okay. Coffee. Have you paid for it?"

"Yes."

"Then let's get out of here." A rowdy group of young men appeared in the doorway, jostling one another and calling each other names that made Merry blush. Clearly they were ending a night of drinking with a meal of deep-fried food.

"Ow," Hannah complained, shaking off Merry's grip on her arm. "Easy, will ya?"

"Easy?" For the first time since she'd been awakened by the phone, anger took the place of fear. "Easy?" She snagged Hannah once more, this time by the wrist. "No one calls me up in the middle of the night, begs me to drive an hour to come rescue them," she paused to catch her breath, which was getting shorter as the baby got bigger, "and then tells me to take it *easy*." She stopped and whirled Hannah around to face her. "We passed *easy* a good hour ago."

Hannah opened her mouth to protest. For a long moment, her lips were just one big O, and then, as if realizing how much better the devil you know could be than the devil that you don't, she shut her mouth and followed Merry to the car.

"How did you wind up at that truck stop?" They had made it past the group of rowdies unnoticed and were headed back down the highway to Sweetgum. Even though Merry had resolved to hold her questions until the morning, she couldn't keep from asking that one. "Where in the world were you going?"

Hannah was looking out the side window, so all Merry could see was the back of head. "Does it really matter?"

"It matters to me," Merry snapped. And to her surprise, she realized she meant it. She cared about Hannah. "I was worried sick when you called. Broke every traffic law in the books racing to get to you."

Merry's tirade was met with silence. She felt tears sting her eyes. What was it about this girl that scared her so? And then she realized exactly what it was. Hannah's life was every fear she'd ever had for herself and for her children all rolled up into one terrifying bundle. And now that Jeff had announced he'd declared bankruptcy, her fears were suddenly much more real. More immediate. More in danger of actually coming to pass.

"Hannah, you owe me an explanation." Merry said the words, but she didn't think she'd actually get a response, so she was shocked when Hannah turned back to face the windshield and started to speak.

"I just had to get away."

"Where?"

"I don't know, okay?" Hannah snapped.

"Who did you have to get away from?"

More silence.

"Hannah? Was it your mom?" Merry kept her eyes on the road, hoping that would encourage the girl to talk. "Did she do something?"

"No. She wasn't even there."

"Then who?"

Hannah burst into sobs. Surprised, Merry jerked the steering wheel of the minivan, almost sending them into the nearest ditch.

"Watch out!" Hannah cried.

"Sorry. Sorry." Merry straightened the wheel and took her foot off the gas pedal. "Everything's okay."

Hannah snorted.

"Tell me who tried to hurt you."

"Gentry. Gentry Carmichael."

"Who is Gentry Carmichael?" Merry had never heard the name in her life.

"My mom's boyfriend. She took off yesterday. I haven't seen her since. And then he came over tonight."

Those words sent a wave of chills through Merry. "Did he try to touch you?"

Hannah's head dropped, her chin almost touching her chest. "He did more than try," she mumbled in abject misery.

Merry put her foot on the brake and eased the van to the shoulder of the highway. She shifted into park and turned toward Hannah, as much as she could anyway considering her bulk. With one hand, she reached across to touch her shoulder. "I'm so sorry, Hannah."

To Merry's surprise, Hannah didn't shrink away. Instead she leaned ever so slightly closer. Merry slipped her arm around the girl and drew her awkwardly across the space between the two front seats. Hannah's first sob slipped softly from her lips, but in a matter of moments she was crying and shaking as if she'd narrowly escaped death. And maybe she had, Merry thought, using her free hand to wipe away the tears running down her own cheeks.

"Do I need to take you to the hospital, honey?" The words almost stuck in her throat, but she had to ask them.

"No. It's not that bad—" She sobbed again. "He just grabbed my—" Fresh tears drowned out the rest of the sentence, but a wave of relief swamped Merry that it hadn't been a worse violation. Later she would find out exactly what had happened, but at least the poor child hadn't been . . . She couldn't even let her thoughts go there.

"I think we'd better get home," she said, patting Hannah's head before shifting back to her seat. "It's all going to be okay."

Hannah gave her a weak smile, probably one of the few times Merry had ever seen the girl do so. "Thank you," she murmured. Merry patted her shoulder again.

"You're welcome."

Ten minutes later they were halfway home, and Hannah had fallen asleep with her head propped against the passenger side door. Merry glanced at the clock on the dashboard. Three thirty in the morning.

Strange how her own life suddenly looked much brighter in the darkness that had almost taken Hannah that night. Yes, she was imperfect as a mother. But she'd always be the kind of mom who would drive for an hour in the middle of the night to pick up someone else's kid. And if that was the kind of parent her new baby was getting, that was fine.

More than fine, actually.

It was something a lot of kids would never have.

Better late than never, Merry thought with a bittersweet smile. That was true for her—in so many more ways than one.

Twenty-Six

Ruthie piled her small amount of luggage on the porch so she could lock the door behind her. She gave the wood a pat, one last expression of affection. She'd arranged to rent her house for the next two years to a young schoolteacher who was a member of the church. The arrangement benefited both of them. The schoolteacher could save most of her money for a future down payment on a house of her own. And Ruthie would know that her home was well looked after in her absence. Assuming she came back at the end of the two years.

Rev. Carson had taken her departure with good grace, although he'd implored her to make a list of all the things she did and how she did them. A pity, really, that she couldn't stay and work with him. He seemed like the kind of preacher who understood both the value and complicated nature of a church secretary's job.

Ruthie locked the door and put the key under a flowerpot, as she'd promised her new tenant. "Good-bye, house." It was silly, she supposed, to actually talk to her home, but after all these years a proper farewell seemed important.

"Why are you talking to your house?"

Ruthie jumped. She'd been so lost in her own thoughts that she hadn't heard her sister coming up the sidewalk.

"Just saying good-bye."

"That's more consideration than you were going to show me." Esther's face was pinched into lines of disapproval.

"I didn't think there was anything more for us to say." Ruthie frowned. "Why are you here?"

"I'm driving you to the airport."

"You don't have to. I called a cab."

Esther pursed her lips. "Yes, I think I do. You can use my cell phone to cancel the cab."

Ruthie would rather have been boiled in oil than accept Esther's offer, but she also couldn't bring herself to say no. "How did you know I was leaving?"

"I happened to stop by the church this morning. Apparently it never occurred to Rev. Carson that you wouldn't tell your own sister you were on your way to Africa for two years."

"You don't need to drive me to the airport."

"No, I don't. But I'm going to."

"All right." Ruthie knew better than to argue with Esther when she used that tone. Besides, now that she was leaving, what could it hurt? She hoisted her duffel bag over one shoulder and grabbed her tote with her free hand.

"That's all you're taking?" Esther frowned in disapproval.

"We're limited as to what we can bring."

"I guess you won't need much out there in the jungle."

Ruthie bit back a laugh. "I'm hardly going to the jungle, Esther. I'll be in a village, like I was before, but it's not far from a small city. No electricity, but that's why I'm bringing solar-powered flashlights." Amazing how an ordinary ten-dollar household object, taken for granted in America, could transform life in the place she was going.

"Do they have running water?"

"Yes, Esther. And I've had all my shots. Remember, I've done this before."

"That was a long time ago."

"Not really." Ruthie's eyes grew misty. "Most of the time, it seems like yesterday."

"Yes, well, you're not as young as you used to be." And then deciding, apparently, not to pursue the argument, she waved Ruthie toward the car as if she were a recalcitrant child. "Come on. You don't want to miss your plane."

The hour-and-a-half drive to Nashville both sped by and dragged on. Esther's Jaguar with its leather interior was comfortable, its low-slung engine eating up the miles with ease. But with only the two of them inside, Ruthie struggled to find topics of conversation. Other than family dinners or other group gatherings, she still hadn't seen Frank alone. Hadn't wanted to, of course, but perhaps she should have tried to put some closure on their relationship. Closure especially on the strange and twisted last few months. Acquiring her visa and her assignment in Namibia with the church-based volunteer agency had taken far longer than she'd expected, in part due to her age.

"How long will you be gone?" Esther asked, breaking the silence between them.

"I signed on for two years. But I might stay longer."

"I can't believe you're doing this just to spite me," Esther snapped, clearly not able to control her temper any longer. "I'm sorry if you think I used you, but it was for a good purpose, don't you think? I assume you didn't want Frank to die either? And you were both being so stubborn—"

"We were being individuals, Esther. Grownups with minds of our own and decisions that were ours to make."

"He was being ridiculous. He had to have that surgery."

"And you made sure he did, no matter what it cost."

"We've already been over this." Esther kept her eyes fixed on the highway.

Ruthie sighed. Why was she even trying to get her sister to see things from her point of view? If she needed any more confirmation that she was doing the right thing, then this conversation did the trick.

"Yes, we have been over this. And neither of us will ever be able to understand the other." She kept her gaze glued to the scenery out the passenger side window. "Still, you don't need to go all the way to

Africa to punish me." Was that regret she heard in her sister's voice? Ruthie fought the urge to put her head in her hands and weep.

"Believe it or not, Esther, my decision has nothing to do with you and very little to do with Frank."

"You're too old to be gallivanting off like this. What if you get sick?"

"They have hospitals in Africa too. Angelina Jolie had a baby there and lived to tell about it."

"It's hardly the same thing."

"Well, I'm not likely to have any babies at my age."

Esther pounded the steering wheel with the palm of one hand. "There's no reasoning with you. Honestly. Well, if you want to throw your life away . . ."

"I already did."

"Excuse me?"

"I already threw my life away. I've been throwing it away every day for the last thirty years."

"Ruthie—"

"Does the truth shock you? It does me too. But your charade taught me something, Esther, that nothing else ever has."

"It did?" She sounded as if she didn't know whether to be frightened or pleased.

"I spent my life waiting for Frank to come for me." She held up a hand to stop Esther from speaking. "I did. It's true, and I'm ashamed of it. But when he finally did act on his feelings for me, I discovered a very important truth."

"Which was?"

"That unrequited love is like a drug. You can get addicted to it." As she spoke the words, she felt a great weight lifting off her shoulders. The very thing she'd always thought had anchored her to Sweetgum had turned out to be a millstone instead.

"That sounds very romantic," Esther said with derision. "I'd simply have called it hanging about, waiting to see if my sister's marriage broke up."

"You're probably right."

"I'm always right."

Except when you're wrong, Ruthie thought, but she knew better than to say it out loud. She didn't want to be dumped on the side of Interstate 65 and have to hitchhike her way to the Nashville airport.

"Well, in any event, if I've thrown my life away, I'm retrieving what's left of it." All those years Ruthie thought she'd been faithful to her family and to her church, indeed to God, serving and loving and trying to bury the longings of her heart. Yes, she thought she'd been faithful. As it turned out, she'd just been scared.

"Will you write?" Esther asked. They were nearing the southern outskirts of Nashville now. Only another twenty minutes or so and they'd be at the airport.

"Yes. And e-mail."

"I don't do the e-mail." Esther sniffed.

"Then I'll write to you and e-mail Alex."

"I thought he wasn't speaking to you."

"Maybe he will when there's an ocean between

287

me and his father." For the first time since they'd left Sweetgum, Ruthie felt tears threaten. "He's the son I never had, Esther. I couldn't stand it if I lost him."

"You won't."

"How do you know?"

Esther didn't answer. Just glanced over at her, that infamous eyebrow arched high as a kite.

"Okay, okay. You won't allow it. Enough said."

"Do you need to make any stops before we get to the airport?"

"No. I'm good."

"I'll miss you, Ruthie." Esther's words came out of nowhere, as unexpected as they were precious.

Now tears choked Ruthie's throat and stung her eyes in earnest. "I'll miss you too, Esther."

It was the closest Ruthie had ever felt to her sister. Which was at once the happiest and the saddest thing she could think of.

Merry peeked around the corner of the bathroom door, careful not to alert the girls to her presence.

"That color has got to go," Courtney was saying as she brushed through Hannah's ratty hair. "Maybe my mom will take us to the salon later. Some highlights would look really good." She pulled Hannah's hair away from her face. "I'm thinking a dark brown base with some caramel strands."

With her face free of the usual heavy makeup, Hannah finally looked her age. "I don't know—"

"And maybe we can stop at the drugstore and pick

up some new makeup. Neutral colors. A smoky eye," Courtney said, sounding like one of those makeover shows on television, "but in a soft gray or brown. Not all that black."

Merry thought Hannah might object, but the curve of her lip, which so often turned upward to express her surly displeasure, remained relaxed and natural. "That would be great. But not until I can pay your mom back," Hannah said.

Courtney paused in the midst of combing through Hannah's hair. "Um, I was thinking I could pay for it, actually."

Merry watched as the girls' eyes met in the mirror.

"I think I owe you one," Courtney said. "A complete makeover. And then we can call it even."

Please, God, Merry prayed. *Soften Hannah's heart the way you've softened mine.*

Hannah reached up to take the comb from Courtney's hand. "Okay. I guess." A grudging agreement, Merry thought, but an agreement nonetheless. She quietly turned around and headed back down the hallway. She'd learned enough over the last few months to know when to leave a miracle alone.

Merry rarely went to Jeff's law office. On the few occasions that she did, he was generally distracted and impatient. She'd always known he didn't multi-task well, and mixing family with his law practice invariably ended with Merry feeling as if she'd drawn the short straw.

Today, though, she needed Jeff as her attorney, not as her husband. He'd been up and gone by the time she'd awakened, as he had been almost every day since he'd told her about the bankruptcy, so they hadn't had a chance to talk about Hannah. Merry had insisted that the girl call her mother to let her know where she was, but there'd been no answer at the trailer. Since it was Saturday, they didn't have to worry about school. But at some point, someone was going to notice that Hannah wasn't where she was supposed to be.

"Morning, Mitzi," Merry greeted Jeff's new paralegal when she entered the storefront office on the Sweetgum town square. She searched the young woman's eyes, wondering if Jeff had told her about their financial situation. The office appeared the same as always—warm but slightly musty, the walls of the reception area lined with law books, their titles etched on their spines in gold lettering.

"Good morning, Mrs. McGavin. I'll tell your husband you're here." Mitzi was pleasant but not chatty. If she knew the state of Jeff's business finances, she certainly wasn't giving anything away. She rose from behind the desk and disappeared down the hallway behind her work area.

Merry waited in the front office for several long moments, her gaze flicking over the titles of the books—all with words like *torts* and *claims* and *penal code.* They were symbols of a large part of Jeff's life, a part that she could never fully share.

She traced her fingers along the spines, wondering if she and Jeff would have grown apart if he'd been a dentist or an accountant. Probably, she admitted to herself with a frown. It wasn't the law that was the problem with her marriage.

"You can go on back," Mitzi said, reappearing right beside her. Merry jumped, a hand flying to her chest. "Sorry, Mrs. McGavin. I didn't mean to scare you." Again, her friendly tone revealed nothing but the most pleasant of demeanors. Suddenly Merry felt sorry for the young woman. Had Jeff given her any indication that she should polish up her résumé and start pounding what little pavement there was in Sweetgum?

"Thank you, Mitzi." Merry made her way down the corridor to Jeff's office. Over the years, she'd become accustomed to his working on Saturday mornings because it was often the only time many of his clients could make an appointment. While Frank Jackson represented the well-heeled citizens of Sweetgum, Jeff tended to take on the working men and women who didn't have the freedom to keep weekday appointments without their wages being docked. Jeff's commitment to fair representation of all of Sweetgum's citizens was one of the things she'd always loved about him. She just hadn't thought through to the financial consequences of taking the less wealthy folks in town for clients.

She peeked around his office door. "Hi, honey."

"Hello." He'd been polite but distant since the day

he'd broken the news about his bankruptcy to her. Most nights he'd fallen asleep on the couch instead of in the bed next to her, and when he did seek out a bed, he often slept in Jake's lower bunk. Having him in bed next to her last night had been the exception rather than the rule. He said he wanted to give her room to be comfortable now that she was so pregnant, but Merry knew that her comfort wasn't the only reason.

"Have you got a minute?"

He looked past her into the hallway. "Where are the kids?"

"Jake's at a friend's house, and Courtney's watching Sarah."

"Oh."

She moved farther into his office, shutting the door behind her and taking a seat across from him. "I need your help."

"My help?" Obviously that wasn't what he'd been expecting her to say. So far she hadn't confronted him about the bankruptcy, hadn't demanded details that he didn't seem to want to share.

"It's about Hannah."

As if on cue, his expression grew stormy. "Look, Merry—"

"I need your *legal* help."

He paused. "Why?"

"I can't let her go back home. Well, she can't anyway because her mother took off. And I don't want her going into foster care either. I can talk to

Theda Farley. She's the Family Services caseworker for the area. You remember her from church?"

"The new redhead who sings in the choir?"

"Yes."

"So what do you need my help with?"

"I think Hannah's going to need a guardian. Someone appointed by the court to make sure her best interests are served." She took a deep breath. Swallowed. "I want you to ask a judge to make you that person."

"Merry—"

"I know it's terrible timing. But, Jeff—" She wouldn't cry. If she did, then he'd just think she was being all hormonal and emotional. "She said her mother's boyfriend touched her last night."

Another shadow crossed his face, but this one was different. It was immediately followed by a look of grave concern. "Should we call the police?"

"No. From what I could get out of her, he just made a grab for her. She ran away before he could do much more."

"How'd she get to that truck stop anyway?"

"I don't know. I couldn't bring myself to ask."

They were both quiet for a long moment. "The thing is . . ." But she couldn't finish her sentence. She wanted to say what she was thinking, but she wasn't sure Jeff would understand.

"What's the thing?"

"The thing is . . . all this stuff with Hannah, it put a lot of things in perspective."

Jeff picked up a pen and started to tap it against the desk. "Merry, just because you've brought a troubled teenager under our roof doesn't mean we're going to have a Hallmark moment. Our problems are still very real."

"I know that." She tried not to snap, but why couldn't he understand what she was getting at? "We have a lot of things to sort out. But, Jeff . . ." She rubbed her belly and felt the baby stir beneath her hand. "We have so much going for us. And I don't mean the house or the country club membership or anything like that." She leaned forward, as least as much as her bulk would allow, and reached for his hand across the desk. *Please let him meet me halfway,* she prayed silently. "We've got the kids and our folks. We both have good educations and the ability to make a living, even if it doesn't turn out to be a lavish one." His hand stayed where it was, wrapped around the pen, but at least he'd stopped the drumming. "We have each other. Even if we've lost our way a little bit."

"We're going to have to start over, Merry." His voice broke when he said her name, and he bit his lip to keep his emotions under control. Merry recognized the response for what it was, an attempt to keep his composure when he really needed to fall apart.

"If we work together, we can make it again," she said. "Just like we did before."

Finally he reached out and took her hand. His

eyes were moist. "I feel like I've failed you. I know how much you love our house, your pretty things."

"Shh." Now that his hand was in hers, she knew that there was hope. And she'd felt hopeless for so long that just a glimmer of possibility was enough to restore her strength and courage. "It's going to be all right." She didn't know how it would, but they'd work it out somehow. "At least we'll be doing it together. I'd rather be poor than lonely, Jeff."

In an instant he was on his feet and moving around the corner of the desk. "Merry, I'm sorry."

"I'm sorry too." But now his arms were around her —or at least as far around her as they could get these days—and she wasn't fighting this battle by herself anymore.

"I wanted to tell you." He tucked her head under his chin and pressed her close. "But every time I tried—Well, it never seemed like the right time."

"This time, we'll do some things differently," she said. She leaned back so she could look into his eyes. "For example, I want to be kept apprised of how your practice is doing. If we need to put austerity measures into place, I want to be the first to know."

"Okay. Deal."

"And when Sarah starts kindergarten in the fall, I can come in and help out—typing, filing, whatever you and Mitzi need. The baby can come too."

Jeff laughed. "I see."

"Do you?" She shook him. Not hard because she wasn't strong enough to shake him too much. Just enough to make sure he was listening. "I don't want to be lonelier in my marriage than I was when I was single." She ducked her head. "And if you ever decide you want out—"

"What?" The look he gave her was priceless. His face was the definition of *incredulous*.

Merry blushed. "I just know that it's . . . easier . . . for men to walk away. And you've been under a lot of pressure—"

"Stop." He put his fingers on her lips. "Do you really think I'd just leave you and the kids?"

"It happens, Jeff. And I know I'm not as young as I used to be." Tears welled in her eyes, and she had to clear her throat before she could continue. "And after this one makes an appearance . . . well, let's just say my body will never be what it once was."

"Merry, what's really going on?" His gaze held hers, and she couldn't look away. "I don't think you believe I'm going to abandon you and the kids."

She shook her head. "No. Of course not. I guess . . . well, I guess I just never realized how vulnerable I would feel. I don't regret being a stay-at-home mom. Not for a minute. But I'm so dependent now, Jeff. Dependent on our marriage. On you."

"And I haven't been acting very worthy of your trust lately, have I?" Regret was written all over his face. "I'm sorry, Merry. More than you can know. And I'm sorry that you felt like you couldn't tell me about the pregnancy."

"And I'm sorry you couldn't tell me about the bankruptcy."

Jeff smiled. "How about we pinkie swear not to hide stuff from each other anymore?"

And then she was in his arms again before they could lock their little fingers together like their children did when making a promise. "I'll come clean if you will," she said.

He looked into her eyes, and just like the first time he'd kissed her good night on her parents' front porch, she thought her knees might buckle beneath her. "Merry McGavin, you are the silliest woman I ever met in my life." He kissed her, full and warm. "And the most beautiful." Another kiss. "And this is the last time we're ever going to have this conversation because from now on we're going to remember that we're a team."

"Okay." The word came out slightly breathless, but between Jeff's kiss and the baby taking up most of the room in her torso, she didn't have a lot of oxygen at her command.

"Now you need to get out of here so I can get to work." He patted her cheek.

"I'll see you later on?"

"Hopefully by midafternoon. Definitely by suppertime." He winked at her. "I'd be home earlier, but I just acquired a new case, and I need to do a little research on family law and custody of surly, troubled teenagers."

The smile that split her face was so broad it almost hurt. "Thank you."

"You're welcome."

"I love you."

"I love you too."

"Bye."

"Bye."

Merry shut his office door behind her, called a cheery good-bye to Mitzi as she breezed through the front office, and headed for her minivan. She felt like Dorothy when she had learned, at long last, the true power of her ruby slippers. Like that fictional heroine, Merry realized with satisfaction that the power to go home again had been in her possession all along. She just had to figure out how to use it.

Twenty-Seven

Eugenie did not make a habit of calling on single gentlemen in their homes. Not on a Saturday afternoon. Or any other day of the week, for that matter. But after Homer Flint's latest phone call, she found she had little choice but to leave the library in the care of her part-time assistant in the middle of the Saturday rush and march straight to the parsonage.

When Paul answered her knock, he looked both surprised and pleased to see her. "Good afternoon, Eugenie."

"It was you."

"What was me?"

"You convinced Homer and his minions to give me a reprieve."

Paul cast a glance over her shoulder up and down the block. "I think you'd better come inside."

"Yes. I think I should." She disliked the smile that teased his lips but chose to ignore it.

He motioned her through the foyer of the old Colonial-style house and into the living room. "I'd ask you to sit down, but as you can tell—"

There wasn't a stick of furniture in the room. "There's no need. This won't take long."

"Our parsonage in Nashville was much smaller." He waved a hand to indicate the rest of the large home that had been purchased by the church in the town's more prosperous days. "My furniture barely made a dent in all these rooms."

"I didn't come to discuss home décor, Paul."

"No, I can see that."

"You did it," she repeated. "Don't deny it."

Paul looked bored with the conversation. "I can't imagine what you're talking about, Eugenie."

"What do you have on them anyway? It must be something spectacular. They were so dead set on Ed Cantrell's niece."

Paul twisted his mouth to keep from smiling. "Well, I did hear that she got a good job with the library system in Nashville."

Eugenie looked at him through narrowed eyes. "That's not easy considering that most systems are laying off people these days, not adding them."

"I suppose that's true." He looked as innocent as an angel. "Someone who used to live there must have had some connections in the city government."

"Paul!"

"Yes, Eugenie?"

Had he always been so infuriating? She didn't remember that from their time together forty years ago.

"How did you manage it?"

Paul let out a long breath and held up one hand. "Okay, okay. Yes, it was me. But I was only acting in the best interests of this community. Your services are still very much required at the Sweetgum Public Library."

"I don't like you interfering."

"No, but I'm sure you like the result."

Well, she couldn't deny that. "That's not the point."

"Actually, it is."

"What?"

"I want you to be happy, Eugenie. If that means your job in the library, then that's what you should have."

Her mouth fell open. It was entirely possible she stopped breathing. What on earth—

"I don't need your help."

"It appears that you do, in fact. If I was the one responsible for Homer's change of heart, would you want me to undo it? Answer me honestly."

"No." The word came out of her mouth on one long rush of air. "No, I wouldn't want you to change it."

He looked over his shoulder, and Eugenie could see the kitchen through the doorway beyond. "I'm afraid I've got a cake in the oven that I need to see about."

She laughed. "A cake?"

Paul stiffened. "Is there a problem with a man baking a cake?"

"No. Of course not." But her reassuring words couldn't disguise the amusement in her tone.

"I think it's a bad idea to laugh at a man who just got you your job back."

"Ha! So you admit it."

And then all the humor drained out of his face, and he looked every one of his sixty-something years. "Yes, I do, Eugenie. I admit to putting some pressure on the city council on your behalf. Now if there's nothing else you need from me . . ." He nodded his head in the direction of the kitchen.

Eugenie felt as if the breath had been knocked from her body. He'd made the very admission she'd come here to demand, but instead of feeling vindicated, she felt bereft.

"Paul—"

"Let's just let it be over, Eugenie."

"But—"

"You've made your feelings clear."

The floor seemed to move beneath her feet, her knees wavering until she thought her legs might give way. "I don't think I have." Heat suffused her cheeks.

"Excuse me?"

She stood up straighter. "I don't think I have made my feelings clear."

She'd had plenty of sleepless nights since that disastrous meal at Tallulah's Café to think about what he'd said to her. And in the privacy of her home and her heart, she'd admitted that he had been right. "You were right," she said.

"About what?" He looked appropriately skeptical.

"All those years ago, I chose to trust my head and not my heart."

"I'm glad you finally realized it." He started to turn away. "If you don't mind letting yourself out . . ."

"I love you." Oh dear heavens, she'd actually said it out loud. Now instead of moving beneath her feet, she wished that the floor would open up and swallow her. She was far too old to be behaving this way. What on earth had possessed her to—?

"Eugenie." He came toward her, scowling. Not a good sign. Her heartbeat was erratic enough to worry Frank Jackson's cardiologist.

"Just let me finish," she said in her best librarian's voice.

"Yes ma'am." He wasn't smiling yet, but there was a hint of humor in his voice.

"I don't really want to do this . . ."

"You do know how to make a man feel like a million bucks."

She put a hand to her chest, hoping to impose some sort of control over her heart. But it was far too late for that, wasn't it? She wanted to laugh and cry all at the same time.

"If you still want to try . . ." Her voice trailed off. She couldn't finish the sentence.

"If I still want to try . . . ?" Paul prompted.

"Then I'd be willing," she said, the words tumbling over one another in her rush to get them out. She wished she'd never come.

"Okay." Now he was smiling, but he was standing clear across the room. She wished he was closer.

"Okay what?"

"Okay, we can try."

In her wildest dreams, which to be honest weren't terribly racy, Eugenie never would've envisioned what happened next. And she certainly never would have expected to be kissed so thoroughly, not at her age, not by the man she'd loved and lost so long ago.

And certainly not in the empty living room of the parsonage owned by the Sweetgum Christian Church.

Everybody in town heard about the preacher and the librarian before she did, Hannah thought, as she paced back and forth in front of the public library. She always seemed to be the last to know anything. So when Miss Pierce had called the McGavinses' house the night before and asked Hannah to stop by after school, she knew what was coming. The librarian had already dumped her on Camille St. Clair. What more could she want? Was she going to kick her out of the Knit Lit Society too?

Hannah was worried. She'd spent a lot of time, and most of her available cash, knitting something for the librarian for *The Wonderful Wizard of Oz* project. They were dust cloths. Or washcloths, she guessed, depending on what someone wanted to use them for. Hannah called them "Auntie Em's Cleaning Cloths." They weren't fancy—just a seed stitch pattern that looked bumpy and worked well for picking up dust or scrubbing out a pot. Seed stitch took more concentration than anything else she'd tried so far because you had to alternate between knitting and purling. Plus, once you finished a row, then when you came back the other way, you had to knit the purl stitches and purl the knit stitches. Hannah had ripped out her first effort time and time again. But in the end it had been worth it. She couldn't think of any better way to say thank you.

Still, Hannah was worried. Miss Pierce had spent a lot of time on the phone last night with Mrs. McGavin after she'd finished speaking with Hannah. Mrs. McGavin wouldn't tell her what it had been about, and secrecy always worried Hannah. It never meant anything good.

While the two women were on the phone, Hannah had taught Courtney to knit. The whole evening had been weird but okay. She never would've imagined that in a million years—her teaching Courtney McGavin anything. They would never be best friends, but Hannah didn't think she'd be getting any lunch trays flipped over on her anytime soon.

Might as well get it over with, Hannah thought. She stopped pacing and instead climbed the few steps to the library door before she slipped inside.

The librarian was behind the circulation desk as usual, scolding an older woman for allowing her dog to chew on the library books she'd checked out. "They're not toys, Mrs. Brewster. They're books."

Hannah bit her lip so the lady wouldn't see her smiling. It was nice to see someone else on the receiving end of the librarian's bossiness for a change.

"Ah, Hannah. There you are." She said good-bye to the trembling Mrs. Brewster and motioned for Hannah to come closer to the desk. "Thanks for coming by."

"You said you had something to talk to me about?" She hated the way her stomach was tied up in knots. Had Dorothy felt this much trepidation when she'd come face to face with the Wicked Witch? Then again, Miss Pierce wasn't a witch. Just a librarian. A few similarities sometimes, but no overall resemblance.

"I've been talking with Merry and her husband," Miss Pierce said.

"So?" She refused to flinch. It was going to be bad news.

"Even though Jeff McGavin is going to be your legal guardian for a while, until your mom can be found, they can't take you in to live with them right now."

Hannah shrugged to hide the disappointment that crushed her chest. It was what she'd expected. Foster care couldn't be that much worse than dodging Gentry. At least she didn't think so, although she'd certainly heard stories—

"So we've come up with another idea," the librarian said. "I wanted to ask you about it and see what you think."

"Like my opinion would really matter," Hannah said, hoping she sounded angry and not hurt, like she felt. Of course the McGavins didn't want to take in a loser like her. They had three perfect kids of their own and another on the way. And though Courtney had been a whole lot nicer to her lately, it's not like she would want Hannah taking over half her room permanently. Even though Hannah was disappointed, she could understand that much.

"Of course your opinion matters," the librarian said, frowning. "Don't be ridiculous."

Hannah started to turn around and leave, but then stopped. Where would she go? She still had a key to her mom's trailer, but the electricity and water had been turned off a few days ago, Mrs. McGavin had told her. And she couldn't exactly go running to the McGavinses' house when she'd just been told they didn't want her there either.

"I have to get to work," Hannah said without turning around to look at the librarian.

"I'm sure Camille can spare you for a few minutes. Do you want me to call over there and tell her you'll be a little late on my account?"

Hannah shrugged. "Whatever."

"Turn around, please," the librarian ordered, and Hannah, despite the fact that she really, really wanted out of the library, did as ordered.

"We've come up with another plan for you." Suddenly, the librarian looked a little nervous. That got Hannah's attention. They were going to send her away. Probably to one of those wilderness camps for troubled teens or a juvenile detention center. She should run. She should run right now, before—

"No need to look so panicked," Miss Pierce said,

exasperated. "We're not planning anything devious. Something along the lines of . . . well, like Dorothy's situation in *The Wizard of Oz*."

What? They were going to throw her in the path of the nearest oncoming tornado? "Mrs. Farley at Family Services said I didn't have to go anywhere I didn't want to."

The librarian's eyebrow arched way up, like a cat's back. Hannah had learned over the last few months to look out when her eyebrow did that. "Oh she did, did she?"

Hannah shrugged.

Miss Pierce blew out a long breath and fiddled with the cuff of her sweater. "Hannah, what I'm trying to say, not very eloquently, is that I'd like you to consider coming to live with me."

In all her born days, those were the last words Hannah had ever expected to hear out of the librarian's mouth. "You want me to live with you?"

"You're right." She waved a hand dismissively. "I'm sure it's not a good idea. I'm far too old and set in my—"

"Would I have my own bedroom? Or would I have to sleep on the couch?"

The librarian looked surprised. *Well, score one for me,* Hannah thought.

"You'd have your own room, of course. But I would expect you to help with household chores. Your grades would need to be solid. I don't demand perfection, but I won't tolerate a slacker either. And

308

you would need to continue your part-time job with Camille at the dress shop. I can give you a little spending money, but not much."

Spending money? Hannah almost laughed. Her whole life, spending money had meant being able to buy a jar of peanut butter and a loaf of bread. Maybe some jeans and T-shirts at the thrift store if she was lucky. If she didn't have to feed and clothe herself, she could buy yarn. The thought made her want to throw up, but in a good way. She might even buy a book or two. A book she could keep for her own and not have to return to the library.

"What do you think, Hannah? Would you be willing to give it a try?"

She couldn't afford to show too much emotion. If people knew how you really felt, they used it against you. At least her mother always had. But she couldn't quite banish the smile that wanted to slide across her face.

"I don't dust," she said. "I just want to be clear about that. That's all I do all day long at that dress shop."

"Fair enough," the librarian said. "But I don't do other people's laundry. So you'll be responsible for your own."

If Miss Pierce only knew. Hannah had been doing her own laundry since she was nine.

"Then I guess it would be okay."

The older woman nodded with satisfaction. "We can move your stuff after work today. I'll meet you at the dress shop. We can drive to the McGavinses' and pick up your belongings."

Hannah nodded, not trusting herself to speak. The librarian glanced at her watch. "You'd better get moving or you'll be late."

"Yes ma'am."

Hannah didn't know why the librarian grinned so broadly when she said that. And then she realized what she'd just done. She'd called Miss Pierce "ma'am." They were getting to her, those Knit Lit ladies. The next thing you knew she'd have a knitting bag of her own to carry around all over the place.

Hannah never would've admitted it to anyone, but she really liked that idea.

Twenty-Eight

The February meeting of the Sweetgum Knit Lit Society came before Esther was ready. Since the day she drove Ruthie to the airport, she'd felt as if one of her limbs had been amputated. She hadn't expected that, of course. Not in the least. She should have been relieved. Grateful even. After all those years of living in the shadow of her husband's love for her sister, she should finally feel at peace. Instead she felt restless and unhappy.

Everything Frank did these days irritated her. Even though he no longer snored, he was still sleeping in the guest room. She hadn't told him about the absence of snoring since his surgery. She would tell him soon. When she was ready.

When she could find the forgiveness in her heart that had always eluded her.

The Pairs and Spares Sunday school classroom was a little chilly tonight, Esther observed as she set her knitting bag on the table and took her seat. She engaged in the usual round of greetings and catching up. Eugenie seemed to sparkle. Hmm. Something was up there. She needed to be more watchful. Esther didn't like to be the last to know anything.

311

Merry too seemed more at peace. Not long until the baby was born. She had that glow of pregnancy that Esther remembered. No amount of Crème de la Mer could duplicate that natural radiance.

Camille, Esther noticed, had bags under her eyes as if she hadn't been sleeping. Esther felt sorry for the girl. No doubt she'd been up in the night with her sick mother. They should hire some help for that shop of theirs. More help than Hannah, of course. The teenager was starting to look like a normal human being, much to Esther's relief. At least her hair color was now a normal dirty blond, and she'd left off that heavy eyeliner.

Then there was the empty chair next to hers. Ruthie's chair. She hadn't expected that chair to haunt her, but it did.

"Esther, how's Frank doing?" Merry asked as they all began stitching away. "Is he keeping up with his cardiac rehab? I know my mother had a hard time getting my dad to do his."

"He's doing fine. Very faithful." Because she nagged him every day. On that point, her plan had developed a hitch. Once Frank had learned of Ruthie's departure, he seemed to slip once more into the funk that had plagued him in those months before the surgery. But Esther would manage that problem, just as she managed all the problems in her life— with sheer determination and the refusal to be bested.

Somehow, though, victory didn't feel as satisfying as it used to.

"Have you heard our news?" Eugenie asked, nodding at Hannah. Esther shook her head, along with Camille. Merry simply smiled. "Hannah has agreed to come and live with me," Eugenie continued.

Esther shut her mouth to keep her jaw from dropping open. "Really?" she finally managed to say. "How lovely." But what she really wanted to say to Eugenie was, *Are you crazy? She'll ruin your life.* But Eugenie looked pleased as punch, and Hannah was smiling shyly and actually tucking that mop of hair behind her ears, out of her eyes.

"Wonderful," Camille said with the enthusiasm Esther couldn't feel. "I'm glad that worked out."

Merry glanced at her watch. "Where's Ruthie? She's never this late."

The moment of truth had arrived. Esther cleared her throat. Opened her mouth to say something and found herself at a loss.

"Esther?" Eugenie looked at her with curiosity, which quickly grew to alarm. "Has something happened to Ruthie?"

"Ruthie's gone."

"What do you mean, 'Ruthie's gone'?" Eugenie said, a horrified look on her face.

"Not gone as in dead," Esther reassured her. "Gone as in out of town. I drove her to the airport."

"Where did she go?" Camille asked, her eyes full of curiosity. "When will she be back?"

Esther's smile hurt. For that matter, her cheeks hurt, her scalp hurt, and her neck definitely hurt.

Facades were heavy armor in the end. They might protect you, but they took a great deal of strength to lug around.

"She's gone to Africa. Namibia, to be exact. She's going to teach in a village school and work on a project to distribute mosquito netting and solar flashlights." Esther only knew that because she'd gone online to read about the program in which Ruthie was participating. Didn't that show love for her sister? Esther detested computers. "As for when she'll be back, well, I think in two years. If she doesn't decide to stay longer."

"Two years!" Merry looked appalled. Almost as appalled as Frank had when Esther told him about Ruthie's departure. He'd been devastated that Ruthie hadn't said good-bye. Esther thought that was for the best. A clean break all around.

A tiny part of her did wish that the clean break hadn't been of her husband's heart. Or perhaps what she really wished was that her husband's heart had never been in the position to be broken in the first place.

"She didn't even say good-bye. Can we write to her?" Camille asked. "Or e-mail?"

"Both. I have the information right here." Esther had asked Frank's secretary to type it up and make copies. She placed the pile of papers on the table. "We'll hear from her all the time. Two years will pass very quickly."

What was that strange gnawing in her stomach?

She'd eaten a good breakfast and her usual salad for lunch. For supper she had cooked an omelet (three eggs and cheese for her, egg whites and vegetables for Frank). There was no reason for the discomfort in her midsection.

"I can't believe it." Merry's eyes welled with tears. "She won't see my baby until he's walking and talking."

"I'm sure she regrets that," Esther said, feeling as if she should offer the necessary comfort to the rest of the group. Or perhaps she was merely comforting herself since she couldn't share the truth of the matter with anyone else. That was the biggest price she had paid, she realized with a start, for the life she had led. She was a social leader, the envy of many women in Sweetgum. But she was also absolutely, totally alone. Especially now that Ruthie was gone.

Esther refused to cry in front of the other women. "Should we discuss the book?" she prompted with false cheer. Not that she'd read it. Not that she'd completed the necessary project. She simply had to change the subject before she fell apart right there in the Pairs and Spares Sunday school classroom.

"So what did you all think of *The Wonderful Wizard of Oz*?" Eugenie asked, as was her custom. There'd never been a shortage of discussion, Esther thought, as the others dived into their opinions and insights.

"I understand why Dorothy needed all those other characters to travel with her. She never would have made it to the Emerald City alone, much less killed the wicked witch," Hannah said, which even Esther had to admit was a mature insight.

"Whom do you think changed more, though? Dorothy or her friends?" Eugenie asked.

Esther looked around the table at the other women as they pondered their answers. Things had certainly changed in the last five months since Eugenie first brought Hannah to a meeting of the Sweetgum Knit Lit Society. Had the teenager's introduction into the group been the catalyst for all the changes? Or was Hannah's presence merely a coincidence?

Perhaps a little of both, Esther thought.

Camille dropped her knitting into her lap. "I know it's not in the book, but I always cry when I see the part in the movie where Dorothy tells the Scarecrow that she'll miss him most of all," she said, and Esther could tell she was thinking of her mother. Esther felt a lump rise in her throat. She'd been close to so few people in her life. Even as she'd resented Ruthie, she'd depended upon her. Though their relationship had never been straightforward, it had been vitally important. Esther understood now. Ruthie was her Scarecrow. Or maybe Ruthie was Dorothy, and she was Ruthie's Scarecrow. Either way, the pain of separation was just as intense.

Esther wondered if Ruthie felt the same, over there in Africa by now, embarking on a new life so far away from all she'd known. But really she was returning to something she'd known and loved long ago. Which was Kansas and which was Oz for Ruthie? There was no way to know. At least not until she saw Ruthie again and could ask her. Until then she'd just have to wonder.

Camille's mother managed to stay awake until Camille returned from the meeting of the Knit Lit Society. She knew her mother would want to hear all about the book discussion and the projects the group had made.

"Hi, Mom." She leaned over and brushed a kiss across her mother's cheek. The room was lit only by a small lamp, the television playing softly in the background. "You shouldn't have waited up," she scolded gently.

Her mother smiled, a faint, soft expression that combined pain and peace into a vague curve. "I know. But I wanted to hear about the meeting."

Camille settled into the chair beside the bed and set her purse on the floor. "Well, we had a good discussion, like we usually do. And you'll never believe what Esther told us about Ruthie." At that moment, her cell phone began to ring in the depths of her bag. "She's gone to Africa to do mission work. Can you believe that?"

"Aren't you going to answer your phone?" her mother asked, nodding toward Camille's purse.

Camille looked down at her feet. She could see the glimmer of pink nestled between her wallet and the notebook she kept that listed her mother's medication along with the dosages. And then her eyes rose to meet her mother's.

"No," she said, with the same combination of pain and peace in her voice that she so often saw on her mother's face. "No, Mom. I don't think I am going to answer it."

These days instead of lunching alone at Tallulah's Café on Tuesdays, Eugenie met Paul. Since no one knew of their previous relationship, Tallulah was sure that her matchmaking was responsible for the happiness of the couple in question. Paul and Eugenie said nothing to disabuse her of the notion either. Their past was their business, and neither of them saw a reason to share it with anyone but each other.

As they left the diner, Paul walked with Eugenie back to the library. They hadn't made it halfway around the square though, when he stopped her and pulled her into his arms, right there in broad daylight.

"Paul Carson? What on earth are you doing?" She could feel the blush firing up her cheeks. "Let me go right now." That's what she said, but what she thought was, *At last.* Paul's arms tightened around her, and she buried her face against his shoulder. She would never grow weary of this, even if her face was on fire.

"I want to ask you something," he said. Eugenie's heart thudded in her chest.

"Ask me something?" she echoed like some silly fool without a lick of sense.

"Eugenie? Look at me, sweetheart."

She hadn't been called that in so many years, and the endearment had the opposite effect from what he'd intended. She could feel more color flooding her cheeks. She kept her head pressed against him and tried to ignore the wonderful way he smelled—the slightest hint of aftershave with a little bit of mint. As if on his way out of the café, he'd eaten one of the peppermints Tallulah kept in a bowl by the door. Come to think of it, he probably had.

"Come on. You can't hide forever." He pulled away, and she had to let him go. She wasn't going to start being a clinging vine at this late date. "There, that's better."

His eyes were full of the love she never thought she'd find again. "Eugenie, I don't see any sense in going on this way. I think it's high time we made our relationship permanent." He paused. "Will you marry me?"

"Paul, this isn't the time or place—"

"I think it's the perfect time and place."

"We're standing in the middle of the town square."

"You haven't answered my question," he said. His hands cupped her upper arms. She finally found the courage to look him in the eye.

"Paul . . ."

"Oh no." A clouded expression covered his face. "Don't start off whatever you're going to say like that. Not with 'Paul . . . '" He mimicked her hesitant elongation of his name.

"We're far too old—"

"Speak for yourself, Eugenie Pierce. I'm not as old as all that, and neither are you."

"I don't know if I can change."

"I never said I wanted you to."

"I've never lived with anyone else." *Except for Hannah,* she added silently. And that had only been a week, hardly long enough to count. Besides, Paul didn't even know about that yet.

"There's a first time for everything," he said.

"Paul, be serious." If her cheeks had been red before, they were the color of ripe tomatoes now. "I've never . . ." She couldn't finish. Thankfully he saved her from having to do so.

"Eugenie, whatever you think the obstacles are between us, I promise we will figure out a way to overcome them. Miracles don't come along every day, you know." He stopped and grinned. "And I say that as a professional miracle-pointer-outer."

"What if it doesn't work out?" There. She had said it, voiced her deepest fear.

His hands fell away from her arms. He frowned. "Well, as much as I'd like to sustain the romantic nature of this proposal, you've raised a valid question. So let's talk about it. What if it doesn't work out, as you say?"

"I've spent a lot of years building the life I have now—," she began.

"Then don't change it."

What? Eugenie's stomach dropped to her shoe tops. "I thought you wanted—"

"Of course I want us to be together. I think I've made myself pretty clear on that count. But no one's offering any guarantees here, Eugenie. Just because we're old doesn't mean that our lives still aren't a minefield of risks. Even if you turn me down, that fact won't change. If you believe you can make your world a hundred percent safe, then you're sadly mistaken."

She had believed that. She'd clung to that idea fiercely until the day he'd walked into the Pairs and Spares Sunday school classroom and turned her life upside down.

"It's time to take a risk, Eugenie." He drew her back into his arms again. "The good news is that you don't have to take it alone."

Yes, it was good news, Eugenie thought. Very good news indeed. The kind she hadn't heard much of since she'd walked out of church all those years ago.

"I'll make a terrible minister's wife," she said.

"The only thing I expect you to be is the town librarian," Paul answered.

"What if I ruin your ministry?"

"I'll find another church. Or retire."

"What if—" But before she could continue her protests, he silenced her with a kiss.

Eugenie had always frowned on public displays of

affection, especially in the town square. But on that cold February day, right in front of the lingering Valentine's display in the big plate glass window of the Rexall drugstore, she indulged in one with the new pastor of the Sweetgum Christian Church.

Contrary to what she'd always believed, the sky didn't fall, but the ground beneath her feet did shake.

Eugenie decided she'd wait until later to tell him he was also about to acquire a teenage foster daughter as well as a new wife.

Epilogue

What with one thing and another, the Knit Lit Society didn't get around to throwing Merry a baby shower until well after the birth of Hunter Joshua McGavin. The Pairs and Spares Sunday school classroom had never looked so festive, Eugenie thought as she scored the sheet cake with a knife, careful that each serving would be topped with a blue icing baby bootie. No one ever wanted cake duty, but Eugenie didn't mind. It gave her a chance to observe the difference that nine months had made in the lives of the Sweetgum Knit Lit Society.

Merry sat behind a pile of presents, opening one while she laughed at something Camille had said to her. Camille had seemed to lose her sparkle for a while, but she was doing better. Her mother wouldn't be around much longer, Eugenie thought. It was a good thing Camille had the Knit Lit Society. When the time came . . . well, Eugenie had no doubt who would be there to support the girl.

Esther was recording the gifts on monogrammed stationery with a fountain pen. Eugenie could see new lines of strain around her mouth, but at least Esther hadn't said any more about that nonsense of divorcing Frank. He was doing well—even starting to jog around Sweetgum every morning. No, the lines must be for another reason besides Esther's marriage. Her concern for Ruthie, no doubt. Even though they all heard from her regularly, they worried. Namibia was a long way away.

Hannah appeared next to Eugenie and reached for two plates of cake. Eugenie opened her mouth to scold the girl and then realized she'd misread Hannah's intent. She wasn't helping herself. Instead she turned and carried the plates to Merry and Camille, setting them down beside each of them. Eugenie bit her lip. Taking in an unhappy adolescent had put some strain on her budding relationship with Paul, but with patience and love they would all make it through.

Eugenie laid aside the knife and smiled as Merry almost squealed with delight over the beautiful little sweater and cap Hannah had knit for the baby. In the blink of an eye, Merry had her arms around the girl and was hugging the life out of her. Camille applauded, and even Esther looked pleased.

They'd all knitted gifts for Hunter Joshua. Eugenie glanced over at where he slept sweetly in his carrier. Even in slumber, he was a busy boy. His little fists opened and closed as if trying to grasp something just out of his reach. His chin and mouth worked up and down like a fish on the bank, desperate for air. Yes, Merry was going to have her hands full with that one.

"Eugenie. Come over here. Merry's about to open

324

your present," Camille called. Eugenie wiped the remains of frosting from her fingers on a napkin and crossed the room.

"All right, all right. Here I am."

Merry carefully slid the beautiful wrapping paper open at the seams, slitting the cellophane tape with her thumbnail. Eugenie's breath caught in her throat. What if Merry didn't like her gift? Or worse, what if she didn't understand its significance?

The wrapping paper discarded, Merry pried the lid off the box and pulled back the tissue paper inside.

"Oh, Eugenie." Was that dismay or wonder in her voice? Eugenie realized she was holding her breath.

"Is that . . . ?" Camille's voice trailed off.

Esther stood up and moved closer for a better look. "It's exquisite," she said, reaching over to finger the delicate garment.

Even Hannah looked impressed. "You must have done that on needles the size of toothpicks," she said. "That'd take forever."

"I did use size 2s," Eugenie said. "But they're a little bigger than toothpicks."

And then Merry was up and out of her chair and in front of Eugenie. "I don't know what to say. Thank you seems so inadequate."

Eugenie knew that Merry was speaking of more than the snowy white christening gown she'd labored over so lovingly and so long. "It should fit," she said, uncomfortable with overt displays of emotion. "I made it a little big. Just in case."

Merry didn't answer, just threw her arms around Eugenie. For a long moment Eugenie stood, rigid. And then her arms found their way around Merry, and she hugged her back. "It was my pleasure," she said, meaning every word. "Every stitch of it."

Hunter Joshua let out a high-pitched wail, which galvanized the women into action. Merry reached for the diaper bag for changing supplies, Hannah bent over him and made funny faces, and Esther cooed and clucked to him as if he were one of her own.

"He's just hungry," Merry said. She produced a bottle from the diaper bag. She turned to Eugenie. "Would you like to feed him?"

Eugenie felt the color drain from her cheeks. She'd never—But a pang of longing seized her. Suddenly she wanted to hold Hunter Joshua and give him his bottle more than anything.

And so a few minutes later, she found herself settled into the rocking chair that had been pilfered from the church nursery for the occasion. The baby lay warm and heavy in her lap, his head tucked into the crook of her arm. With her free hand, she held the bottle, teasing his lips until he took it and began to suck noisily. Eugenie laughed. She was going to have to brush up on her knowledge of the boyhood classics. You never knew. Someday this young man might show up in her library in need of straightening out.

Looking around the room, Eugenie realized that the Sweetgum Knit Lit Society was now held together by much more than her proddings and persuasions. They were bound together by more than their books and knitting even. Somewhere in the last year, they'd been stitched together by love. And that love, more than anything else, would keep them coming back to the Pairs and Spares Sunday school classroom for a long time to come.

Basic Shawl Pattern

By Nanette Mathe

Yarn: Any bulky weight yarn—approximately 600 yards

Hint: Combine two or more strands of a lighter weight yarn to obtain the look and yarn weight desired. If knitting with more than one strand, the shawl will require approximately 600 yards of each yarn. Be sure to knit a swatch to test the needle size to obtain the right gauge.

Gauge: 14 stitches and 20 rows equal 4 inches

Needles: 13 (American) or size needed to achieve the gauge

Hint: If you want to add fringe to the shawl, cut it first. Then you can simply knit the shawl until you run out of yarn!

Fringe: Cut a piece of strong cardboard or mat board 8 inches. Wrap yarn loosely around the board. If wrapped too tightly, the fringe will shorten when it is cut. To put a piece of the fringe on every other row, approximately 175 strands are needed. After wrapping, cut strands on one end only—they will be 16 inches long. Set aside.

Shawl: Cast on 3 stitches.
    Row 1: Knit
    Row 2: Knit 1, yarn over, knit to end

***Repeat row 2 only* until piece measures 35 inches from cast on edge.** At 35 inches there will be 143 stitches on the needle. If you have yarn left, or want a longer shawl, knit until your yarn is gone. Be sure to save enough yarn to cast off!

Hint: When starting a new ball of yarn, attach at the beginning of the row. Leave a tail of at least 8 inches of yarn before knitting the first stitch. After knitting the row, tie the two tails together close to the edge of the shawl. These strands will become part of the fringe. Trim to desired length when the rest of the fringe is in place. This way, the ends of the yarn will not need to be buried in the knitting and the shawl will be reversible.

Cast off all stitches loosely. If the cast off is too tight, the shawl will gather, or bunch at the top!

Attach one piece of fringe at each end of every other row. To do this, fold each piece of fringe in half. Using a crochet hook, pull the fold halfway through the edge of the shawl. Open the fold and thread the two ends of the fringe into the opening. Keeping the two ends together, gently slide the fold up to the edge of the shawl. Trim the fringe if desired.

Shawl Variations

- Create a striped shawl by changing colors. Stripes can be equal in length, created by knitting the same number of rows in each color or unequal in length, created by not knitting the same number of rows. Adjust yardage by number of different colors used: for example, if three colors are used, 200 yards of each color will be needed to knit the shawl.
- Create a subtle striped effect by adding a very thin strand of metallic thread every few rows.
- Leave the fringe off of the shawl.

Enjoy!

Readers Group Guide

1. In the novel, Eugenie chooses classic novels for the group to read that feature heroines whom she hopes will inspire fourteen-year-old Hannah. What qualities do you see as being consistent in many fictional heroines? What qualities does your ideal heroine possess? As real life and fiction often play out very differently, what does it mean to you to be an everyday heroine? Who are some heroines of literature that have remained memorable to you?

2. Hannah, while stubborn, angry, and guarded, has an impact on each of the members of the Knit Lit Society, despite the differences in their ages and status in Sweetgum. What character do you think she impacted most? What new friends in your life have encouraged unexpected personal growth?

3. What role, if any, does faith in God and family play for each of the characters in *The Sweetgum Knit Lit Society*?

4. Sisters Esther and Ruth have a complex relationship. If you walked in Ruth's well-worn Birken-

stocks, would you have handled the situation with Esther and Frank differently?

5. When faced with the threat of a dramatic change in situation, Esther doubts her own ability to adapt. What factors have been personal motivators to adapt within changing situations in your own life? How do you respond to change?

6. Which character in *The Sweetgum Knit Lit Society* do you most identify with? Which heroine of the classic girlhood literature the Sweetgum women read do you most identify with?

7. Women often find comfort and guidance in small groups such as the Knit Lit Society. Why do you think this is? How have small circles of women impacted your life?

Center Point Publishing

600 Brooks Road ● PO Box 1
Thorndike ME 04986-0001 USA

(207) 568-3717

US & Canada:
1 800 929-9108
www.centerpointlargeprint.com